Payoff

Payoff

DOUGLAS CORLEONE

 Minotaur Books 🐾 New York

PAYOFF. Copyright © 2014 by Douglas Corleone. All rights reserved. Printed in the United States of America. For information, address St. Martin's Press, 175 Fifth Avenue, New York, N.Y. 10010.

www.minotaurbooks.com

The Library of Congress Cataloging-in-Publication Data is available upon request.

ISBN 978-1-250-04073-2 (hardcover)
ISBN 978-1-4668-3601-3 (e-book)

Minotaur books may be purchased for educational, business, or promotional use. For information on bulk purchases, please contact Macmillan Corporate and Premium Sales Department at 1-800-221-7945, extension 5442, or write specialmarkets@macmillan.com.

First Edition: August 2014

10 9 8 7 6 5 4 3 2 1

FOR MY DAUGHTERS,
MAYA KAILANI & KYRA SKYE

Here is true immorality: ignorance and stupidity; the devil is nothing but this. His name is Legion.

—GUSTAVE FLAUBERT

Part
One

THE KIDNAPPERS
OF CALABASAS

Chapter 1

The nightmare opened with a sound she heard at least a dozen times a day. On the north side of the house, there was a door used by the servants. The door opened onto a vestibule that guests had to pass through to reach the staircase that led to the main floor of the house, one floor below her bedroom. The door had a distinctive squeal. She'd been meaning to ask Manny to oil the hinges for weeks. Now she was relieved that she had forgotten. That sound gave her time, maybe just enough time to get to Edgar's handgun. Because she was suddenly certain that sound could mean only one thing—someone was inside the house.

Emma threw her legs over the side of the bed and instinctively fell into her slippers. When she stood she was nearly overcome by a wave of dizziness. She planted her right foot and steadied herself, took a deep breath, and moved like a shot toward the walk-in closet.

As she rose on tiptoes to reach the high shelf of the closet, she listened for footfalls on the stairs, but the rest of the house remained quiet. When she'd left Olivia's room not twenty minutes ago, her teenage daughter was sound asleep in her bed.

Please stay there, sweetheart. No matter what you hear.

Emma hefted the small steel gun vault off the shelf, turned, and set it on the edge of the bed. She spun the first of the three dials on the combination lock, fixed it into position, then moved on to the next—*8, 2, 1*—her and Edgar's wedding anniversary.

No question now, as she lifted the lid, that there were footsteps on the stairs, heavy footsteps, not the steps of a lone intruder attempting to maintain stealth, but the steps of two or three individuals moving as quickly as their legs allowed.

Emma removed Edgar's .38 Special from the vault's foam-lined interior. The revolver was loaded, as always, and felt heavier in her hand now than when she'd practiced with her husband at the gun range.

She caught a glimpse of herself in the mirror above the dresser as she moved toward the closed bedroom door. She would have liked to retreat to the master bath to slip her spa robe over her lavender nightie, but there wasn't time. The footfalls had reached the main floor.

Emma curled her long fingers around the door handle. Cursed herself for leaving her cell phone downstairs, charging in the kitchen, for not insisting on having a landline in the bedroom.

Deep breaths. Olivia is safe upstairs. You won't let them reach her.

She twisted the handle and slowly opened the door. Instantly nausea struck and she nearly vomited at her feet. Looking down from the second landing, she watched three masked men turning the corner, single-file, and heading with long, purposeful strides straight for the stairs that led up to her bedroom.

A clipped shriek escaped her lips, and the first of the men looked up. Beneath his black ski mask, the visible flesh around his eyes was painted black.

Emma raised the .38 in both hands and aimed for the center of his chest.

As she squeezed the trigger, a fourth man blew out of the door to the home office she'd recently set up across the hall. The revolver discharged as he rammed his right shoulder into her midsection, slamming her against the doorframe.

Emma's body tumbled into the bedroom, and as soon as her head smacked against the hardwood floor, she realized she'd dropped the handgun.

Through the open door, she could see each of the three men reach the top of the steps and turn toward the stairs leading to the third floor.

Olivia.

"Please, no!"

The fourth man—the one who had lain in wait in her office—delivered a powerful blow to her temple, knocking her face hard against the floor. She immediately became disoriented, the ringing in her ears reminding her of the times she sat on the green shag carpet in her grandparents' living room watching Woody Woodpecker or Bugs Bunny cartoons, when all of a sudden Woody or Bugs or Elmer Fudd was interrupted by an earsplitting pulse, followed by *"This is a test of the Emergency Broadcast System. This is only a test."*

Emma attempted to lift her head but the room spun as though she were drunk, a fuzzy white frame rapidly closing over her vision.

She bit down hard on the tip of her tongue, tasted the tang of blood in her mouth as she tried to keep herself from falling into a faint.

Olivia needs me.

The fuzzy white frame began receding but then she felt a hand grab her by her hair and drag her backwards as she shrieked. The heels of her bare feet bounced against the surface of the hardwood floor.

She screeched as the intruder pulled a hood over her face.

She was shrouded in blackness, a gloved hand closing tightly around her throat.

Upstairs, Olivia screamed, and Emma felt her entire body shudder.

Help. Please someone help us.

Emma's mind reflexively turned to the next morning, to the sun rising high in the California sky, and Manny arriving through the same door the intruders had entered. She envisioned the majordomo trudging upstairs, none the wiser that anything had transpired while he was gone.

Until he reached the second landing, that is, where her bedroom door would no doubt remain ajar. He would rap lightly, afraid to wake her even though he knew she never slept past five.

"Mrs. Trenton," he would call with his thick Spanish accent.

There would come no reply, of course. Concerned, Manny would push open the door to make certain nothing was wrong.

Here he would find Emma sprawled out on the hardwood floor—strangled, though he wouldn't know it yet—a black hood still covering her head as though she were the executioner rather than the executed.

"Mrs. Trenton," he would say again as he approached her.

Manny would kneel over her and feel for a pulse. Then, as he often did, he'd make the sign of the cross, dip into his pocket for his cell phone, and dial 911.

Once he was sure the authorities were on their way, Manny would walk out of the bedroom and hurry up the stairs to check on Emma's daughter.

Oh, please, no, not Olivia . . .

Chapter 2

When Emma came to, she was seated in an upright position, her back propped against the wall. Which wall she couldn't be sure, because the hood still covered her face. She didn't know how much time had passed, whether it was day or still night.

She was parched.

Her throat burned.

Her head throbbed.

But she'd survived. Which surely meant that Olivia . . .

"Olivia."

Her voice was hoarse. There was no response. She tried to move, then realized both her wrists and ankles were bound tight.

"Olivia?" she said again.

She felt a presence standing over her.

"Who's there?"

Smoke permeated the hood, caused her to cough violently.

Is there a fire? She was sure she was going to suffocate.

"Olivia!"

Emma tried to maneuver her body in such a way that she might be able to stand, but she only raised her lower half slightly, then fell hard to her knees, cursed at the surge of pain.

A low throaty male laugh emanated from somewhere not far away.

They're still here. The sound confirmed it.

The man who'd laughed rattled off something in Spanish.

Emma's response was automatic, her voice cracking with every syllable. "What, what did you say? *Please,* in English."

Another man replied to the first, also in Spanish. He sounded far off, too far for them to be in any part of the house other than the great room.

Then some light from the French doors should be penetrating the hood. I should be seeing red, not black. Christ, could it still be dark out?

Never in her life had she felt so disoriented—and that, in and of itself, was utterly terrifying. She could feel the small blond hairs on her bare arms standing on end.

Without warning, one of the men ripped the hood off her head, jostling her neck. A sharp pain traveled south through her shoulders, and she had to keep herself from crying out.

The room was black, the windows and doors covered with dark sheets she didn't recognize. She blinked repeatedly, hoping it was just a matter of time before her eyes adjusted. But the intruders had effectively blocked all light from seeping into the room.

"What do you *want*?" she cried.

She wondered why her mouth wasn't gagged or sealed with tape—but then, what did it matter how much noise she made? Their closest neighbors would have to strain to hear cannon fire coming from their house.

The Trentons' estate rested in the hills of Calabasas, an exclusive city in Los Angeles County, surrounded by towns such as Woodland Hills and Malibu. Tucked in the heights of the southwestern San Fernando Valley and the Santa Monica Mountains, Calabasas was a place where people valued their privacy and paid seven, sometimes eight, figures to ensure it.

"*Where's* my daughter?"

Emma glanced down at her wrists and realized they were bound together with zip ties, the strong plastic fasteners used by police during riots and protests. The darkness prevented her from seeing her ankles, but it felt as though they were bound by the cables as well.

She was sweating profusely but felt goose bumps running up her bare legs. She looked down and noticed a tear in her nightie, her left breast slightly exposed.

So much flesh. I feel like one of those pathetic girls in Edgar's movies.

Edgar was in Europe for the premiere of one of his studio's films at the Berlin International Film Festival. These men must have known her husband was away, which meant they were most likely professionals. Professionals didn't kill, did they? They took what they wanted and left.

So why are these bastards standing around?

Emma could make out only two silhouettes, meaning the other two men may have been doing just that, searching for and snatching valuables.

Or raping my daughter.

The abhorrent thought flew at her like an errant arrow and struck her square in the chest.

"*Where's my daughter?*" she cried again, helpless to keep the words from pouring out.

She's only fifteen! she wanted to shout. But that was the mindless drivel Edgar's writers would put in their victim's mouth. The intruders wouldn't be persuaded by calls for morality; they'd laugh and spit in her face and beat and rape whomever they pleased.

"*Oh, god, please let us go. Take whatever you want, just please leave us alone.*"

Emma knew these words were no more useful, but they'd flooded out of her mouth as though released by a dam. The longer she sat here, she knew, the less control she'd have over what spilled out of her lips; she was sure it was just a matter of time before she said something that would get both her and her daughter killed.

If they were going to kill us, they would have done so already.

"Please, just . . . Just show me my daughter. *Please.*"

A gloved palm shot out of the darkness and struck her full-force in the face. Her nose took the brunt of the blow and instantly felt numb, blood flowing freely from both nostrils over her lips, onto her chin, spilling onto the front of her nightie and puddling in her lap.

So much blood, she thought in a panic. *But it's only a broken nose. It's nothing. You can't bleed to death from a broken nose, can you?*

Her lips stung.

Her front teeth felt loose.

The inside of her mouth was cut and she was swallowing blood.

When she spoke again her words were horribly garbled. "Please, tell me what you want, I'll tell you exactly where it is."

One of the masked men knelt before her. She looked into his eyes, which appeared black in the lightless room. The mask contained a hole for his mouth; the harsh stench of cigarettes emerging from between his lips caused her to dry heave.

Slowly, the man whose face was merely an inch or two from hers ran his gloved hand up the inside of her right thigh and she shivered. He stopped just shy of her crotch, squeezed her leg firmly, then reached into her nightie and cupped her partially exposed left breast.

Emma's busted lower lip trembled.

Tears welled in each eye.

Her throat constricted.

In a thick, smoky accent, the man said, "What we want, you will tell us where it is?"

Her entire body already shaking, she did her best to control her neck and summon it to nod.

"Yes." Her voice was little more than a hiss.

The corner of the man's lips turned up in a grin as he leaned into her so closely that the wool of his mask brushed up against her broken nose, making her itch.

"But what we want," he said softly, "we already know where it is."

Chapter 3

Several minutes later Emma's eyes widened to the point of strain as the masked man brandished a blade at least a foot long and as sharp as the horror-film prop displayed prominently in Edgar's den. With her heart pounding harder than it did during even her most strenuous workouts, she closed her eyes and felt the steel being pressed lightly against her throat, dragged slowly from left to right, stopping dead center, then moving down her chest, between her breasts, slicing through the sheer material of her nightie.

She held her breath.

Allowed tears to stream down her cheeks.

Forbade herself to make a sound.

The man said, "How much cash will we find in the safe in your husband's movie-picture room?"

She opened her eyes, exhaled, watched the blade retract leisurely from her body.

"I don't know," she whispered hurriedly. "Forty, fifty, maybe sixty thousand dollars."

"That is not enough."

"There's jewelry," she said, her breathing uneven. "Lots of jewelry hidden behind the—"

"—behind the painting in your precious little office, yes. It is lovely and we will take it, but I am afraid it is still not enough."

Emma grimaced. "How much do you want?"

"We require something that will fetch us eight and a half million dollars."

She said, "We have *nothing* like that."

"No?"

"No. Take the cars. There are four of them. The yellow and black one is a Bugatti Veyron; it's worth almost three million dollars."

The corners of the man's lips dripped like melting candle wax into a frown. "Why do you need such a car?"

"I don't. It's my husband's. Please, take it. Just leave, that's all I want. Please."

"Can I sell that vehicle for eight and a half million dollars?"

He was playing with her. Her head felt like a lead weight and she didn't know how to answer. Why were they taking their damn sweet time?

Because they know no one is coming to help us. Christ, how did they disable the goddamn alarm?

"No," she said. "I told you we have nothing like that. There's the cash, there are the cars, and there's my husband's movie memorabilia."

"This movie . . . memorabilia," he said, pronouncing each syllable as though it were its own word. "It is important to your husband?"

Her husband, Edgar, was the CEO and chairman of Carousel Pictures. This man had to know that. Why did this son of a bitch care whether that crap was important to *Edgar*?

"Yes, very."

"Your husband will pay to have it back?"

"Yes, Edgar will pay any price to have it returned."

The masked man tilted his head as though he was suddenly curious. "Eight and a half million dollars, even?"

Emma didn't know how to respond. Clearly it wasn't a serious question. Edgar's stuff had *some* monetary value, but mostly it was sentimental. Edgar hardly kept anything in the house. Especially in recent months, since their marriage began teetering on the precipice of divorce. Surely much of his wealth was hidden. Technically, the Trentons were worth north of ten million. But Emma doubted he maintained anywhere near that much in their bank accounts.

"I don't know," she conceded. "He'll pay, I don't know how much, but a lot."

"A lot," he repeated. Over his shoulder he said something in Spanish. Whatever he said caused the other man in the room to laugh.

"How about *you*?" the man said. "How much would Mister Trenton pay for *your* life?"

She scoffed, then immediately regretted it. "You'd have to ask him. Shall I get him on the phone?"

His lips curled in an uneven grin. "That will not be necessary. I can reach him in Berlin if I need to."

A thought occurred to her and with it a glimmer of hope. It had to be coming up on dawn here in California, which meant that the banks would soon be opening in New York. And it was already midday in Western Europe.

"Edgar can wire the money to you right away if you'd like." She could hear the desperation in her own voice, but it was no matter. These men knew she was desperate.

The man in front of her motioned to the other, and the other approached. This one was carrying a large black case, the mere sight of which induced in Emma an irrational terror.

"What is that?" she cried.

The man sitting on his haunches in front of her took the case and set it on the floor. He clicked open one of the latches, then another. "It is a carrying case for a bandola. You know what it is, a bandola?"

Her mind reached. "It's a mandolin."

"No, not exactly." He lifted the lid of the case. "It is a string instrument, yes, so you receive some points, Missus Trenton."

She searched the man's face. He appeared to be smiling. Then her eyes fell on the open case, and her stomach lurched. She became short of breath, couldn't seem to draw in any air at all. The man in front of her paid no attention as she struggled for oxygen.

All the while, she surveyed the contents of the case. There were stun guns, another knife, a handgun that looked to be a .22. There was a crowbar. But what frightened her most were the medical supplies. In a transparent plastic box topped with a wide red cross sat a syringe, a blue liquid chemical, a variety of pills, and latex gloves.

"What are you going to do with me?" she cried.

"We are going to play a little game I call 'My Husband Loves Me, My Husband Loves Me Not.'"

The man removed the transparent box from the case and opened it in front of her. Across the room, a laptop monitor lit the area around it with an unnatural glow.

The man kneeling before her removed the jar containing the blue chemical, held it up to Emma's wet eyes. "Do you like frogs?" he said.

Emma didn't reply, her eyes transfixed on whatever it was in that jar.

"You are trying to decipher what I am holding," he said.

Again she said nothing.

Over his shoulder the man said, "Tell me when you have him on the line." To Emma, he said, "We are contacting your husband, just as you wish."

He then used the syringe to pierce the foil covering the jar and extracted a significant amount of the blue liquid. He removed the syringe, eyed the tip, flicked it with his fingernail as she'd seen Dr. House do hundreds of times on television.

"It is very important to eliminate the air bubbles," he said. "Very important. Even when you are administering poison."

Chapter 4

I have Edgar Trenton's assistant," the man with the laptop said. It was the first time Emma had heard him speak English.

To Emma, the man kneeling in front of her said, "That would be Valerie, yes?"

Emma bowed her head, yes.

"Your husband is fucking her, no?"

She swallowed hard. "Yes."

"And yet you remain married to him."

"For the time being." Her voice had leveled out; she felt a numbing sensation swelling in her gut. The fear was somehow subsiding the more they spoke—in the same way that pain faded when you were about to pass out.

I'm going into shock.

"Ah, I see. Because of your daughter, yes? When your daughter is of age, then it is '*Adiós*, Mister Trenton. Leave the gun. Take the cannoli.'" He chuckled at his own words. "Probably I should have waited a couple years until you were in charge of half his finances. I get the feeling you would be far easier to persuade than your husband."

"You want my husband to wire you money from Berlin."

It was his turn to ignore her. Instead of offering a reply, he reached for Emma's left forearm and twisted it hard. Pain shot upward from her bound wrist.

"Keep your arm like this. Do not move it."

He removed one of the latex gloves from his kit and tied it tight around her arm, just above the elbow. Then he reached back into the bandola case and removed a packet of matches.

Emma squinted to read the cover, to no avail.

He removed one of the matches and struck it against the pack. The match lit, the reflection of the flame flickering in her captor's eyes as he scanned her arm.

In a few seconds the match was nearly burned down.

"There she is," he said quietly.

"Who?"

"Your vein."

The masked man blew out the match, and the smell of burnt sulfur blended with her blood and his cigarette breath. With one gloved hand he held her left forearm; with the other he held the syringe a few inches over the vein.

"Do we have Edgar?" Although he was speaking to his fellow intruder, his eyes never left Emma's arm.

"Valerie is looking for him. He is apparently in a theater but she does not know which one."

The man with the syringe sighed. "Tell this Valerie that we do not have all night."

The one with the laptop turned. "If one of them becomes suspicious, they will contact the authorities."

"So then, we are on a clock." Looking into Emma's eyes, he whispered, "Ticktock, ticktock, ticktock."

"Please," Emma said.

The man shook his head. "I am afraid we are going to have to start without your husband."

"Start what?" she said, the fear creeping back into her voice.

He held up the syringe. "This is the venom of an amphibian known as *Dendrobates tinctorius 'azureus.'* It is a species of poison dart frog known for its color, which is azure or bright blue." He tilted the syringe so that she could see the liquid moving inside. "Their venom is toxic to humans. However, the frogs rarely cause casualties unless the venom comes into contact with an open wound or sore. See, it takes a large dose of the venom to cause death in humans, and the dart frogs, despite their name, have no way of injecting their target." He paused, holding the syringe in front of her eyes. "This, in case you are wondering, is considered a large dose."

Without another word, he punctured Emma's skin with the tip of the syringe, pressed down on the plunger, and watched the blue liquid travel up her vein.

She cried out, but the man slapped a gloved hand over her mouth.

"Quiet," he said. "The venom has an immediate effect. You are no doubt feeling it already in your nerves and muscles."

Emma's eyes went so wide, she could feel them bulge from their sockets. She fought against her restraints.

"Within minutes," he said, "you will be completely paralyzed. And then, one by one, each of your vital organs will begin to shut down."

Emma felt the venom going to work, something alien traveling through her veins, shutting down nerves, numbing her, freezing her muscles. She felt a terror so raw, she thought it would stop her heart.

Her body slumped forward.

Her thoughts broke into millions of tiny fragments.

Her cells were losing their struggle for life.

"There is little time for me to administer the antidote," the man said. "I will do so only if your husband agrees to wire the eight and a half million dollars to my Cayman accounts immediately."

He looked back at the man with the computer. "Of course, first his lover Valerie will have to locate him, and she does not appear to be having much success."

The man with the computer said, "Valerie says Edgar is inaccessible. She cannot reach him, because of security, regardless of the emergency."

The man in front of Emma carefully replaced his items into the bandola case. The matches he slipped into his front pocket. Then he closed the lid of the case and locked it.

He looked her in the eyes. "I am sorry, Emma. I am afraid we are out of time."

Across the room, the laptop snapped shut, extinguishing the glow of the monitor and throwing the room back into complete darkness.

Emma tried to move her lips but she couldn't speak. The man rolled her onto her back, her neck lolling so that she could see the stairs the intruders had used to enter her home, only now she saw everything entirely upside down.

Footfalls again filled the house. The other two men were descending the stairs from the top floor to the floor with the master bedroom, then the final ten steps leading down into the great room. In the darkness, she could barely make out their black boots.

The man with the laptop joined the others. The man with the bandola case sank to one knee, kissed his gloved fingers, then placed those fingers against Emma's bloody lips. "Farewell, Emma."

He stood and moved to join the others. Her eyes followed his every step until he reached the stairs. With no small degree of effort, Emma raised her gaze to meet his for one last time.

When she did, she saw that the two men from upstairs were carrying something together. It appeared to be a body wrapped in a sheet. The men turned to descend the stairs leading back to the vestibule and the door that led outside.

A sound she didn't recognize emanated from Emma's throat.

All four men stopped and looked back at her.

The man who had done all the speaking took a step forward. "Emma would like to say good-bye to her daughter," he said quietly to the others.

He reached into his pocket and plucked from it his packet of matches. He tore one off and struck it against the flint. With one gloved hand he ripped the sheet off, revealing Olivia's face in the blush of the flame.

The flesh around Olivia's eyes was crimson.

Her mouth was gagged.

Her shoulders were bare.

She was awake, her entire face a mask of terror.

The match slowly burned down till the flame reached the man's gloved fingers and extinguished itself.

It was the last Emma saw of her daughter, Olivia.

Chapter 5

Never ask for a loan or a favor. Both have to be repaid, and without fail, the interest will be far greater than you could ever have anticipated.

So it was with Edgar Trenton, chairman and CEO of Carousel Pictures in Burbank. In another lifetime, I'd asked the studio mogul to extend me a courtesy. Instead he granted me an outright favor, and I'd been in his debt ever since. Today that debt was about to come due.

Years ago, after my six-year-old daughter, Hailey, was stolen from our home in Georgetown and my wife, Tasha, took her own life, an opportunist named Will Collins wrote a book about the abduction, the subsequent investigation, and the whole sordid aftermath. The book did about as well as Collins's previous attempts at bestseller-dom, which was to say, his publisher was able to move a paltry three thousand copies. The book was a bust. How could it have been anything but? The story had no ending, no resolution. My daughter was never found and the authorities stopped looking. By the time the book was published, people had lost interest.

Of course, that was a risk all true crime writers took, from Truman Capote to Ann Rule to Diane Fanning. If you wanted to write about a crime, you had to get involved early; then it was up to law enforcement and twelve men and women in a jury box to see that your story contained closure. If any of them failed in their task, so did your art. At least in terms of book sales. Not so with movies.

Movie studios like Carousel Pictures simply inserted the words BASED ON A TRUE STORY in the opening credits; then they had license to end the film however they liked. Carousel optioned Will Collins's story for something to the tune of five thousand dollars, a real steal if the studio ultimately buys the rights and makes the picture. But then, that rarely happens. Far more often, the option expires and no studio ever picks it up again. The author's dream of seeing his work on the silver screen dissipates like a cloud of smoke and then it's back to the old drawing board. Or keyboard or legal pad, or whatever writers use these days.

But some authors get lucky. A bigwig like Edgar Trenton reads the book on the toilet and loves it, thinks, *We could do something about that awful ending, retrofit it Hollywood style.* He sends it to a down-in-the-mouth screenwriter, who salivates at the thought of making fifty grand for adapting someone else's sweat and agrees to draft a script. A hundred and ten pages later, the bigwig receives the script, reads it, and typically tosses it aside if not directly into the trash bin. Once in a while, however, the studio exec will fall in love with the script; he'll see his own genius in it. After all, he's the one who rescued the book from the remainder piles. He'll send the script out to major agencies like CAA and William Morris and tell them it's a hot property. "See if Daniel Craig or Clive Owen or Ewan McGregor wants to play this character Fisk. No? All right, then get me Jason Statham."

Once a big star is attached, the film has a hell of a good shot at moving forward. Suddenly, you have a talented director with a proven track record, someone like Arthur Baglin, and everyone else is on board. That was the case with Will Collins's masterpiece, *Unfathomable: When the Daughter of a U.S. Marshal Went Missing in Our Nation's Capital.*

The U.S. Marshal was me. The daughter was mine. But the story was ultimately owned by Edgar Trenton.

Until I paid him a visit and convinced him to let it go.

I offered to pay him, of course. Five grand for the option, another fifty for the script, and whatever other costs he'd incurred.

He flatly refused payment. "This can't be about money," he'd told me. "Because if it is, regardless of how much you pay me, I'm getting the raw deal. We have Artie Baglin directing. We have Jason Statham in negotiations to play you. This picture could conceivably make the studio a couple hundred million worldwide. No, if I'm going to scrap the film, I'm going to do it as a favor to you. Because I'm also a father with a little girl, and I can only imagine what you've already been through."

I told him I appreciated the gesture but that I didn't accept favors.

"I'd much rather pay you," I said.

But Edgar Trenton wouldn't budge.

So, he'd done me a favor. And I walked out of his office on the lot in Burbank feeling as though I'd scored one hell of a good deal.

And I had, no question about it.

That is, until this morning, when I received a telephone call from Edgar, and he told me that his own daughter, Olivia, had been taken by four masked men during a violent home invasion in Calabasas, California, less than six hours ago.

Chapter 6

Twenty minutes after I touched down at LAX, a limousine took me north on the 405 past Santa Monica and West Hollywood to the Ventura Freeway and the hills overlooking the Pacific Ocean.

The size of the Trentons' estate in Calabasas didn't surprise me; before trying to persuade Edgar not to film the Fisk family's tragic story, I'd researched how much studio execs earned. Even the studio execs with flawed track records, such as Edgar's. Suffice it to say, money would never be an issue for him. At least not in the way it was for 99 percent of the country.

I also wasn't surprised to find no police presence, though I'd hoped Edgar came to his senses. But no, he'd received a very specific demand for eight and a half million dollars and no involvement of the authorities, and he was hell-bent on following the kidnappers' instructions to the letter. With the notable exception of contacting me, of course.

"Please, Simon," he'd pleaded over the phone. "I can't go this alone."

When I stepped out of the limo onto the circular driveway, Edgar Trenton was there to greet me. He'd gained a couple dozen pounds since I first met him, and his salt-and-pepper hair had lost its pepper.

We shook hands and I said, "Before you show me anything, I

have to repeat the advice I gave you over the phone. Let me bring in the feds."

"Simon, I hate to have to say this, I really do. But there's no time to mince words, and it may be the only thing I can say to make you understand." He paused and looked me square in the eye. "We only met because I've read your story. I know it inside and out. And though it pains me to ask, what exactly did the feds achieve for *you* when Hailey was snatched from *your* house?"

One thing about the players in Hollywood, they knew how to tug at your heartstrings. How many hours I sat up in bed in the black of night second-guessing the decisions I'd made in those first ninety-six hours of Hailey's disappearance, I'll never be able to calculate.

"All right," I said. "We do this your way, for now."

"Follow me."

Leaving my single piece of luggage in the trunk of the limo, I followed Edgar around the side of the grand house, to a door he said was used almost exclusively by the help.

"*Almost* exclusively?"

"Occasionally we ask guests to use this entrance. Particularly if we're throwing a large party. Otherwise the driveway in front of the main entrance can become severely backed up."

I pulled on a pair of latex gloves and examined the door, which was made of a sturdy light oak with an oval of beveled glass centered in its upper half. No sign of forced entry. Hadn't been dusted for prints, because Edgar insisted the intruders were all wearing gloves.

"Who besides you, your wife, and your daughter has a key?"

"Well, there's Manny. He's our majordomo."

"Your what?"

"Our head servant. He's in charge of the other male servants— the driver, the chef, the gardener."

"He's the butler."

"Yes, he's the butler."

"What's Manny's last name?"

"Villanueva."

"He's here in the States legally?"

"Oh, yes. Emma's fastidious about who she hires. Every employee has to either be a citizen or a permanent resident. All of their documents—copies of birth certificates, social security cards, passports, green cards—are on file in her office upstairs."

Quickly he added, "Don't get me wrong, we're not prejudiced. This is Southern California, after all. We believe all foreign-born people, documented or undocumented, should be able to seek better lives for themselves here in America. They should be permitted to obtain driver's licenses, their children should be entitled to an education."

He paused, lowered his voice though there was no one else outside. "It's just that in our last house, when we lived in Beverly Hills, we had this young woman, Sofía, who took care of Olivia, and she was detained in a federal facility after being stopped for a minor traffic infraction. Olivia absolutely loved her, and I spent tens of thousands of dollars on an immigration attorney, and in the end, nothing could be done. It was just a terrible experience, so since then—"

I cut him off. "Where is Manny originally from?"

Edgar turned, squinted as he gazed down at the Pacific. It was late in the day, yet the sun still hung high in the sky. "Panama, maybe? I'm not really sure, but it'd be on file."

"Any other servants have a key?"

"No, Manny's always the first to arrive. If he has the day off, we make arrangements to let in the maids and other staff."

"You pay Manny well?"

Edgar nodded. "Of course. He's the majordomo, he makes six figures. The other servants don't earn quite so much, but their pay is competitive with other households in L.A. County."

"All right. You'll give me access to all their files, then?"

"Of course."

"I may need to interview them."

He hesitated. "That may not be wise. They're good, hard workers, but I don't know that I'd take them into my confidence."

"That's just why I may need to interview them." I added, "Don't worry yourself about it. We won't alert them to what this is all about until we absolutely have to." I stepped away from the door to survey the ground, looking for shoe or boot prints or at least trampled grass. "I take it that no one but your driver is working today?"

"We called everyone scheduled to work and told them they wouldn't be needed until further notice."

A skipping-stone walkway led from the main door to this. It looked as though it had been recently cleaned. Not necessarily in the last twenty-four hours, but not a scuff mark or speck of dirt could be seen. Likewise, every blade of grass stood tall and green. At the bottom of the drive, there was a gate with what looked like a working camera. How did these men get from the road to the door without kicking up some dirt or knocking down some grass?

As I walked down the hill, I thought of the day I returned from Romania to learn that Hailey had been taken from our property. I remembered all too vividly pacing the length of our enormous backyard, trancelike, looking for some clue, some hint of what might have happened to our daughter, of who might have been responsible. As terrified as I'd been that day, my belief that we'd eventually learn the answers to those questions never once wavered. Whatever happened, I'd thought, whoever took her, it was only a matter of time until we knew.

Eleven years later, I was still no closer to learning my daughter's fate. For me, there was no hope of closure, and that knowledge continued to eat at me night after night after night.

Before I realized it, I'd wandered a good hundred feet from Edgar's house. I turned and started back toward the door used by the intruders.

I said, "Let's have a look inside, then."

Chapter 7

The interior of the Trentons' home was every bit as vast as I'd anticipated, the sparse traditional furniture making it appear even more so. The great room was airy with few walls, but every wall possessed its own bookcase, each bookcase loaded with a variety of books, not just hardcovers but also trade and mass market paperbacks, fiction as well as nonfiction. For the first time I realized that Edgar's finding Will Collins's *Unfathomable* wasn't necessarily dumb luck. The Trenton family either read a good number of books or made one hell of an effort to make it appear as though they did.

A lithe redhead, as striking as she was tall, entered the room. She held out a slender hand and I took it lightly in my own as I looked into her fiercely intelligent green eyes. Her irises were surrounded on all sides by red cobwebs, no doubt from hours of constant crying and a deprivation of sleep. From what Edgar told me over the phone, she'd survived a night of pure terror, and I couldn't help but admire the fact that she was standing here at all. I'd expected to be speaking with her from a bedside chair.

"Mrs. Trenton," I said, "I'm terribly sorry to be meeting you under these circumstances."

"Please, no need for formality. Emma is fine."

I bowed my head. "Simon."

"Where shall we start?" Edgar said.

I replied, "With the ransom demand."

"Yes, right." Edgar excused himself and moved toward the stairs.

"Where did you find the demand?" I asked Emma.

"It was in our mailbox."

I felt Edgar's eyes on me as he walked up the stairs. Victims didn't like to be questioned separately. Dividing couples made them feel as though the authorities thought they were at best forgetful or untrustworthy, and at worst, suspects.

"How long after the intruders left did you find the ransom demand?"

"I don't know exactly," she said. "I had no sense of time after they left. They arrived sometime after midnight. Within a few minutes, they'd knocked me out, either with a choke hold or a punch to the temple, maybe chloroform. That was in my bedroom. When I came to, I was here in the great room, propped up against that wall." She pointed to the wall directly across from the French doors. "It was pitch black in here. They had dark sheets tacked up to cover every window. I don't know how long I was awake before they put me out again and fled."

I stepped forward and studied her bruises, the worst of which appeared on her left temple. Her eyes were black and blue, no doubt from a blow to the nose. Her voice was rather nasal and didn't match her face, so it was safe to assume she'd broken a small bone or two in the nose. In my experience, the bones in the nose healed on their own. But the strike to the head warranted a visit to the hospital, and I told her so.

"After all this is over," she said, shaking off the idea.

"I don't want to frighten you, Emma, but a blow to the head requires diagnostic testing, even if you feel fine. You could be suffering a brain bleed and not *know* it until you collapsed. The damage by then could be irreversible, or you could die."

"I'm aware of the 'talk and die' syndrome, Simon. Edgar and I are dear friends with Liam Neeson, and I absolutely adored his wife, Natasha. They were in this house more times than I can count."

Emma was speaking, of course, of the lovely actress Natasha

Richardson, who had died following what seemed like a minor fall on a ski slope in Quebec. For a solid hour after the spill, she had looked and felt perfectly fine; then came a sudden and severe headache. Two days and two hospitals later, the forty-five-year-old British beauty had passed.

Before I could say another word, Edgar was on his way down the stairs, holding the ransom demand in his ungloved hand. I sighed but there was nothing I could do. Over the phone, I'd warned him to preserve the crime scene for the police, not to touch anything at all without gloves, but he clearly hadn't heeded my advice in this regard either. The sheets Emma had just told me were covering the windows when the masked assailants had been here were now neatly stacked on the floor. Even the evidence in Emma's own body—the alleged blue poison—was probably long gone.

"So, Emma," I said, "roughly what *time* did you discover the ransom demand?"

"A short time after dawn. Before I even called Edgar, I ran outside and looked around for Olivia."

"What caused you to check the mailbox?"

She shrugged. "The little red flag was raised. I knew it hadn't been up the previous evening, so I ran the rest of the way down the drive to the mailbox and opened it." She motioned to Edgar. "This note was inside."

Edgar handed me the single sheet of paper, which appeared to contain text printed from a computer.

E. Trenten:
Sorry we missed you. O. will be returned to you for 8.5m US. Instructions to follow. If you involve law enforcment there will be no deal. We will than simply return O.'s head.
   Obrigado.

I set the letter down on a small table. "I take it from our conversation that you intend to pay them."

Edgar motioned to the ransom note as though the answer were obvious. "Of course I intend to pay them."

"It's not always as simple as it seems, you know."

"What other choice do I *have*?"

Do I *have,* I noted. *Not "we," plural, but "I," singular.*

I stared down at the ransom demand again. There were two misspellings for "Trenton" and "enforcement." Also, the author used "than" when he should have used "then." Yet the language was sophisticated, idiomatic. *Sorry we missed you.* It was the kind of language you'd find on a note from your cable guy or UPS driver. *Instructions to follow.* That too sounded like something out of an American movie rather than the words of a real kidnapper. But then, kidnappers watched American movies too, I supposed.

Obrigado means "thank you" in Portuguese. Why give anything away? Unless it was intentional. Like the misspellings.

I looked up at Edgar and answered his question. "Right now, unless you've changed your mind about bringing in the authorities, we have no other choice but to go over everything that happened last night."

"And then?"

"Then comes the hard part," I said. "We wait."

Chapter 8

Start from the beginning of the evening," I said to Emma. "Be as detailed as possible."

Sitting on the sofa across from me, Emma uncrossed her legs and leaned forward, her eyes closed as she tried to conjure the seemingly meaningless details of the previous night. Edgar placed an arm around her and delivered an awkward kiss that clipped her upper right ear. He had to be at least fifteen years older than his wife, which in Hollywood, probably wasn't any stranger than an age difference of a couple of months in the heartland. Certainly it wouldn't have surprised anyone that a man of his means could land a woman of her caliber. And they'd been married sixteen years, which meant he'd been a reasonably young man of forty-five when they became engaged, and she'd been going on thirty. Back then, Emma had aspired to become a film actress, while Edgar was rapidly climbing the executive ladder at Carousel Pictures.

"Nicholas, our driver, dropped Olivia off from school at about three," she said. "She came upstairs to my office, gave me a quick kiss, then went to her room as usual. Neither of us had any plans for the evening."

"What were you doing while you were in your office?" I said to keep the conversation flowing.

Emma seemed a tad embarrassed. "I was working on a short story."

"Emma's a wonderful writer," Edgar added. "She has a few stories out on submission right now, to publications like *The New Yorker* and *The Paris Review*. Once a few of her stories are published, she intends to continue work on her novel."

She waved him off, said, "Please, Ed, let's focus." She drew a deep breath, then continued. "I finished what I was working on about an hour and a half later, then I went to Olivia's room and knocked on her door. She didn't answer, so I tried the handle, but it was locked, which is a fairly new thing."

Edgar shrugged. "She's fifteen, Simon. What can you expect?"

"Anyway," Emma said, "when she finally responded, she sounded as though she'd been sleeping. I asked her to come to the door, but she said she was in bed. This is another new thing; she's been taking naps in the afternoon."

"If only we could all afford a daily siesta," Edgar said.

"So, I told my daughter, I didn't mean to disturb her, I just wanted to know what she'd like for dinner. She said she'd really been craving a Double-Double from In-N-Out Burger. I asked her, 'What about the whole vegetarian kick you've been on?' She said she'd been cheating anyway, and she needed a break from pizza and salads. So, I said, 'Fine, In-N-Out it is.'"

I said, "Aside from her increased desire for privacy, how has your relationship been with your daughter?"

Emma was quick to say, "It's been wonderful." She thought about it. "You know, we argue over the usual things. Curfew, cleaning up after herself. Staying in touch while she's out of the house, though that hasn't been a problem recently—she's finally enjoying spending more time at home. The one thing we *have* argued about over the past few weeks is how much time she spends on the Internet, the social networks and such."

"I have the same argument with my assistant Valerie." Edgar's words elicited a sharp look from his wife.

"Olivia's computer," I said, "is it still upstairs?"

"No," Emma said, "it's gone. They took it. It was a top-of-the-line

MacBook. They took that, her iPad, her iPhone, her iPod—everything they could get their filthy hands on."

"At least a couple of those items have locator applications," I said.

Edgar said, "We thought of that. We contacted Apple first thing. They told us that her computer, phone, and iPad have all been wiped clean. There's no way to locate them."

"Do you have Olivia's passwords? E-mail? Facebook? Twitter? Whatever else?"

Emma shook her head.

"You mind if I have a colleague attempt to crack them?" I said.

"Of course not," Edgar said. "So long as he's discreet."

"She," I corrected him. "And yes, she is very discreet." I removed my BlackBerry from my pocket. "Before I place this call, tell me what else was taken."

"My jewelry," Emma said. "A couple of Edgar's Rolexes. The money from our safe."

"How much?"

Edgar said, "About thirty thousand."

Emma turned to him. "That's all that was in there?"

He said, "I haven't counted every bill recently, but yeah, that's about right."

"You gave them the combination?" I said to Emma.

"I offered it."

"They knew the combination, then?"

"Either that, or Olivia gave it to them. We trust her completely. She has the combination in case of an emergency."

I nodded. "Anything else taken?"

Edgar said, "My gun."

"This is the .38 you told me about over the phone?"

"Yes."

To Emma, I said, "Edgar tells me you went for the gun when you heard the intruders entering."

Her jaw shifted.

Her nostrils flared.

Her emotions were rising to the surface again.

"That's right," she said. "I went to the closet in our bedroom, took the gun vault from the high shelf, and placed it on the bed. I entered the combination and removed the gun. Then I opened the bedroom door. And I saw—" She swallowed hard. "—*them*. They were running up the stairs toward me."

"What did you do next?"

"What I've been taught to do," she said. "I aimed dead center at the first man's chest. But just as I squeezed the trigger, another man rushed out of my office and tackled me."

"So you got a shot off?" I was surprised Edgar hadn't mentioned that to me.

"I did. But because the other man tackled me, the shot went wide."

I stood, motioned to the staircase. "Show me where the bullet struck."

"That's just it," Edgar said. "She can't."

"I *heard* the weapon fire," she insisted. "I *felt* the recoil."

"Yet we've searched the entire house up and down," Edgar said, shrugging. "There's not a single bullet hole to be found."

Chapter 9

Following an exhaustive back-and-forth, Edgar stood and held out his hands, palms up, facing me. "She was knocked to the ground and then knocked out a few seconds later." Emma scoffed.

He turned to her and said, "I'm not saying you're lying, sweetheart. I just think it's possible you're mistaken."

I had a couple follow-up questions for Emma about the shot she was sure she'd fired, but I preferred to ask them outside Edgar's presence.

"All right," I said. "Emma, would you put together a list of your daughter's online accounts? E-mail addresses, Facebook profile, Twitter handle, and anything else you may know about."

She pushed herself off the sofa. "Of course."

"Edgar," I said as she shuffled away, "tell me about the alarm system."

He shrugged. "Well, for one, it doesn't work unless it's turned on."

"Who would have been responsible for turning it on?"

"With me away, Emma would've been responsible. Manny always asks before he leaves for the day, but we usually tell him we'll take care of it."

"And last night?"

"Emma says she *thinks* she turned it on. But then, she also thinks she fired a shot when there's no bullet hole in the house."

"Who besides Manny and your immediate family possesses the code?"

"No one that I know of. But we were never particularly careful about it. Someone could have seen one of us enter the code. We have several guest bedrooms; sometimes people stay overnight."

"And the camera outside?"

"Outdated. It's really just for show. It works, but it doesn't record unless we put a tape in, and I can't remember the last time we did. Security was never an issue, Simon. This is Calabasas; there is virtually *no* violent crime. Maybe the occasional domestic dispute. Property crimes are rare, and if someone were looking to rip someone off, they'd have plenty of bigger and better homes to choose from in Malibu or Brentwood or Bel Air. This is something we never could have imagined."

Tasha and I had felt very much the same way, living in Georgetown, and I'd been a U.S. Marshal at the time. I'd not only *known* the worst of humanity; I'd also dealt with it on a daily basis.

Emma returned with a list of Olivia's online accounts, and I excused myself to make my call. Kati Sheffield was a thirty-four-year-old FBI computer-scientist-turned-mommy. Four years ago, when she became pregnant with her first, she quit the Bureau to stay at home. It didn't take long for her to discover that her services were in great demand among private investigators like yours truly. Now Kati was pregnant with her third, and maintained a booming small business to boot. All of it on the down low, of course. According to Kati, her husband, Victor—a detective with the Connecticut State Police—didn't even know what she did to earn money. *Some* detective, I thought.

"Hey, Finder." The code name she'd given me.

I glanced at my watch, added three hours. "Good evening, Breaker. Mind opening a few doors?"

I could hear her toddler, Miles, singing along with the television in the background. *Mickey Mouse Clubhouse*, if I wasn't mistaken. My own daughter, Hailey, had adored Mickey Mouse before she was taken. But then, it was silly of me to pain myself like this every time I heard *M-I-C-K-E-Y* or the "Hot Dog!" song. After all, what kid didn't love Mickey Mouse?

"Happy to," Kati said. "When do you need them open by?"

"Before the carriage turns back into a pumpkin would be nice. They belong to a teenage girl, so it shouldn't be too difficult."

"I'll do my best. Give me what you got."

I gave her everything on the list, then said, "So you're even working nights? And how is it that Sherlock doesn't know?" *Her* code name for her husband, Victor, not mine.

Kati had the kind of smile you could hear over the phone. "I'm pretty sure he thinks I'm having an online affair. Last week I caught him downloading a book about the psychology of cybersex to his Kindle. He said it was for a case."

"Maybe it was."

"He's currently assigned to the Welfare Fraud Unit."

"Oh. Sorry, Breaker. By the way, how are you feeling?"

"Fat, hungry, tired, fat, and nauseous."

"First trimester still?"

"Just started the second."

"It gets better, doesn't it?"

"I'll have to let you know; it's different with every pregnancy. I'll call you once I've opened the doors, Finder."

"You're a gem."

I stuffed the BlackBerry back into my pocket and returned to the great room. I asked Emma if she remembered anything else about the intruders that she and Edgar hadn't already shared. But no, all she knew was that they were Hispanic, couldn't tell from where.

"I can't tell a Mexican accent from a Puerto Rican accent from a Portuguese accent," she assured me with some embarrassment. "The one who did most of the speaking, he had dark brown eyes, but I couldn't tell you anything about his skin color, because the flesh around his eyes was painted black. His lips were darker than most. Not as pink. The one with the computer spoke with a barely audible accent. The other two, I didn't hear speak at all. They were all of average weight and height, as far as I could tell."

"Nothing else distinguished them? Any scars? Tattoos? Maybe a limp?"

She thought on it. "The only real clue I tried to look for was on the pack of matches the leader removed from the bandola case. It was a dark matchbook with yellow and green lettering, but I couldn't make out the words."

I'd already done a bit of research on my BlackBerry while waiting for my flight at the airport. The bandola is a South American instrument, played primarily in Venezuela and Colombia. The blue dart frog whose venom the assailants claimed to have poisoned Emma with is also found in South America, in southern Suriname and the northern to central parts of Brazil. These could be two valuable clues. Or they could be attempts at misdirection, like the misspellings in the ransom note and the use of the word *obrigado*.

I wouldn't know until I knew.

Edgar ran a hand through his thinning hair. He was sweating despite the chilled air in the room. "What now, Simon? What do we do?"

I pointed toward the stairs, said, "Next thing I'd like to do is pay a visit to your daughter's room."

Chapter 10

Olivia's bedroom didn't look anything like the room I'd slept in as a teenager. That shouldn't have come as any surprise, yet somehow it did. The sheer size of her room gave me pause. It was larger than the studio apartment I currently kept in D.C. The room boasted a huge walk-in closet. Beneath our feet was another hardwood floor; above our heads, a vaulted ceiling with a decorative ceiling fan. As opposed to the traditional style found in the rest of the house, Olivia's room was ultramodern, every piece of furniture bathed in a light pink with the occasional sprinkle of silver. The walls and bedding were bright white, almost blinding with the waning sunlight bleeding through the blinds on the massive windows.

I scanned the hardwood floor for blood or scuff marks but it seemed immaculate. The sheets were clearly kicked around but didn't necessarily show signs of a struggle.

On one of the nightstands next to her bed was an eight-by-ten-inch framed photograph of Olivia standing between her mother and father on the red carpet in front of the old Grauman's Chinese Theatre. Olivia appeared older than her fifteen years in the way that daughters of the Hollywood elite often do. Her long, silky brown hair cascaded like a waterfall across her bare shoulders. Her eyes were a crystal clear blue that you'd think existed only in paintings. Her slender body hadn't fully developed, yet she posed in a way that told anyone viewing the photo, *Don't you dare think of me as a child.*

But she *was* a child. A child in danger. A child who needed to be found at any cost.

"Don't take these questions the wrong way," I said, "but does Olivia use any illegal drugs?"

"I'm sure she smoked pot," Emma said. "We've joked about it. But nothing harder, to my knowledge."

"I think she may have tried LSD," Edgar said.

"What makes you say that?" I asked.

"She watched my Blu-ray of *Fear and Loathing in Las Vegas* recently, and she was laughing for two days straight."

"Any prescription drugs?"

Emma shook her head. "She'd been taking the antidepressant Paxil for several months, but she stopped that not long ago."

"Why did she stop the Paxil?"

"I think so that she could drink alcohol."

"She drinks often?"

"No, not often. Just at parties, and I'm sure she drank while she was away."

"Had Olivia been on any trips recently?"

"Just one, a couple months back. She and a few of her female friends flew to the Caribbean."

"Which islands?"

"The Cayman Islands."

"Where did they stay?"

Edgar said, "The Ritz-Carlton on Seven Mile Beach in Grand Cayman."

"Anything unordinary happen during the trip?"

"Not that we know of," Emma said. "She came home thrilled, said she had the time of her life."

"How about between then and now? She make any long-distance phone calls or talk about anyone she met while she was abroad?"

"No," Emma said. "She didn't mention any boys, if that's what you mean."

"She stopped taking the Paxil before or after the trip?"

"After, I believe. Maybe just before, I'm not sure. But the doctor I spoke to—her pediatrician, actually—told me that her stopping the Paxil abruptly is probably what was causing the afternoon sluggishness and occasional nausea."

"Any vomiting? Maybe an eating disorder?"

"No, I don't think so. Just the nausea. It would come and go."

"Did she lose any weight?"

"No," Emma said. "If anything, she gained a pound or two since the trip."

Edgar added, "Of course, she'd been starving herself before the trip to look good in her swimsuits."

"Did Olivia keep a photo album of the trip?"

"No," Emma said. "Her camera's digital, one of those tiny Nikon COOLPIX that Ashton Kutcher pitches. The photos she doesn't like she deletes, the others she posts on Facebook."

If Kati came through, I'd have access to those by tonight.

"Mind putting together a list of her friends, Emma?"

"Not at all."

"Star the names of the girls she went to Grand Cayman with, please. And any addresses and phone numbers would be helpful."

"Of course."

Emma grabbed a pen from her daughter's desk and stepped into the hallway, heading in the direction of the stairs.

Edgar turned to me. "I'm trying to remain strong for her, Simon, but I have to tell you, I'm absolutely petrified. What if we never get Olivia back?"

I could tell Edgar what that felt like. I could describe for him in great detail the way an ordinary mind began to perceive everything around it quite differently. How paranoia became a constant state. I could tell him he'd never experience another truly happy day from now until the end of his existence, how it would simply be impossible because that part of the brain responsible for happiness had been irreparably damaged, if not utterly destroyed, the moment his daughter was stolen from this house.

"Right now, Edgar, we have to focus entirely on getting her back. It does none of us any good to even consider the other way around. We have a window now, and that window is constantly shrinking. Whatever measures we take, they begin as soon as Emma returns to this room with my list."

"But the ransom demand—"

"Until you receive word from the kidnappers, there isn't anything we can do on that end. But that doesn't mean we have the luxury of sitting around and doing nothing to find your daughter until we hear from them."

"All right, Simon. Tell me, what do we do next?"

On the second floor of the house, one floor below us, a telephone began ringing.

"That's in my den," Edgar said, moving toward the door.

I followed him down the stairs and into a room filled with Hollywood memorabilia. Costumes, awards, weapons, autographed pictures all vied for the eye's attention, but just now it was our ears that were leading the charge.

"Restricted," Edgar said, pointing to the caller ID. He lifted the receiver and held it between our heads so that I could hear. "This is Edgar Trenton," he said.

"Are you alone?" The voice was synthesized, just as you'd expect to hear in a Hollywood movie.

Edgar looked in the doorway, where Emma stood trembling. "My wife is here."

"No law enforcement?"

The voice of the man on the other end didn't sound as though he were surprised to hear that Emma was alive. They'd never meant to kill her.

"No law," Edgar said. "Tell me what I need to do to get my daughter back alive and unharmed."

"Do you have a pen and paper?"

Edgar tossed aside some folders on his desk and found a Sharpie.

He uncapped the marker and tested it on one of the folders. "I do," he said. "I have a pen and paper ready."

"Listen carefully," the voice said. "Take down every word I say. As I explained in the letter, if you fail to comply exactly, I will mail you your daughter's head in a plain brown box. Is that understood?"

Edgar's face lost what little color it had. His right hand began shaking and he had to plant the left on his desk to steady himself. He looked as though he might collapse.

In the seconds that followed, there was complete silence.

Then somehow Edgar Trenton finally gathered himself and managed a stammering yes.

Chapter 11

We had only forty-six minutes.

Edgar's bank apparently remained open till 7 P.M. "There's a new look to bankers' hours," he explained as we hurried up the hill toward his neighbor's drive. "With deregulation, you get increased competition among financial institutions. Banks are competing with brokerage houses and credit unions. They're treating their businesses more like retail operations than professional services groups. 'Open late' is just the newest hook."

Edgar finally ceased his nervous rambling. His eyes were hooded and I could tell he was tired. Soon as he received Emma's call, he'd taken a private jet home from Berlin. Even if he'd slept on the plane, there was little doubt he was jet-lagged.

Over the Pacific, the sun was dropping from the sky, leaving us in an eerie dusk as we approached his neighbor's gate. Edgar rang the bell impatiently, propping himself up against a stone pillar.

The intercom squawked to life. "Ed, is that you?"

Edgar looked into the camera. "Yeah, Freddy, I need a favor."

There's that damn word again.

"Sure, Ed. What do you need?"

"I need to borrow your Ducati."

Freddy hesitated. "Are you serious?"

"As an aneurysm. Look, Freddy, it's my friend who'll be driving it.

There's no time to explain. If anything were to happen, you know I'm good for it."

"Of course, Ed. It's just a matter of liability."

"*Damn it,* Freddy, this is urgent."

"Does your friend have a motorcycle license?"

"I do," I said.

There was a long pause. "All right. Wait there, I'll bring it to the gate."

"We're in a hurry," Edgar said.

A few minutes later I followed Edgar's black Ford Escape down Prado de las Flores on Freddy's silver Ducati. Last time I drove a motorcycle was roughly a year ago, heading east on the autobahn out of Berlin. The sound of the engine made me think of this beautiful woman, Ana, a lawyer from Warsaw whom I deeply cared about but would probably never see again.

Life, it's full of unfairness.

I passed the Escape as soon as we merged onto the Ventura Freeway. I had to make it to West Hollywood well before Edgar in order to get into position. The kidnappers wanted Edgar to reach Wells Fargo just before it closed, so that there would be fewer people inside. They chose a branch in West Hollywood because of the darkness and chaos outside. That was where the kidnappers would be driving around with Olivia, ready to release her upon completion of the final wire transfer.

Or so they said.

The kidnappers wanted $8.5 million wired equally into four Cayman accounts. Because of Olivia's trip, Edgar's brows had risen when he heard "Cayman," but that was probably no more than coincidence. All criminals banked in the Cayman Islands. Some legit people too, I assumed.

"I need to know my daughter's alive," Edgar had barked into the phone after jotting down the instructions with a black Sharpie. "Let me speak to her."

"I will do better," the synthesized voice said calmly. "I will let you see her."

"When? How?"

"When you step inside the bank, go straight to the front window and look outside. My man will be driving a black Dodge Charger west on Sunset Boulevard. Your daughter will be in the backseat, directly behind the driver so that you can see her. Come alone. We will be conducting countersurveillance. If anyone is watching you, we will kill her."

The plan was for me to park inside an underground garage, just hidden from the street. When I received word that the Charger was coming, I'd start up the ramp and fall in line a few cars behind them. The Ducati would provide me enough flexibility so that I wouldn't lose the Charger, even if it took an abrupt turn off Sunset.

"I'm walking up the block now." Edgar's voice came through crystal clear on my earpiece. "Traffic going west on Sunset is flowing steadily. The Charger will have room to maneuver, so be sure to stay on top of them."

"Copy."

I was parked on the ramp and ready. From the breathlessness in his voice, I could tell Edgar was moving much faster than he was used to. My watch confirmed that he still had six minutes before the bank locked its doors.

"I'm about to enter the bank," Edgar said into his Bluetooth.

"Copy." I revved the engine on the Ducati, steeled myself.

"I'm turning toward the front window."

My stomach burned.

My teeth grinded inside my helmet.

My right arm needed steadying.

"And there they are, Simon."

The Ducati took off like a bolt. At the top of the ramp, I caught air and landed hard, made a sharp right west onto Sunset, and scanned the traffic for the Charger's distinctive taillights.

There you are, you bastard.

Edgar had insisted on going forward with the transactions, which—thanks to numerous flops and various bad investments—would virtually wipe him out. I couldn't argue. If somehow I lost the Charger and couldn't get Olivia back to him and Emma, I wouldn't be able to live with myself.

Hell, I could barely live with myself as it was.

I remained four cars behind the Charger, which wasn't making any unusual moves. I could see the back of Olivia's head, directly behind the driver. I couldn't see her arms but I assumed they were bound.

"The first transaction's completed," Edgar said five minutes later. "We're beginning the second."

Sunset went on forever. Traffic moved at about thirty miles per hour. The kidnappers had vowed to drop Olivia off on the boulevard wherever they were when they received confirmation of the final transaction.

"How do I know you'll let her go?" Edgar had demanded.

"What would I want her for?" the synthesized voice said. "I know you cannot pay any more."

Those words were enough to convince Edgar but not me. Something about the entire situation felt wrong. Why choose Edgar Trenton as your mark in the first place? There were plenty of Hollywood heavyweights up in those hills with much younger daughters, little girls who would be much easier to control.

"The second transaction is complete. We're beginning the third now."

"Copy."

There were other things about the Trentons' story that troubled me. Whatever had happened later, Emma *should* know whether she'd fired the gun. And why did the intruders bother with Olivia's computer, iPad, and iPhone, when the pot they were after was so much larger? The jewelry and the thirty grand in cash, too—these were things that could potentially be traced. A job of this magnitude, it was typically all or nothing. Why fret over the small stuff? Why take on any unnecessary risk?

"The third transaction is complete. We're beginning the fourth and final transfer, Simon."

"Copy."

And why the elaborate show for Emma Trenton? They didn't get anything from her, nor did they attempt to. All they really did was provide her with information.

Or misinformation.

We'd passed through Beverly Hills and Bel Air and were about to enter Brentwood when suddenly the black Dodge Charger made a razor-sharp right off Sunset and headed for the 405.

"Edgar," I shouted. "They're taking off. Stop the final transaction."

Last thing I heard was Edgar crying out, saying something about it being too late, and please, Simon, don't lose them.

Then reception cut out, and I accelerated, taking the Ducati upwards of ninety as I hit the San Diego Freeway heading north.

Chapter 12

The headlight on the Ducati cut through the darkness as I kept my eyes fixed on the Charger's taillights. The Charger weaved through the light traffic, making full use of the broad freeway, momentarily riding a Volvo's back fender before slicing onto the right shoulder and passing. The driver crossed three lanes in a shot, then accelerated to speeds well over one hundred. The Ducati had enough power to keep me on his tail, but only in a James Bond film can a chase like this end well. I needed to involve the LAPD as soon as possible, but there was no way to reach for my phone and remain vertical. I stole glances into the autos I passed, hoping to spot someone punching in 911, but there was no way to tell. Drivers who held up their smartphones had probably just tapped the record button so that they could upload the video to YouTube when they arrived home.

I'd memorized the Charger's Arizona license plate, but a hell of a lot of good it would do if I lost the Charger itself. No doubt the car was stolen, certainly the plates. With the eight and a half million safely in these kidnappers' Cayman accounts, Edgar and Emma Trenton would have no hope of ever seeing their daughter, Olivia, again.

From the far left lane, the Charger shot across the freeway toward the Skirball Center Drive exit. A beige SUV banked to the right to avoid the Charger and ran up against the right guardrail, throwing up a shower of sparks. I zigzagged through a half dozen vehicles, but I'd been far enough behind the Charger to catch the off-ramp without causing any major collisions.

With no cars in front of it, the Charger picked up speed. We had a length of open road to light it up, but it wouldn't last. Any moment now, we'd hit a fork, with either path leading straight to the treacherous Mulholland Drive.

The Charger bore left at the fork and busted a wide U onto Mulholland, causing a minivan to screech to a stop at a green while its pissed-off soccer mom leaned on her horn. As I passed her, I made the gesture for her to get on the phone, but she mistook it for the finger and flipped me the bird right back.

Here Mulholland was a two-way, two-lane road with a forty-mile-per-hour speed limit, meaning, unlike on the wide 405, there was literally no room for error. Once we crossed over the freeway, old-fashioned telephone poles stood sentinel on either side and the speed limit dropped to twenty-five. We were doing well over ninety.

The road bent hard to the right, and a sign warned of an upcoming traffic light. The light was red but we both blew through it. Mulholland then curved to the left and we stormed past a private high school.

I ached to attempt a pass, but visibility around these curves was zero, and there were too many spots where the Charger could hop off Mulholland. The son of a bitch had picked a hell of a road for a chase.

In the backseat, the girl turned 180 degrees and chanced a look back at me. I thought I could see her scream, but that was probably my imagination.

As we flew past a Presbyterian church, I strained to listen for the sounds of police sirens over the roar of the Ducati's engine.

Despite Mulholland's terrifying twists and turns, the driver of the Charger continued to accelerate. After a short while I decided I had no choice but to try to pass him, slow him down, force him into a decision of fight or flight before he killed himself and Olivia.

He was probably armed. If I could get him to take a shot at me, he'd have to divide his attention between the Ducati and the road.

On the right, a surreal view of Los Angeles blew by us. We were now high above the city, careening past deadly drop-offs. I needed to wait until the road was covered on the right by trees. If I made my move too soon, the Charger would inevitably soar off a cliff.

Although a sign indicated a sharp left turn ahead, the Charger didn't slow.

Something the size of a fist formed in my throat as I glimpsed the glow of a pair of oncoming headlights rounding the curve just ahead of us.

I pulled back on the bike and braced myself as the Ducati fell into a slide. My eyes remained glued to the Charger as its tires tried to lock but spun helplessly along the gravel.

The oncoming vehicle was a monster, a yellow Hummer that had no place on Mulholland at night. I yanked my head aside just in time to miss the rear wheel as it threw gravel up against my face-plate.

I released the bike and hit the blacktop hard and rolled, cutting up every part of my body, hoping only to spare myself broken bones.

The Charger glided through the green-brown brush toward the cliff.

I heard a young woman's scream.

I may have screamed myself.

Then my body came to a jarring halt at the side of the road, and the Charger took flight, turning end over end as it plunged down the side of the mountain.

Chapter 13

The sound of the crash hit my ears almost instantaneously and I knew the Charger had come into contact with something—a thick tree, maybe a boulder—that prevented its free fall down the mountain.

I ripped off my helmet. Ignoring the pain coursing through the lower half of my body, I leapt to my feet and hobbled on a badly strained ankle through the brush toward the edge.

I could finally hear sirens but they were far off. I looked down the mountain. The Charger hadn't fallen all that far, its momentum stopped by a large brown rock, but the engine was on fire, the flames clawing their way toward the gas tank. The tank would probably explode before the first responders reached us. There was nothing to do but to try to pull Olivia from the wreckage before the blast.

If the blast took me with it, so be it. At least I'd have tried.

I took a step back, leapt over the side of the cliff, throwing my feet out in front of me to slow my fall. I skidded a bit faster than I would have liked, my left leg burning as it slid down the rock, but before I could bitch about it, I found myself at the rear bumper of the fiery Charger.

The fierce heat did its damndest to keep me away.

With my right arm shielding my face, I pushed myself to my feet and went around the rear toward the driver's side, trying to catch a glimpse of Olivia, but I couldn't see her.

I did see blood. Lots of it. And when I reached the side of the vehicle, I found the driver crawling out the open door. I grabbed him by the back of his jacket as he wailed, and tossed his body aside like a luggage-thrower on the tarmac at Reagan National. I dropped painfully to my knees and dug to find the lever to push the front seat forward. My fingers brushed against a broken bottle, then slid through a warm liquid.

Got it.

The front seat flew forward. As I kicked my heels into the dirt to stand, a female form fell out of the backseat and into my arms.

I lifted the body so I could look at her.

There was nothing left of her face but a scarlet mask of muscle and skull. The body itself was broken, the bones in her arms, in her neck, in every spot I touched, were pulverized, utterly shattered.

As the sirens neared, my chest flooded with a deep hatred for those with such a naked disregard for human life.

I pressed my fingers against Olivia's limp neck to seek a pulse but it was futile. Inundated with grief, I felt for Olivia as though she were my own daughter.

When the flames began to lick at my face, I stepped back, wanting to roar, the rage in me hot enough to melt the polar icecaps.

But I still had a clock to beat. The LAPD were closing in, and if this driver was still alive, I needed to talk to him. How else would I be able to find and kill every last bastard involved in this?

Choking on the thick black smoke, I set Olivia's body down and turned to look for the spot where I'd tossed the driver. He was alive and conscious but he hadn't gone far. I stepped toward him.

The driver lay on his stomach, inching his way up the mountain like a slug.

I dropped to one knee, rolled him over, and shouted over the noise, "What's your *name*?"

Blood dripped from his forehead down his face, but I could see enough to know that he was a good-looking kid. Or at least he had been ten minutes ago.

"Help me," he pleaded.

Perfect English. Well, as perfect as it can be with windshield glass lodged in your jaw.

I repeated, "What's your *name*?"

"P-please," he managed.

Roughly, I went into his back pocket and found a wallet. I opened it, pulled out a California driver's license. With my eyes tearing and stinging from the intense heat, I could just make out the information: Jason Gutiérrez of Ellenwood Drive, Los Angeles.

Twenty-four years old. From the looks of him, he wasn't going to see twenty-five.

"Who do you *work* for?" I said as I replaced the license.

"P-please," he muttered. "Pray with me."

I pulled another card from his wallet: Member, Screen Actors Guild. Hadn't even expired yet.

The sirens were coming up Mulholland.

"*Who* kidnapped the girl?" I shouted.

"Wha—? What girl?"

I replaced the SAG card, found a California registration for the Dodge Charger. The car was registered under his name.

"The young lady in the backseat of your car," I said, barely hanging on to my last shred of patience. "*Who* kidnapped her?"

"She was—" He choked on the blood in his throat. "She wasn't kidnapped, she's my girlfriend."

My eyes widened as I pulled a picture from the kid's wallet. "Olivia was your *girlfriend*?"

Through the smoke, I stared at the picture hard, tried to reconcile the face in the photo with the face I'd seen in countless pictures hanging in the Trentons' home.

"No Olivia," he mumbled. "Jennifer."

He was telling the truth. The picture was of Jason and some other Caucasian girl. A beautiful brunette like Olivia, same perfect cheekbones, same thin body frame, but several years older.

"Christ," I said.

"They . . . hired us."

"They?" I searched his eyes. "Who's *they*?"

"I don't . . . Someone on the Internet . . . He hired us. . . ."

"Us? Who's *us*?"

"Me and . . . Jennifer."

"Hired you and Jennifer to do *what*?"

Blood spilled over his lip, down his chin, and he looked away.

"Hired you to *do what*?" I repeated.

"Dri . . ."

I lifted his head in my hands, placed my ear as close to his mouth as I dared.

"Drive," he whispered.

I looked in his eyes again. "Are you saying that's Jennifer back there by the car?"

Tears streamed down his face, cutting through the dirt and the blood. "Yes . . . My girl . . . Jennifer . . ." He was hyperventilating. "Is she—?"

"She's dead," I said. "Whose plates are those?"

Trembling, he said, "They gave me . . . Left them . . . My mailbox . . ."

"What were your instructions?"

Jason started to fade. I lifted the lids of his eyes with my fingers, repeated the question.

The sirens were closing in.

"Drive . . . Slowly past Wells Fargo on Sunset . . . There will be . . . Be a man in the window. Make sure he sees you. . . ."

The red and blue lights of the patrol cars lit the sky above our heads as a helicopter approached fast from the south.

His voice became a low growl. "They said, if anyone follows you . . . *Drive* . . . Do whatever it takes, don't let them catch you or you won't get the second half of your money. . . ."

A spotlight hit me full in the face. I threw up my arm to shield my eyes.

"Please," he said, crimson bubbles forming atop his lips, popping, spilling scarlet down his neck. "Pray with me to God for—" He swallowed, coughed, spit up more blood. "—for forgiveness."

I took his hand in mine. "God's not here," I said softly. "Only me." With my other hand, I lifted his head so that he could look me in the eyes. "And no matter whose daughter that girl was, I can't forgive you for this."

His body jerked.

He was going into shock.

His mouth was moving but no words were making it through his lips, only blood.

A pair of cops started down the cliff.

"I just want . . ."

I waited.

"Wanted to act," he managed. "Just wanted . . . a role."

"Well, now you've got one," I said as the helicopter shone its searchlight on us, and the last glimmer of life left Jason's eyes for good. "Now you get to play dead, kid."

I lowered the lids of his eyes and stood just as the first of the uniformed officers reached our position.

Chapter 14

Evidently the soccer mom who flipped me the bird hadn't dialed 911 after all, because the LAPD bought my story that I'd been enjoying a leisurely ride along Mulholland when I saw the Charger ahead of me driving erratically then go off the cliff. It didn't hurt that Jason had a half-full bottle of Wild Turkey stashed under the front seat.

The yellow Hummer hadn't stuck around.

The Ducati was totaled.

Sorry, Freddy. Life, it's full of unfairness.

I checked my BlackBerry for reception and was surprised to find it was strong up here. I wanted to call Edgar before he saw this bloodbath on the news. So I excused myself and began limping away from the cops. As I did, I overheard one of them say that they hadn't yet been able to reach Jason Gutiérrez's next of kin, because there was no one at his home. His neighbor told police he lived alone; his mother lived somewhere just outside San Diego.

"Simon," Edgar answered his cell, "tell me you have Olivia."

"It wasn't her in the Dodge Charger, Edgar."

"But I *saw* her, Simon."

"It was a ruse."

"A ruse? *Why?* What would they have to gain by that? They know I have no more money."

Edgar was right. It wasn't clear what they had to gain, unless they thought Edgar wouldn't actually go through with the wire transfers. But then, if Edgar didn't make the transactions now, he never would, so to what end were they keeping Olivia?

Of course, it could be that a mistake was made. That Olivia had struggled or tried to escape. Or that one of the kidnappers had gotten too rough with her, and now she was dead.

Or it could have been that obtaining the money wasn't their primary objective, and that the entire ransom demand was nothing but strategy, a way of buying time to get Olivia out of the country.

But why?

I thought of the Lindsay Sorkin case in Europe last year and I shivered. I couldn't become involved in another nightmare like that.

But then, what choice did I have now? I was *already* in, neck deep.

On the other end of the line, Edgar was crying. "Does this mean she's gone, Simon? Tell me the truth. Does this mean my daughter's dead?"

"Not by a long shot, Edgar." I inhaled deeply, struggled to maintain my voice. "I'm at the scene of an accident right now. The kidnappers hired the driver of the Charger and his girlfriend to drive past Wells Fargo while you were in the window. Then they were supposed to hop on the 405 and lose anyone who might be following. They made the mistake of jumping onto Mulholland and accidentally went off a cliff. Both the driver and his girlfriend, Jennifer, are dead. But before Jason died, I was able to extract some information from him. His computer may hold the key to discovering who it was who hired him. I need to get to his house, and fast."

"Of course, Simon. Where does he live?"

"Eagle Rock. It's a town next to Glendale."

"I'll have Nicholas pick you up. Where are you on Mulholland?"

"Just have him follow the flashing lights." I looked back at the cops, standing around, cracking jokes about drunk drivers. "Oh, and don't send the limousine, Edgar. I want to remain inconspicuous."

"Understood."

Soon as I hung up with Edgar, I saw that I had a missed call from Kati. She never left messages, so I called her back.

"Hey, Finder."

"What have you got for me, Breaker?"

"All doors are wide open."

"That quickly?"

"A fifteen-year-old girl? Come on, Simon. All her passwords are the same."

"What is it?"

"*E-A-R-F-A-L-1.*"

I sounded it out in my head. "What the hell is that supposed to mean?"

Kati's infant, Lacey, was screaming her head off in the background.

"I don't know, maybe nothing. Maybe it's a misspelling of the word 'earful,' as in she gets an earful from her parents when she misses curfew."

"Maybe."

"Are you all right, Finder? You sound—"

"I'll be fine."

I heard a *ping* in the background on Kati's end.

"You won't believe this."

"Try me," I said.

"I just received an instant message inviting me for a session of cybersex."

"No kidding."

"No kidding," she said. "And get this—it's from Sherlock's ancient AOL account, LawDawg72."

"Probably he wants you to know it's him."

"No, Sherlock doesn't know I know this handle. I hacked into his PC when we first started dating." She sighed. "He's testing me, trying to prove I'm cyber-cheating."

"You're trouble, Breaker."

Ping.

"Gotta go, Finder. Sherlock just asked me if I've ever taken part in a threesome."

"So?"

"So, let's just say I have. But he wasn't involved."

"Oh. Well, good luck with that."

As I stuffed the BlackBerry back into my pocket, I watched the horizontal bodies of Jason and Jennifer rise up the hill toward the waiting ambulance, sheets covering each of them from head to toe.

Had I really only arrived in Los Angeles hours ago?

If so, how many bodies would be draped in white sheets before all this was over?

My mind drifted back to the Lindsay Sorkin case, and my time in Poland and Ukraine last year. It caused me to shiver.

From the corner of my eye, I caught a vehicle rounding the bend. The goddamn thing looked like a futuristic bumblebee on wheels.

One of the cops stepped into the middle of the road and held out a hand, causing the vehicle to stop. The cop went around to the driver's side, and the driver lowered his window.

After a moment, the cop turned his head left and right, apparently searching for someone.

"Christ," I said when his eyes finally locked on me.

The cop motioned me over. As I approached, the cop said with a smirk, "Mr. Fisk, your, ah, ride is here."

"Christ," I said again as I went around to the passenger side.

I opened the door and settled into the softest gray leather on the planet.

"What the hell is this?" I said to Nicholas.

"It's a Bugatti Veyron, sir," Nicholas said, straight-faced. "Mr. Trenton paid more than three million dollars for it."

"Christ," I said a third time.

So much for remaining inconspicuous.

Chapter 15

Jason Gutiérrez lived in a small blue ranch home on Ellenwood Drive in Eagle Rock. The houses on the block were dark but I could see neighbors peeping out their windows as the three-million-dollar Veyron cruised by.

"Drop me at the end of the block and disappear," I told Nicholas.

"When shall I pick you up?"

"Never."

I stepped out of the Veyron and waited till it rolled away to start my walk. The area behind the row of houses was pitch black, a wooded mess directly behind them. I skirted the edge of the trees, counting the houses as I moved. Jason's would be the eighth one in from the end of the block.

The rear of Jason Gutiérrez's house was as dark as the front, a high silver fence keeping trespassers out. Making as little noise as possible, I climbed the fence and dropped down on the other side, my right ankle politely reminding me that I'd already been in a fairly awful motorcycle accident tonight.

I waited for the pain to abate, then looked up, pleased by my spot of luck. The sliding glass door was slid open, leaving nothing but a screen door between me and the interior of Jason's house.

As soon as I started for the door, however, a series of menacing barks broke the silence, and I broke into a run. From the sound of its bark, the beast was either a Rottweiler or a dinosaur, but I wasn't sticking around to find out. I made for the screen door as fast as my strained ankle allowed me.

From the corner of my left eye, I caught the monster rounding the edge of the house and I lowered my head and pushed myself harder, convinced that the damage of the beast's bite would be far worse than a snapped ankle.

No time to play with the handle, I flung myself toward the screen and tore it right off its frame. Quick as I could, I leapt back to my feet and slid the sliding glass door into place. The Rottweiler ran full-force into the door and squealed.

"Sorry, pup," I said.

I was sure the Rottweiler would continue barking and biting at the glass now slick with saliva. But the dog simply picked itself up, whimpered, and walked away, its head down as though it were embarrassed.

I knew the feeling.

I turned and looked down at the stained carpet and decrepit couch. Jason Gutiérrez had been a starving artist and I couldn't help but feel for him. Takes a hell of a lot of guts to pursue a life you'll love at the expense of things like food and clothes and health insurance. In the six years Tasha and I watched Hailey grow up, we'd vowed to support our daughter in whatever she wanted to do in life.

Tasha's parents had money—so had my father—and the three of them were miserable wretches all their lives. Not that there weren't musicians and actors and poets just as foul. But I figure, even if you're going to walk through life with a heart hard as stone, you may as well sing some songs, put on a play, maybe recite a poem or two.

The ranch was a single floor with two bedrooms, only one of which couldn't pass for a closet. The larger was Jason's room. In it was a double bed with sheets older than me and a small desk that was propped up on one side by yellowed and tattered screenplays. Atop the desk sat a laptop that had probably lived through the Y2K scare.

I opened the laptop and turned on the power, waited forever as the old boy tried to boot. I'd half expected a telephone modem and was relieved to find the computer was already online. I pulled down Jason's browser history and scrolled through the dozen Web addresses, nine of which led to amateur porn sites.

One address brought me to Lycos, which was apparently Jason's search engine and e-mail network of choice. His e-mail address was already entered and his password was represented by eight black dots, meaning Kati's services wouldn't be necessary. I logged right in.

Jason had a couple hundred e-mails floating around his in-box. Fortunately, most were from Jennifer Channing, presumably the girl who died in his backseat tonight.

As I scrolled through the e-mails, one subject line immediately grabbed my attention. It was a reply to an ad on Craigslist.

I opened it. The sender's Yahoo e-mail address appeared to consist of nine random numbers; I jotted them down but didn't expect to learn anything from the free account. The body of the message was simple.

In need of your services for one night. Call (310) 555-5105.

I took down the number and reached across the desk for Jason's landline. Was it possible that the kidnappers were still in the dark about what had happened this evening? Would they actually take Jason's call? I lifted the receiver. Heard a dial tone. Good, Jason had at least been paying his phone bills.

I dialed the number.

"The subscriber you have called is not able to receive calls at this time."

"All right, then." I replaced the receiver and entered the number into my BlackBerry so that I could try again later. I still had a bit of a job to do at Jason's computer.

I pulled up Facebook, typed in Olivia's e-mail address, then her password, "EARFAL1."

"In," I said aloud. "You're brilliant, Kati."

Breaking into someone's Facebook account for the first time is like arriving at a new amusement park. You don't know where to go first. I was tempted to go through her photos, but in my experience, a picture wasn't always worth a thousand words. So I began at the top of her Timeline.

It became clear right away that even her best friends didn't yet suspect she was gone. The list of Olivia's gal pals was still fresh in my head.

There was Bethany, who'd posted on Olivia's Timeline this morning: *We need 2 go shoppingggg. Retail therapy.* ☺

Then there was Lola: *Wanna go to the GYM this after noon. C'mon girl its been awhile. Maybe we'll see U-no-Who.*

Alysia wrote: *Don't freek but I made the appt. I love love love love love love love you.*

Made the appointment for what?

Patience is not one of my strong points, and I already felt the itch of frustration in my gut. Without context, everything here was cryptic. And every hour that ticked by decreased my odds of ever finding Olivia alive.

I clicked on the section marked "Photos," went straight for the album titled "Cayman Va-cay."

Damn. There were hundreds of pictures. If I studied each one, I'd be here till dawn.

I started scrolling through them. Olivia and the three other girls—Alysia, Bethany, and Lola—on Seven Mile Beach in bikinis; dressed to the nines at nightclubs they were probably too young to get into; poolside with cocktails; sitting down to dinner at five-star restaurants; posing with an iguana the size of one of my arms.

As I was looking through the photos, Olivia began feeling real to me, like someone I'd known for years. Different from when I looked through a few of the photos Emma had given me. Gazing at all these pictures, this was almost like seeing her and her friends in real time. The bats were already going to work on my gut.

Finally, a few pictures with boys.

Now we're getting somewhere.

The trip had taken place a couple months back and the photos were uploaded in chronological order. I suspected each girl had brought her own camera, but right now there was no way to know.

In most of these photos, Lola was paired with a handsome dark-skinned boy who may have been a native to the island. Alysia was with a blond-haired, blue-eyed boy who may well have been from California. And Bethany—well, it all depended upon the hour and the night. From the looks of it, Bethany had posed with every guy on the island who looked under the age of forty.

Olivia didn't appear to be with anyone. In every photo, she was smiling for the camera but alone. In a couple of the pictures, her eyes were fixed on something or someone just outside the frame.

Except at this one nightclub. Here it looked as though most of the photos had been cropped. Olivia was always situated on the right end. Someone was apparently standing next to her yet didn't make the final cut. Definitely a male. In one photo I could see a black shoe, in another a large shadow.

Then the kicker. A right arm. Either very tanned or brown to begin with, I couldn't tell. The arm was snaked around Olivia's thin waist and all I could see was the hand, the wrist, and very little of the forearm. On his wrist was what looked like an expensive gold Rolex, but for all I knew, it could've been a fake.

I continued scrolling. Noticed that the photos seemed to skip an entire day.

Interesting. I jotted down the date.

Ten minutes later, I noted the hour. Wondered if it was too late at night to pay a visit to Olivia's three *amigas*.

Chapter 16

Three dead ends. After returning to the Trentons' estate to shower and change clothes, I'd asked Edgar for permission to speak to Olivia's three best friends. I visited each of their houses just after dawn. Each set of parents insisted one of them be able to sit in on the questioning, which made the mission all but impossible.

Each of the girls claimed not to know anything about the boys depicted in the photos, not even their first names. They'd only spoken to them at the clubs; no one had spent the night with a member of the opposite sex the entire trip. None of the four girls were sexually active, of course. At least not in front of their parents.

As for the missing day—a Tuesday—Olivia had been ill, which was to say she'd been suffering a five-alarm hangover. The four girls had stayed in two rooms at the Grand Cayman Ritz-Carlton. Olivia bunked with Alysia, Lola with Bethany. But during those missing twenty-four hours, Alysia had crashed with Lola and Bethany because Olivia wanted to be left alone. The girls had dropped by Olivia's room to check on her several times that day, but Olivia didn't answer their knocks. However, Alysia *had* received text messages from Olivia throughout the day, informing her that Olivia was alive though still not feeling so well. The following morning, Olivia met her three friends for breakfast and the trip proceeded as planned.

The most I got out of any of them was that "U-no-Who" was a

personal trainer at the gym the girls went to and the purpose of the appointment Alysia had set up.

"We were going to get tongue rings," she told me. In the same breath she turned to her father and apologized.

Malibu, I decided, was a hell of a place to get answers from teenage girls. I'd much rather question kids in the slums.

Back at the Trentons' estate, while icing my strained ankle, I interviewed each of the servants whom Edgar had called in. Manny Villanueva seemed genuinely heartbroken, as did the maid, Karmela Garza. The driver, Nicholas Artenie, was angry with me for having lied to him about the purpose of my visit from the moment I stepped off the plane. The gardener, Raúl Corpas, and the chef, Luis Rivera— neither of whom spoke English—both asked for their attorneys, which didn't surprise me. They'd seen enough episodes of *Nancy Grace en español* to know that anyone in the United States can be vilified by a nasty cable news commentator without a shred of evidence pointing in their direction.

After the interviews, while Raúl and Luis stood outside, waiting for their attorneys, I sat down at the dining room table with a visibly tortured Edgar and Emma and discussed how best to move forward.

"At this point," I said, "we've got to involve the FBI and the LAPD. The kidnappers have all your money, so there's no possibility of working with them anymore. It seems clear now that they're not going to voluntarily give up your girl."

"But *why*?" Emma cried. "I don't underst—"

"I know. That's something I'm going to attempt to figure out. Because once we know the 'why,' it may well lead to the 'who' and the 'where.' And *that's* how we're going to get Olivia back."

"So, you're not leaving us," Edgar said.

"Of course not. Why would I? I've been working this for less than a day."

"I don't know. I just assumed that once the FBI got involved—"

"Don't get me wrong. I won't be working with the feds. That won't do anybody any good. They've already got the best and the brightest. They don't need me. They're going to attack this case from one angle, and I'm going to attack it from another."

"How much do you need to continue this investigation? Besides what we've given these bastards, Emma and I have a few hundred thousand socked away in a savings account."

"Look, Edgar, I'm not motivated by money. But I'm not allergic to it either. There may be a significant amount of travel involved, and airfare isn't cheap. Neither are hotels. I don't eat often and I don't eat fancy, but I do eat. And I drink a hell of a lot of coffee. I'll also need to rent transportation when I get to wherever I'm going." I leaned back in my chair. "Speaking of which, tell your neighbor Freddy I'm really sorry about the Ducati."

Edgar pushed away from the table and said, "Let me go get you a check, Simon."

That left me alone with Emma for the first time since I'd arrived in California.

I said, "Is there anything you left out that maybe you didn't want Edgar to hear? If so, tell me now. I promise to keep it in confidence."

"No," she said. "Of course not. What makes you—?"

"How is Edgar's relationship with his daughter?"

"Fine. I mean, he spends too much time at the studio, but that's nothing new. He has no more or less time for her now than he did the entire time she was growing up."

"How about your relationship with your husband?"

Emma hesitated.

I said, "Any infidelity on either side?"

She lowered her eyes to the table.

I said, "Edgar had mentioned a former babysitter of Olivia's, a Sofía who was ultimately deported after a long immigration battle. When I took a look at her file, I noticed that her face had been scratched out of a few of her pictures."

Emma looked up at me, trying to control a slight twitch in her lip. "That would be my handiwork."

"Anyone else?" I said. "Anyone more recently?"

She nodded. "Edgar's been sleeping with his assistant, Valerie, for at least the past six months."

"Does he know that you know?"

"I think so. Pretty much everyone knows. People who work in the movie industry generally aren't quiet types."

"Any talk of divorce?"

"Not yet."

"But you're considering it."

"Of course."

"Have you taken any actions in that regard?"

She said, "I've spoken with a lawyer."

"Did you pay the lawyer?"

"Yes, of course."

"By check?"

"No, with cash."

"What's the lawyer's name?"

"Ernie Byers in Beverly Hills. He's the best. He represents all the big agents and entertainment lawyers in their divorces." She added, "Or their husbands or wives, depending on who gets through his door first."

"Is there a prenuptial agreement in place?"

"No. Ernie said I'd be entitled to half. He didn't think Edgar would even contest it. California law is pretty clear."

I heard Edgar's footfalls as he started down the steps.

Quickly and quietly, I said, "When you fired the .38 at the assailants, did the recoil feel *any* different than it had when you fired the gun at the range?"

She bit down on her lower lip, which was already swollen. "I don't know. I hadn't really thought about it."

"Well, think about it," I said.

I pushed my chair away from the table and stood up just as Edgar stepped into the great room. He handed me a check and I stuffed it in my pocket without looking at it.

"You must be exhausted," Emma said to me. "You haven't slept. Would you care for some coffee, Simon?"

"Espresso, if you have it."

"Of course. I'll be right back."

I turned to Edgar. "Last night when we were in Olivia's room, we got interrupted by the phone call from the kidnappers. Would you mind if I had one last look around?"

"Not at all. Would you like me to come up with you?"

"No need, Edgar. Stay down here and rest. I'll call down if I have any questions."

Chapter 17

I slipped on a pair of latex gloves and stepped back into Olivia's colossal room. Her parents had already inventoried it, so I didn't need to spend much time going through her drawers. The only thing on the list that had surprised me was Olivia's U.S. passport.

"That's a good thing, right?" Edgar had said. "It means they don't intend to take her out of the country."

I wasn't so sure. Leaving Olivia's passport seemed to me like another attempt at misdirection.

I found Olivia's passport in her top desk drawer. I flipped through it, then stuffed it in my pocket. If I located Olivia in another country, she'd need her passport to come home with me.

Next I got down on my hands and knees and examined every inch of the hardwood floor. I then checked every inch of her walls, including the areas behind her furniture and framed posters and those inside her walk-in closet.

Nothing out of the ordinary.

Time to go.

As I stepped out of the room, I flipped the switch to extinguish the light but shut the ceiling fan off instead. I turned it back on, watched the blades slowly pick up speed again.

While I did, my eyes locked on the ceiling around the fan. The base of the fan seemed to be wobbling. Looked as though it could come crashing down at any moment. Whoever put that ceiling fan up there had done an awful job. But that didn't mesh with anything else about this house, except maybe the squeaky door downstairs.

I hate heights but I wanted to examine the base of the fan. So I moved the armoire just below it. I flipped the switch and waited until the fan stopped spinning; then I removed my shoes and socks and climbed on top of the armoire.

Two of the screws on one side of the fan were loose. I was able to unscrew them with my fingers. Carefully, I shifted the base in order to feel around inside, hoping I wouldn't electrocute myself. I felt around and felt only wires.

I was about to replace the base when I heard something shift inside it. Sounded like something metal. I reached my hand inside the base and pulled out what looked like a large diamond pendant. If it was real, it was worth a fortune.

I replaced the base and the armoire, then started the fan to make sure it was working.

Then I went downstairs and showed Edgar and Emma the pendant, asked if they recognized it. Neither of them did.

"Do you have a small hand mirror you don't mind me destroying?" I said.

Emma went to retrieve one.

"Where the hell did you find it?" Edgar said.

"It was hidden in the base of Olivia's ceiling fan. When Manny comes back to work, he'll need to screw the base in properly. It's dangerous as it is now. Could fall on someone."

Emma returned with the hand mirror. I set the mirror on the table and ran the diamond across its center.

The mirror split neatly in half.

"It's real," Emma said, puzzled. "Could this be what the intruders were looking for?"

I didn't think so. But it could well have had something to do with why their daughter was taken.

"If you don't mind, I'd like to borrow this," I said, holding up the pendant.

Edgar hesitated, but Emma stepped forward and said, "Of course. Anything that might help get Olivia back to us."

I placed the pendant in my pocket. Edgar's eyes followed it all the way.

"It's safe with me," I assured him.

He nodded and forced a smile, and I suspected he was thinking about his neighbor Freddy's Ducati.

Before he changed his mind, I said, "Would you have Nicholas bring the car around?"

"Certainly." Edgar pressed an intercom button and gave the order.

"The moment we pull away, I'd like you to call the FBI field office on Wilshire Boulevard." I recited the telephone number. "Tell them everything, leave nothing out."

I started for the front door, dragging my lone suitcase behind me.

"Don't you think you should be around when they arrive?" Emma asked. "They're bound to have questions for you."

"I don't doubt it," I said. "But over the past twenty hours, I failed to report a serious crime, I provided the LAPD with a false accident report, and I burglarized a dead man's home. I'm no use to you if I'm in custody."

I turned the handle and opened the front door, let the Los Angeles sunshine fully fall on my face for the first time since I'd arrived. This was the only part of L.A. County, it seemed, where the sun was never snuffed out by smog.

"Where are you heading to, then?" Emma said.

"I've got a flight leaving from LAX in less than an hour." I added, "Best to keep that bit of information to yourselves. When the feds first get here and find this wreck of a crime scene, they're not going to be too happy."

"We won't say a word," Emma assured me. "But where *are* you going?"

"I'm beginning where your daughter went two months ago and where your money went last night." I started down the steps past Raúl and Luis and watched Nicholas pull the car around the long circular drive.

Over my shoulder I told Emma, "I'm heading to the Cayman Islands."

Part Two

THE BANKERS OF GEORGE TOWN

Chapter 18

The moment my plane touched down at Owen Roberts International Airport in Grand Cayman, I turned on my BlackBerry and clicked on the browser. My thumb worked as fast as it could, first booking a return flight to the States for ten days from now, then reserving a room at the Grand Cayman Beach Suites. During the flight, the overweight businessman sitting next to me had explained that getting through customs could be a bitch here in the islands. I'd need to show proof of a hotel reservation and a return ticket. Thanks to a practiced thumb, by the time the plane emptied out, the problem had been solved.

At the airport I rented a black Jeep Wrangler with a GPS. It was only two hours later here than in L.A., and I wanted to get started right away, but I decided to check in at the Grand Cayman Beach Suites first to establish a base. The resort was located on Seven Mile Beach, just a shell's throw from the Ritz-Carlton.

I had only the one piece of luggage with a couple changes of clothes. I tossed the suitcase on the room's king-size bed, then hurried downstairs to the Tommy Bahama store I'd spotted on the way up. If you're going to run around a Caribbean island asking questions about a missing girl, it's best not to look as though you've just flown in from Washington, D.C.

I showered and dressed in a relaxed fashion befitting the island, then headed out on foot in the direction of the Ritz-Carlton. My first objective was to establish a time line, particularly for Olivia's missing day. It was possible, of course, that Olivia's abduction had absolutely nothing to do with her vacation in Grand Cayman. But in my years as a U.S. Marshal hunting down fugitives and then as a private investigator retrieving children from noncustodial parents abroad, I'd honed my instincts to a razor-sharp point. And for the past twenty-four hours, my gut had been telling me that this island held the clues that would ultimately lead me to Olivia and her kidnappers. I wasn't about to start second-guessing myself now that every second counted.

The last Ritz-Carlton I'd entered was in Berlin. It was about a year ago, when I'd been hired by an American couple, Vince and Lori Sorkin, to find their six-year-old daughter, Lindsay, who'd been stolen in the middle of the night from their hotel room in Paris. Early in the case, I tracked the kidnappers back to Germany, where I'd paid a visit to my old friend Kurt Ostermann, a private detective who aided me on a previous case that had all gone to hell. Years ago, we'd been searching for a twelve-year-old named Elise Huber, who'd been taken from the States by her estranged father. When we finally found the two, the girl became frightened and ran. We gave chase, and poor little Elise Huber ultimately darted into the street in front of a night bus and suffered critical injuries. Unbeknownst to me, the girl eventually died from those injuries, and I was wanted by German authorities. Before Ostermann knew what I was doing in Berlin, he'd summoned the police to his office. Once Ostermann changed his mind about turning me in, the Berlin Ritz-Carlton became our hideout—and the place where I'd suffer several years of missed guilt all in the span of a few hours.

Before taking on the Lindsay Sorkin case, it was my policy not to become involved in "stranger abductions," cases in which the kidnapper was not one of the child's biological parents. The reason was simple: I couldn't bear to relive the days following my own daughter's abduction. Since becoming involved in the Lindsay Sorkin investigation, I'd been seriously rethinking my policy concerning "stranger abductions." It wasn't that I felt the pain of Hailey's disappearance any less. On the contrary, since my involvement in the Sorkin investigation, I'd been experiencing the torment of Hailey's kidnapping even more. Because I'd been reminded of the pure evil that exists in this world, the selfishness and greed and indifference that permits individuals to justify in their own minds bringing harm to an innocent child.

As long as that wickedness exists, how could I pretend otherwise? How could I turn away other parents whose children may have fallen victim to such malevolence?

I'd come to the conclusion that I couldn't. Not without adding guilt to the overabundance of excruciating emotions that already plagued my every day.

I had convinced myself that I was taking on the Olivia Trenton case to return a favor to a studio executive who'd agreed not to film the agonizing story of my family's destruction. But as I stepped through the doors and into the lobby of the ultra-plush Grand Cayman Ritz-Carlton, I realized that the Lindsay Sorkin investigation that had started in Paris and ended in Minsk was just the beginning of what would become a new chapter in the life and career of Simon Fisk.

"May I help you, sir?" said the balding concierge.

"Yes, I'd like to speak to the person in charge of security at the resort."

"Your name?"

"Patrick Bateman."

"One moment." The concierge picked up the phone, punched a button, and spoke quietly into the receiver. When he hung up, he said, "Please have a seat in the lobby, Mr. Bateman. Someone will be down to speak with you in a few moments."

As I moved toward one of the sofas, I scanned the front desk, which was bustling with guests. There were at least three young people working the desk, two of them male. I made a mental note to have a talk with them. Given the comeliness of the four California girls who'd stayed here two months back, I had a feeling these young men would remember them.

I took a seat and pulled out my BlackBerry, opened the browser again. I typed in "breaking news" and clicked on the link to CNN .com. The first headline read:

TEENAGE GIRL ABDUCTED DURING VIOLENT
HOLLYWOOD HOME INVASION

I didn't need to read any further. The news had broken, which meant the Trentons had phoned the authorities, and the FBI was on the scene. The thought brought me some measure of relief, yet Edgar Trenton's words continued to claw at me: *We only met because I've read your story. I know it inside and out. And though it pains me to ask, Simon, what exactly did the feds achieve for* you *when Hailey was snatched from* your *house?*

He was right, of course. If we rested Olivia's fate solely in the hands of the Federal Bureau of Investigation, we'd do so at her peril.

"Mr. Bateman?"

I looked up, although even with me sitting, the man standing in front of me was at eye level.

He held out his hand, said, "Thomas Mylonas, director of security."

Mylonas stood no taller than five feet two inches. He was bald except for prematurely gray peach fuzz that stopped a few fingers above the ears. His eyebrows, however, were bushy and black. His white button-down shirt seemed painted on. Mylonas was a guy who spent plenty of time at the gym and wanted to make sure everyone who looked at him knew it.

"What can I help you with, Mr. Bateman?"

Mylonas seemed like the type of guy who'd get off taking part in a life-and-death investigation, so I decided to play it straight.

"I don't know if you've been watching the news over the past couple hours, but a fifteen-year-old girl was snatched from her home in L.A. the night before last. Her name is Olivia Trenton and she stayed at this resort with three of her girlfriends about two months ago."

"Okay." The look he gave me was noncommittal. Maybe I'd misjudged him.

"I'm a private investigator hired by the family," I said. "I'm trying to rule out the possibility that Olivia met her abductors while here in the islands."

I knew that if I put it any other way, I'd risk scaring him off. No resort wants its name associated with a violent crime, especially the abduction of a teenage girl. Since the Natalee Holloway disappearance in Aruba nearly a decade ago, officials in the Caribbean islands had acted with extreme caution when discussing matters of security with outside investigators or the press. The islands in the Caribbean relied heavily on tourism to fuel their economies. In the Cayman Islands, tourism accounted for roughly three quarters of its gross domestic product and foreign currency earnings. The industry here was aimed at people just like the Trentons—upscale visitors from North America interested in unspoiled beaches, scuba diving, deep-sea fishing, and ultra-luxurious accommodations like the Ritz.

When a territory like the Cayman Islands received bad press, tourism took a hit, leaving only a single pillar of economic development still standing—international finance. The Cayman Islands' tax-free status—and its reputation for discretion, rivaled only by Switzerland—attracted banks and other companies to its shores like excrement attracted insects. (No offense to insects or excrement intended.)

Mylonas said, "So, what specifically can we do for you, Mr. Bateman?"

I stood, lowered my upper body, and spoke quietly. "I'd like to view your security tapes for the period of Miss Trenton's stay at the resort."

Mylonas actually chuckled, which could easily have earned him a cracked jaw, back when I first started this job, following Hailey's disappearance.

"I'm sorry, Mr. Bateman, but are you an attorney?"

"No, as I told you thirty seconds ago, I'm a private investigator."

"I see. Then I'm afraid I can't help you. In order for me to turn over security footage, I'd have to receive a court order."

"I'm not asking you to turn anything over, Mr. Mylonas. I'm only asking you to allow me to view very specific footage. With you standing on—I mean, *over*—my shoulder, if you feel it's necessary."

"I understand. But I still require a court order."

"Look, Mr. Mylonas, a young girl was stolen from her home by four masked intruders. I'm asking you man-to-man to do me this . . . favor."

Just saying the word "favor" made my teeth hurt.

"I'm sorry, Mr. Bateman, but there's nothing I can do. I'm sure that tomorrow morning, you will be able to find yourself a reputable attorney, who will file the proper paperwork with the court and—"

"Tomorrow morning," I said.

"Yes, tomorrow morn—"

"How about tonight?"

Mylonas held up his watch. "It'll be very difficult to find an attorney on the island working this late at—"

"No, Mr. Mylonas, what I mean is, how about tonight I come back here with every television reporter, newspaper journalist, and two-bit blogger on this island, and we feed into CNN and MSNBC and Fox News and tell viewers in the United States and all around the world that the missing California girl is believed to have been targeted for abduction two months ago at this very resort, the Grand Cayman Ritz-Carlton, and that the director of security, Thomas Mylonas, is refusing to aid—no, is *obstructing*—the investigation by withholding video footage that may identify the girl's kidnappers."

I felt the heat rising up my neck and spreading to my cheeks, and

I realized I'd inadvertently raised my voice and attracted the attention of several onlookers.

"Mr. Bateman, I do symp—"

"Mr. Mylonas, *nothing* you can possibly say will mollify me other than the words, 'I'd be *happy* to show you the footage. Right this way, please.'"

My eyes never left his as I removed my BlackBerry from my pocket, opened the browser, and typed in "Cayman television." Using my peripheral vision I clicked on the top link and was brought to the page for CITN Cayman 27. I scrolled down to the number for its news hotline, memorized it, then closed the browser and began punching the number into the phone.

Mylonas eyed the BlackBerry all the while, staring at it as though it were a ticking time bomb.

"All right, Mr. Bateman," he finally said, sweat forming above those bushy black brows. "I'd be *happy* to show you the footage. Right this way, please."

Chapter 19

I don't understand," Thomas Mylonas said, staring into his monitor as I stood looking over his shoulder. "The entire day is missing. Somehow it's been erased."

"Has this ever happened before?"

"I've been with the resort for fourteen years, and in that time we never failed to locate even a minute of footage from any one of our cameras, let alone an entire day from every camera in the resort."

I exhaled. In a strange way, this was more than I ever could have hoped for. This proved I was in the right part of the world, that I would be able to track down Olivia's whereabouts if I could only piece together that missing day.

I asked, "Were there any incident reports filed during those missing twenty-four hours?"

"Let me check." Mylonas tapped away at his keyboard and seemed relieved when the reports of that day appeared on the screen. "According to these records, there were three," he said. "A slip-and-fall by an elderly American lady in the lobby. She claimed the floor was wet, but security checked the area and found it to be completely dry."

"Go on."

"The second incident occurred in the water. A very intoxicated man, also American, complained that he was stung on the foot by a jellyfish. Our staff pointed out the various signs warning swimmers of jellyfish. The man then pulled down his bathing suit, exposing himself, and proceeded to urinate on his own foot in front of twenty or so guests. Police were called to the scene."

"And the third?"

"A fifty-one-year-old Frenchman suffered a heart attack in his room. His wife dialed the front desk. Medics were called to the scene. The man was taken via ambulance to George Town Hospital, where he was pronounced dead on arrival. There's a note here that says that a bottle of Cialis found in his room may have contributed to his death."

"Okay," I said, "I'm going to have to do this the old-fashioned way. I assume you have a record of every resort employee who worked at some point during those twenty-four hours."

"Yes, of course."

"I'll need those names."

Mylonas allowed me the use of his office for the interviews. I began with the personnel presently on duty—security, housekeeping, doormen, the concierge, the front desk. That took me through the night and got me no further than I'd been when I boarded the plane at LAX.

It seemed clear to me that it wasn't only the security tapes that had been purposefully erased; someone, I ventured, had wiped a number of minds clean with Cayman currency.

The question was who?

Mylonas, who had been about to go home when I arrived, remained with me, aiding me whenever he could, calling down to room service to keep me high on espresso.

"In a half hour, there will be a shift change," Mylonas informed me as the sunrise began to creep through the blinds in his office.

"Thank you," I said. "Mind if I jump on your computer while I wait?"

"Go right ahead, Mr. Bateman."

"And another favor," I said. "Have someone gather for me the menus from every restaurant in this resort."

"The breakfast menus?"

"No, no," I said. "All of them. Please."

Once I was alone, I logged in to Olivia's Twitter account. I rubbed my eyes and began scrolling down to the dates she was in Grand Cayman. Actually, I knew from a cursory scan earlier that Olivia didn't tweet while she was here. Just when she returned. Two days after returning home, she tweeted silly things like, "Funniest Moment in Grand Cayman: When Bethany's boob popped out of her swimsuit at Rum Point."

Olivia's tweets would help me establish *where* the girls had been, if not when. The "when" I'd have to sort out for myself. It was possible that nothing from the missing twenty-four hours made it into Olivia's tweets, but I had to explore every avenue.

Mylonas returned with the menus and set them down on his desk in front of me. "There are five restaurants at the resort," he said. "The morning shift has started to arrive. The doormen usually arrive first to change into their uniforms."

"Thank you," I said.

I returned to Olivia's tweets.

Best Name for a Village in Grand Cayman: Hell.
Best Italian Food in Grand Cayman: Ristorante Ragazzi.
Best Snorkeling Excursion: Stingray City (But Scary!).
Best Lunch Entrée: Polenta (CI $24.00).

I swung my chair around when I heard a rap at the door. A stocky young man entered the office and sat across from me. He was dressed in a Billabong T-shirt and board shorts, so I assumed he was a doorman who hadn't yet changed into his uniform. He was deeply tanned, his light brown hair buzzed short, except for a few strands highlighted blond and standing at attention in the center of his forehead.

He reached across the desk and offered his hand. "Jon Krusas."

"Patrick," I said. "Nice to meet you."

"What can I do for you, Patrick?"

Krusas was incredibly cordial, and I supposed that came with a decade or so of opening doors and seeking tips. I liked him right off the bat.

"How long have you been here, Jon?"

"In Grand Cayman? About six months. I transferred here from the Ritz in Battery Park."

"You're a New Yorker."

"Jersey boy, actually." He smiled. "But I don't advertise it."

I leaned forward, resting my elbows on the desk. "Let me get straight to the point, Jon. Two months ago, four teenage girls from Los Angeles flew down here for about a week. The night before last, four men broke into one of the girls' homes and terrorized her and her mother, before kidnapping the girl." I pulled Olivia's picture out of a manila envelope. "Her name is Olivia Trenton. She's fifteen years old."

I immediately caught the flash of recognition in his eyes.

"You've seen her on television?" I said.

"We don't have a TV."

"We?"

"My roommate and I."

"But you've seen this girl before?"

He hesitated, stared at the picture some more while he considered his answer. "Sure, I remember her and her friends."

"Think carefully, Jon. Did you see these girls with anyone else while they were staying at this hotel?"

"No, they pretty much stuck to themselves."

"They didn't bring any guys back to their rooms?"

"Not that I saw." Krusas shifted his bulk in the chair, stared down at his hands, then looked at me.

I reached into the manila folder and pulled out more pictures. "Do you recognize this nightclub?"

"Sure, that's the Next Level. It's across from the Marriott."

"You go there?"

"Sometimes. On Mondays. Monday is all-you-can-drink night." The way he said it made me think Jon Krusas made sure he got his money's worth.

I showed him another picture. "Recognize any of the guys in this group shot?"

The big man's face sank. He parted his lips but then just blew out air. "No, I don't think I've seen any of those guys before."

"No? Are you sure? They're not locals?"

"They could be. Like I said, though, I've only been here for six months."

"It's a small island, though."

He nodded, looked at me with piercing blue eyes. "It is."

"All right, Jon. If you remember anything, you'll be sure to get in touch with me through Tom Mylonas."

"Sure thing." He pushed himself out of the chair, the energy he'd come in with suddenly drained.

I made a note next to his name, memorized his home address.

As he stepped out into the hall, Jon Krusas turned back and looked at me. "How old did you say that girl Olivia is?"

"Fifteen," I said.

"She seemed older," he said, shaking his head.

Then he disappeared down the hallway.

Chapter 20

Following a brief nap in my room at the Grand Cayman Beach Suites, I headed downstairs with my manila folder, intending to return to the Ritz-Carlton to continue my interviews, which had thus far proved fruitless.

Earlier I'd spoken to Edgar, who assured me that there had been no progress on their end. The kidnappers never contacted him again, and the FBI seemed more concerned with why he arranged to pay the abductors eight and a half million dollars instead of calling the feds. Agents were reinterviewing the Trentons' staff and Olivia's friends, but they too were running into dead ends. So far, no suspects or persons of interest had been named.

Meanwhile, the clock continued ticking. The longer Olivia remained missing, the greater the chance she'd never be found.

Downstairs, I checked my watch. It was that awkward time between breakfast and lunch, when no one seemed to be serving food. I wanted something simple, just a grilled ham and cheese sandwich I could eat on the run.

There was an upscale restaurant on-site called Hemingways. I'd passed it yesterday and spotted a club sandwich on the menu. Thought maybe the chef could throw one together fast before they began serving lunch.

I walked toward the restaurant and double-checked the lunch

menu posted outside. A club sandwich cost ten Cayman Island bucks, which was roughly $12.20 American.

I was about to head inside when something else on the menu caught my eye. While speaking to Olivia's friends, I'd put together a list of all the restaurants they'd eaten at for breakfast, lunch, and dinner. Hemingways wasn't on the list, and this was the type of restaurant you'd remember. Maybe one of the girls could have forgotten, but certainly not all three.

Yet there under the section titled *Entrées* was the dish Olivia had tweeted as her favorite lunch—polenta. The dish was marked with a green *V* for "vegetarian" and was priced at CI $24, just as Olivia had posted. The ingredients were tomato, onion, fennel, mushroom, spinach, and mozzarella.

Which meant that Olivia had most likely visited Hemingways for lunch on that missing Tuesday. The girls said they'd eaten all their other meals together.

I stepped into the restaurant, a bright and airy place with tables both inside and out. Cool trade winds blew gently in from the sea. Day or night, this restaurant gave off an air of true romance.

A fifteen-year-old girl wouldn't have come here alone.

A young hostess smiled when she saw me approach. Her jet black hair was pulled back in a tight bun and she wore glasses with thick black frames, which made her look like the naughty librarian you saw in ads for LensCrafters.

"I'm sorry, sir. We don't open for lunch until eleven thirty."

"I realize. Actually, I was wondering if I might have a quick word with you and perhaps some of your colleagues." I reached into the manila envelope and produced a picture of Olivia. "Do you recognize the girl in this photo? She would've been here for lunch on a Tuesday about two months ago."

"Yeah, I recognize her. In fact, the guy who waited on her just walked in behind you."

I turned and saw a man in his mid- to late twenties in black slacks and a white button-down hurrying toward the entrance to the kitchen.

"Wait here," the hostess said. "I'll go grab him."

My stomach began to swell with excitement and I discovered I wasn't hungry anymore. This could be just the break I was searching for.

A couple minutes later, the waiter stepped out of the kitchen with the young hostess trailing him. She had a look on her face like she'd just been told her mother was dead.

"Hello," the waiter said, his eyes pinballing from me to the terrace to the entrance and back to me again. "My name's Chuck." He didn't offer his hand. "How can I help you?"

I held up the picture. Before he even looked at it, he was already shaking his head of curly brown hair.

"You waited on this young lady a couple of months back," I said. "It would have been a Tuesday in mid-December."

"No, I didn't. I've never seen her before. Selma must have been mistaken."

I looked over his shoulder at Selma, the hostess, who immediately dropped her gaze to the floor.

"All I need to know," I said, "is who this girl was here with."

"I wish I could tell you," Chuck said. "But she was never here."

"She was, though," I said. "Two months ago, for lunch. She ordered the polenta."

"Then I must not have been working. I've never seen that girl before in my life."

"You work here full-time?"

"Yes, sir."

"You've been working here awhile?"

"Three years."

"You must have waited a lot of tables during that time."

"Sure."

"Is it possible you waited on this young lady and just don't remember her?"

"No, sir. I've never seen her before. She's never been inside this restaurant."

"Well, which is it?" I said.

"Excuse me?"

"You've never seen her, or she's never been here before."

Chuck took a deep breath. "*If* she's been here, I didn't see her, and I've certainly never waited on her before."

"Selma?" I said. "Who was this young woman with when you saw her?"

"I'm sorry, sir," she said. "Like Chuck told you, I must have mistaken her for someone else."

I studied the waiter's face and I saw fear in every feature; it seemed to ooze out of his pores. The question was why. Had he seen Olivia's photo on television? Had he been threatened? Or was he in on the abduction?

"I have a few more photos I'd like you to take a look at," I said.

"I'm sorry," Chuck said, "but we really need to get to work."

"You don't open for lunch until eleven thirty."

"There's a lot of prep work to be done." He finally locked his eyes on mine. "Please, sir," he said. "Try to understand."

The pleading in Chuck's eyes seemed to answer my question.

He hadn't simply seen Olivia's picture on television, but he wasn't a part of the kidnapping plot either.

Chuck had clearly been threatened.

But by whom?

"All right, then," I said. "How about as a consolation prize you run into the kitchen and throw together a ham and cheese sandwich for me?"

Chapter 21

Heading back to the Ritz-Carlton, I decided to take the scenic route—along Seven Mile Beach. Heralded as one of the most perfect beaches in the Caribbean, Seven Mile was actually a five-and-a-half-mile stretch of golden powdery sand along the West Bay.

Today, the beach was less crowded than I'd been told to expect, the fierce Caribbean sun and the presence of jellyfish combining to keep vacationers by the swimming pools or in the shade.

I passed a few families, parents with their eyes locked on the water instead of on their paperbacks, hoping their children didn't get stung. Lifeguards sat alert at their stations, and I considered stopping to chat with one. Maybe closer to the Ritz-Carlton, I'd have more luck, but unless Olivia had found herself in trouble in the water, I doubted a lifeguard would remember her.

As I walked, favoring my right leg, I spotted a number of snorkelers, who apparently didn't give a damn about the jellyfish. There were four or five kayaks out in the water, along with a couple bright yellow WaveRunners, which I'd seen available for rent at each of the large resorts.

Nearing the resort, I nodded to a skinny old man wielding a metal detector. His flesh was brown and leathery, his white beard long and unkempt. He could have been a vagrant, but something about the way he carried himself told me no.

"Any luck today?" I said.

The old man stopped, wiped the sweat from his forehead, and said, "If it wasn't for bad luck, I'd have no luck at all."

"Is treasure hunting just a hobby," I inquired, "or could you use a few dollars for lunch?"

He took a step forward as though he were about to take me into his confidence, and his unfortunate scent answered my question before he did. "No, I could use a couple bucks to eat," he conceded.

I reached for my wallet and dug out a twenty.

"Wow, thanks," he said with a slight lisp. "You a Brit?"

"I'm an American."

"Oh, me too. You sound like a Brit."

"Good ears," I said. "I was actually born in London, brought to the States by my father as a young boy. How about you?"

He waved it off, said, "I'm from all over. I was in the U.S. Army. Lived in Germany, Japan, did stretches in Nam and Korea. Were you ever in the service?"

I shook my head. "Law enforcement. Used to be a Marshal."

"Oh, you're the guys who chase after fugitives."

On that last word, I saw that he had hardly any teeth.

"That's right." I pointed to the metal detector. "Find much loot out here?"

"Oh, yeah. Not bad. Small things, you know. Little bracelets, those thin little necklaces, maybe a tiny charm in the shape of a heart or a clover. But the price of gold being what it is, sometimes I make enough to eat."

"And if you don't?"

"Then I hit the street, ask folks for spare change. Sometimes, I get lucky, some guy wants to show off in front of his young lady, hands me some paper money. Usually though, it's just coins. Once in a blue moon, someone offers to buy me a sandwich. Takes me over to the deli, buys it himself to make sure I don't touch his money, spend it on booze." He shrugged, offered a great smile—one for those rare magazine pieces on the plight of the homeless. "I don't mind, though. I like to eat even more than I like to drink."

"What's your poison?"

"This is the Caribbean, chum. What do you think?"

"So it's rum," I said.

The old man seemed to salivate. "Rum."

I followed his gaze as he turned toward the sea.

"You wanna talk about treasure," he said, "you get yourself some diving gear and head out there."

"Is that so?"

"Oh, yeah. Hundreds of ships were sunk around the Cayman Islands. What do you think? We got Cuba as a neighbor, and Cuba used to be the last stop for ships setting out for the Spanish Main."

"The conquistadors lost some ships here, then."

"You better believe it. Five hundred years ago, the conquistadors like that fellow—what's his name, Cortés?—were sailing from the Gulf of Mexico to Europe, carrying shiploads of Aztec plunder. Back in the '70s, a young American couple from Georgia found bars of silver, gold, platinum; emeralds and diamonds; rings, bracelets, elaborate crosses. Pulled up a few hundred pounds of treasure. These were *amateur* divers, mind you. They weren't looking for nothing but fun."

"That's incredible," I said, stuffing my hands in my pockets.

"That's not the half of it," the old man said. "Turns out, the ship that wrecked was the *Santiago*. It had been missing since 1522. They found a coat of arms on a colossal ring, and guess whose name was on it?"

"Whose?"

"The frigging Ponce de León family. You've heard of him, right? Juan Ponce de León?"

"Sure, the Spaniard who discovered Florida."

"Right. While looking for the Fountain of Youth, they say." He paused, regained his train of thought. "Well, the captain of the *Santiago* was his brother Rodrigo. Turns out, Rodrigo had accompanied Cortés to Mexico, and his ship was lost right here off Grand Cayman."

"Amazing."

"I'll say. There's hasn't been another find like that, at least not that I know of. But divers find pieces all the time, sell them to this dealer out near Rum Point."

"Is that so?"

"That's where I sell what I find. Mine have no value except for the gold, but Barney, he gives me a good price because I'm out there all the time. He has some magnificent pieces discovered by professional divers."

My hand closed around the heavy pendant in my right pants pocket. "Diamonds?" I said.

"Oh, sure."

"Might you recognize a piece if I showed you one?"

He turned away from the ocean and shielded his eyes. "If I've seen it before, I'll probably recognize it."

I pulled out the diamond pendant I'd found in the base of Olivia's ceiling fan and held it out in my palm.

The old-timer tried to whistle but it didn't go too well. "Oh, yeah. That's a beauty. That monster was sitting in Barney's store for at least fifteen, twenty years. Only recently I saw it wasn't there no more." He looked up at me, a bit suspicious. "Hey, if you don't mind my asking, how did you get ahold of it?"

"It's owned now by a young girl named Olivia back in the States. I'm trying to find out who bought it for her."

"She won't tell you?"

"She's not around anymore."

"Oh, okay. Well, Barney, he'd be able to tell you who bought it."

I placed the pendant back in my pocket. The old man gave me the name of the store, described it in detail, and I reached into my wallet and handed him a couple hundred dollars.

"Oh, you don't have to do that," he said. "That's too much. I only need about half this to eat good for a month."

He tried to hand some back to me but I waved him off.

"It's all right," I said. "Spend whatever's left on rum."

Chapter 22

Rather than continuing on to the Ritz-Carlton, I returned to the Grand Cayman Beach Suites, took a shower to rinse away the sand and sweat, then dressed and headed across the street to the lot where I'd parked the Jeep Wrangler.

It was a winding twenty-five-mile trek from George Town to Rum Point, one of the most remote parts of the island. The point itself was known for its secluded white-sand beach and superb snorkeling. Casuarina trees towered overhead, providing badly needed shade and trunks nifty for hanging hammocks. The trade winds here at Rum Point offered some further relief from the broiling Caribbean sun, yet it remained tempting to bolt through the grass and into the calm green shallows.

Another temptation was the aroma of burgers sizzling on the grill at the Wreck Bar and Grill. Back at Hemingways, Chuck had denied my request for a ham and cheese sandwich, so I was starving. I stopped by the Wreck Bar and ordered a burger and a Coke.

While I sat eating at one of the picnic benches, I glanced at the parking lot and spotted a muddied beige Ford Explorer parked a few spaces away from my Jeep. The driver remained at the wheel, and the engine continued running. The driver's face was covered by a copy of this morning's *Caymanian Compass*.

I made a mental note of the license plate and finished my burger.

As I stood to toss out my trash, a second man jumped into the passenger side of the Explorer, and the SUV backed out of the space, turned the wheel, and peeled out of the parking lot, spinning a few heads.

I walked past the Wreck Bar and gift shops and made for the small stone building that housed the Cayman Grande Boutique. The jewelry shop looked just as the old man on Seven Mile Beach had described it, right down to the display of black coral jewelry in the front window.

A bell rang above my head as I entered.

A tall red-faced heavyset man who looked to be in his mid-sixties stood up with a scowl rather than a smile on his face. "How can I help you?" he said in a tone that sounded as though help would be the last thing he offered me.

"I'm looking for Barney," I said, knowing from the old vagrant's description that this was Barney.

"Yeah? Well, I'm Barney. Who are you?"

"My name's Patrick Bateman. I have a rare piece that was purchased here a couple months back."

"I can't reveal the names of my customers," he said.

I stopped just shy of the counter. "I didn't ask you to."

"Well, then what do you want from me?"

"I just want to confirm that it was your piece."

"Tell you the truth, I wouldn't recognize it if it was, so you're wasting your time."

"I think you might recognize this piece," I said. "It's pretty unique."

He shook his head. "No, sir."

"Don't you want to at least take a look at it?"

"Not particularly."

Barney was staring out his window over my shoulder, and I got the feeling I knew where the passenger of the beige Ford Explorer had been while the driver was reading his paper.

I removed the pendant from my pocket and held it up to let the light hit it. It was a serious piece and it was tough to look away from, even for Barney, who'd probably seen it every day for ten or fifteen years and now wanted nothing to do with it.

"I've never seen that piece before."

"No?" I shrugged. "All right, then. Would you consider buying it?"

Barney shook his head again. "No, sir. Not interested in the least."

I made a show of looking around the store. There were literally a dozen or more signs hanging on every wall, every showcase, reading:

WE BUY ALL JEWELRY—GOLD, SILVER, DIAMONDS.

"Who did you sell this diamond to two months ago, Barney? Just give me a name and I'll leave. You'll never hear from me again, and I'll never tell anyone where I received the information."

"I'm going to have to ask you to leave," he said.

I took a step forward. "Not before you give me a name."

"Leave now, or I am going to call the police and have you physically thrown from the premises."

"Call the police," I said. "They may want to ask you some of the same questions I'm asking you."

"I mean it, mister."

"I mean it too, Barney."

He saw something in my eyes then that told him I wasn't going away easily. He took a step back from the counter, said, "Okay, okay. Let me just check my receipts."

He knelt below the register.

When he stood up, he was holding a .357, pointing it directly at my face.

I didn't flinch. "Who threatened you, Barney?"

"Mr. Fisk, I'm going to give you to the count of five to get out of this store and off my property, or I am going to blow a hole in your face so wide that from the neck up you'll look like a stick figure."

"How do you know my name, Barney?"

"What's that? You told it to me when you walked in here."

"No, Barney, I didn't. I told you my name was Patrick Bateman. You just called me Mr. Fisk."

"Well, then you're a damn liar, aren't you? And if you don't get the hell out of my store right now, you're going to be a dead damn liar."

Barney cocked the hammer. Probably an unnecessary step for the weapon he was pointing at me, but it brought the point home. This .357 wasn't for show. Old Barney here wouldn't hesitate to use it if I persisted.

I squeezed the diamond pendant in my palm, turned, and walked out of the store.

Felt as though it were twenty degrees hotter outside than it was when I went in.

Chapter 23

As the saying goes: Give a man a gun and he can rob a bank. Give a man a bank and he can rob the world.

The Cayman Islands are the fifth-largest banking center on the planet. Why? For starters, the Cayman Islands levy no taxes on profits, capital gains, or income on foreign investors. In other words, the Cayman Islands are a tax shelter. Secondly, bankers in the Cayman Islands know how to keep secrets.

Aren't offshore financial centers that shelter multinational corporations from paying their fair share in taxes harmful to the global marketplace? you may ask. Not according to the International Monetary Fund. The IMF has deemed the system of banking "regulation" in the Cayman Islands "effective" and noted that "the overall compliance culture within Cayman is very strong, including the compliance culture related to AML (anti-money laundering) obligations."

Difficult to comprehend? Suffice it to say that the International Monetary Fund is full of shit.

But I wasn't in Grand Cayman to protest its banking policies. I was here to find a teenage girl who'd been stolen from her home in California. A girl whose life now hung in the balance.

Finding Olivia meant finding her kidnappers. And one way to find Olivia's kidnappers was to find the eight and a half million dollars Edgar Trenton had wired to the Cayman Islands in order to get his daughter back.

The bank Edgar wired the money to was called I & E, and it was located in George Town, across the street from the terminals where cruise ship passengers were let off. I parked the Jeep Wrangler on the street and headed toward the bank, thinking this may well be my most futile effort in any case to date.

If I couldn't get Barney and a young waiter at Hemingways to talk, I sure as hell wasn't going to have any success with a Cayman banker.

When I entered the bank, I was told to have a seat. For thirty minutes, no one came near me, no one so much as looked in my direction. It was as though I was a leper. When I was finally brought to a desk, I informed the gentleman of the situation, gave him everything but my real name. He barely masked a smirk before asking me to leave.

As I made for the door, one of the young tellers was calling it a day and she stepped outside just in front of me. She had short, mousy brown hair, and compared to the rest of the Caymanian bankers, she was severely underdressed. When we both rounded the corner, she turned and smiled at me.

"You were asking about the missing girl," she said quietly through her teeth.

I nodded.

"I can't be seen speaking to you," she said. "Do you know where the Grand Old House is?"

"The restaurant? I just passed it, I believe."

"Park there. Then walk over to Smith Cove."

"Smith Cove?"

"It's a tiny, rocky beach surrounded by trees. You can't miss it. Meet me there in ten minutes. If anyone sees you there, leave."

She hurried off down the street before I had a chance to thank her.

As instructed, I parked the Jeep at the Grand Old House, which seemed to be hosting a rather lavish wedding. I kept my head down and walked in the direction of Smith Cove, which my GPS said was just a few hundred yards farther south.

Smith Cove looked straight out of a Nicholas Sparks movie. Gin-clear water lapped onto a small stretch of sand, fine white powder that felt like cotton under my bare feet. I sat on the edge of a rock, sweat causing my white Tommy Bahama shirt to stick to my back. Above my head were multicolored leaves, hanging from an old and beautiful tree. To complete the scene, the sun was just beginning to set, throwing a pink-orange hue over the placid Caribbean Sea.

For a few moments, I sat there thinking of Ana. Was it even possible for Smith Cove and Warsaw to exist on the same planet?

"Mr. Bateman?"

I turned and saw the young woman from the bank staring down at me. "Actually, my name's Simon. Simon Fisk."

"Louise Dietz. Don't come up, I'll step down." Louise sat on the rock next to me, both our feet dangling. She spoke before I could. "I was at the bank when the first of the wire transfers came in."

"Were they expected?" I said.

"I don't think so. It certainly didn't seem so. As soon as they started, my supervisor hurried me and another teller out the door."

"Do you know whose accounts the money went into?"

"I don't. But from what I overheard, the money wasn't remaining at our bank. It was just passing through, moving to Zurich within minutes."

"Zurich, huh? No surprise there."

"I wish I could help you more, I really do. Problem is, I have zero security clearance at I and E. It's just that you seemed desperate and I wanted to at least confirm that the money made it here."

"I *am* desperate," I said. "And I appreciate your effort."

"What do you have in the envelope?" she said. "Pictures of the girl?"

"And others."

"Can I see?"

"Of course."

I removed the photos, which had been roughly handled over the past twenty-four hours. Each picture was now marred by creases and fingerprints.

"Do you recognize her?" I said.

Louise shook her head. "Just from TV."

"How about any of the other girls?"

"No." She flipped to the first photograph taken at the nightclub. "This is the Next Level," she said.

"Yes."

She reached the photos with the boys, said, "Him I know."

I looked over her shoulder. Louise was pointing to the blond-haired, blue-eyed guy, the one I thought could be from California.

"He's a local?" I said.

"Yeah. Well, kind of."

"Kind of?"

"His name's Kellen. He lives on the island part-time."

"You know him from the bank?"

"I know his father from the bank. They're originally from the U.S., but now they live in Costa Rica. His father works for a big land developer out there."

"Well, that's a start. Do you know his last name?"

"I don't remember it. It's something simple, but I can't wrap my mind around it."

"So, Kellen comes to the bank with his father?"

"Just once. But I've hung out with him. I went on a couple dates with his roommate."

"His roommate? So you know where Kellen lives?"

"I've never been to their place. But I know it's an apartment in George Town. That's where Kellen stays when he's on-island. Otherwise, he's in Costa Rica."

"So, Kellen has just the one roommate?"

"Yeah."

"What's his name?"

"Jonathan."

"Know where I can find him?"

"Sure," she said. "He works as a doorman at the Ritz-Carlton."

"No kidding," I said. "Goes by the name Jon?"

"Yeah, everyone calls him Jon but me."

I'd told Jon it was a small island. And for him, it had just gotten a whole hell of a lot smaller.

Chapter 24

'd memorized Jon Krusas's address from his employment file
after I interviewed him. He'd started his shift at the Ritz-
Carlton early this morning. It was now getting dark, so I
wanted to try him at home. That way, if Kellen *was* on the island, I'd
likely catch them both off-guard—and hopefully get some answers
before it was too late. Before the trail went cold.

The apartment building was unimpressive, looked very much
like a dormitory you'd find at any midsize American college. Which
meant that security probably wouldn't be much of a problem for me.

The building seemed to hold at least a few dozen apartments, so
I waited patiently for someone to exit, rather than buzzing intercoms
haphazardly. Jon Krusas and his part-time roommate, Kellen, lived
on the third floor. Apartment 3E.

A young couple started their way up the path toward the building.
They were both carrying multiple grocery bags. When they reached
the entrance, the male fumbled for his keys. Given the aloofness of
nearly every Caymanian I'd met, I didn't want to appear too helpful
and friendly, lest I seem out of place. So I let him struggle.

When he got the door open, I held it for him. Not a word of thanks.
If I weren't breaking in, I'd have been offended.

I took a hot, smelly stairwell up to the third floor, avoiding the
elevators. As I approached apartment 3E, I heard the theme music
to *Friends*. I took a chance with the knob and it turned in my hand.

"Hello, Jon," I said, closing the door behind me. "Hope you don't mind my dropping in, but I thought we might continue our talk."

Krusas was standing in front of an ironing board in his underwear. Tightie-whities and a wife-beater. Not a good look for anyone, but particularly unpleasant on him.

He looked up, lifted the iron off his shirt, and considered the cord, which led to an electrical socket in the small kitchen, no doubt gauging the hot iron's use as a weapon.

"Won't be effective," I told him. "You might singe one of my forearms, but you won't accomplish anything except making me mad, and you don't want to do that." I pointed to the ironing board. "Set the iron down and take several steps to your left, slowly."

He did as he was told and I moved toward the kitchen and unplugged the iron, never taking my eyes off him.

"You lied to me," I said.

His lips parted, but he didn't say anything.

"About having a television," I added. "If I'm not mistaken, Chandler Bing is about to get locked in an ATM vestibule with a lingerie model during a citywide blackout."

He stole a glimpse at the television, nodded.

"Have a seat on the couch," I told him.

He sat.

I said, "Tell me about your roommate, Kellen. He was in the photos taken at the Next Level."

Krusas shifted his considered weight. "I met the girls at the Ritz the day they arrived. I had no idea how old they were. They were traveling by themselves, they had IDs that said they were eighteen."

"Go on."

"So a couple days later, when they were about to head out to lunch, I told them my roommate and I were going to the Next Level that night. I asked them if they'd like to meet us there."

"What did they say?"

"They said they'd think about it." He paused, peered up at his ceiling. "But they showed up."

"And what happened at the club?"

"Nothing. We all danced. Drank. Took some pictures."

"Why aren't you in any of the photos?"

He frowned. "Because I was the one taking the pictures."

"Kellen hooked up with Alysia?"

"Yes."

"And Lola?"

"Some local. He's native to the island, but I don't know him. I mostly hang with people in the service industry."

"How about Bethany?" I said. "Who was she with?"

"She danced with everyone. She wasn't interested in anyone in particular; she just wanted to have a good time."

"Which leaves Olivia."

He nodded.

"You hooked up with her?"

"No, she wanted nothing to do with me. That's why I was *taking* the pictures instead of posing for them."

"But in some of the photos, it appears Olivia *is* with someone and he's been cropped out."

Staring at Krusas's thick wrists, I knew it wasn't him.

"Those must have been taken later in the night. Once it was clear that Olivia wasn't into me, I tried to get Kellen to come with me to another club. But he wanted to stay with Alysia." He added, "Again, I thought the girls were eighteen."

"So you left and Kellen stayed," I said.

"That's right."

"Did Kellen bring Alysia back here later that night?"

"I don't know."

"You don't know? Well, did he come home?"

"I don't know. I haven't even spoken to Kellen since that night."

"So Kellen didn't come back here?"

"Like I said, I don't know. Because *I* didn't come back here. I got picked up for a DUI. I spent the night in jail. You can check with the Caymanian police."

"That would've been in your file at the Ritz-Carlton."

"Only if I reported it."

"But you didn't."

"No. I had two DUIs in Arizona, where I first worked for the Ritz, then another two in New York, when I worked at Battery Park. That's why I was transferred. If it happens here, I'll be fired."

"So you've had a falling-out with Kellen?"

"Yeah, he was the designated driver that night."

"He moved out?"

"Some of his stuff's still here. I'm pretty sure he just went back to Costa Rica. His dad pays most of the rent on this place. Look, I moved in here because I got a great deal. But we weren't close friends. We never even spoke when he was in Costa Rica, just when he was here in the islands."

Something about the way Krusas was speaking about Kellen troubled me.

"Do you think it's possible, Jon, that Kellen had something to do with Olivia's abduction?"

He shrugged his wide shoulders. "I don't know."

"You don't know? What gives you doubt?"

He scratched behind his ear like a stray before finally dragging his gaze up to meet mine. "I've heard rumors over the past two months."

"Rumors about what?"

"That Kellen may be involved with a Costa Rican gang that's involved in the sex tourism trade in San José."

Five minutes later, Krusas stood in the doorway to Kellen's bedroom while I went through Kellen's things. There was nothing to be found, unfortunately. Nothing at all.

The last name Kellen had given Krusas was Smith, but he didn't think that was genuine. And there wasn't time for me to stick around to attempt to obtain the name from Louise or anyone else at I & E Bank. If what Krusas was telling me was true, Olivia was fast running out of time. If I didn't hurry, she could be gone forever.

"Why did you lie to me twelve hours ago?" I said as I stepped back into the living room.

He lifted his shoulder and spoke softly. "You remember what happened when that American girl went missing in Aruba ten years ago? The Aruban cops picked up five or six guys and kept them in jail while that monster Joran van der Sloot just continued telling lies. I was scared. I realize the truth usually comes out in the end. But what happens in the meantime? Nuts like Greta Van Susteren tell the world what to think and everyone rushes to judgment. I'm a doorman. I'm overweight and I drink too much. But I just want to live my life. I don't want to be infamous."

I turned and opened the front door.

"I hope you find her," he said as I stepped into the hall.

I looked back at him, thought about our meeting at the Ritz this morning. "For your sake, Jon, you better hope I don't find her twelve hours too late."

Chapter 25

Early the following morning I arrived at Juan Santamaría International Airport in Alajuela, just outside of San José. I collected my suitcase and the duffel I'd purchased back in Grand Cayman, then rented a silver Toyota Land Cruiser and made my way into the city.

With its mix of baroque and neoclassical architecture, Costa Rica's capital reminded me a lot of Madrid. Of course, in a way, San José was emblematic of every major European city—due in large part to its hellish morning traffic.

While I waited, breathing in the black fumes of the public bus idling in front of me, I dialed Edgar Trenton on my BlackBerry.

"Simon," he said in a hushed tone, "where are you?"

"Edgar, are you alone?"

"Yes, I'm outside. Raúl's here, but he doesn't speak English. Now, where are you?"

"Costa Rica."

"Have you been watching the news? The FBI's named *me* a person of interest. The media are having a field day."

"Have you brought in a lawyer?"

"Of course. Seymour Lepavsky, one of the best criminal defense attorneys in L.A. But it's not prosecution by the Justice Department that I'm worried about, Simon. It's the prosecution that's occurring on the twenty-four-hour cable news networks. I'm the *lead* story, and they're going to keep digging and digging and digging until they've dredged up every last damning detail about my life."

"What are they saying?"

Edgar inhaled as though it might be the last breath he ever took. "I've been having an affair with my assistant, Valerie. She's a very young girl and now news about our relationship is everywhere. They're saying Emma knew about the affair and that she was going to leave me. Emma apparently went to see this notorious divorce lawyer, Ernie Byers, in Beverly Hills. I had *no idea,* you have to believe me, Simon. But they're claiming that I knew that Emma was aware of the affair and that I knew she'd gone to see Ernie. I hadn't, I swear. But no one seems to care. They're calling *me* a liar and they're calling *it* motive."

Made sense. I'd been close to coming to the same conclusion.

"Simon, they think I arranged this entire thing in order to stash the eight and a half million, so that Emma couldn't get half the money in the divorce."

"But they have no evidence, Edgar. Have your lawyer consult with your publicist and release a statement saying—"

"The feds are claiming *to have* evidence, Simon. The bandola case? The one my wife described? It washed ashore near Gladstones restaurant on the Pacific Coast Highway in Malibu. My gun—the .38 Emma says she fired—was inside the case."

"So?"

"So, they're saying it was *loaded with blanks.*"

There it was, something I'd been wondering ever since Emma told me she'd fired a shot inside the house. It was why I'd asked her if she felt any difference in the recoil. Blanks will do that, discharge with substantially less force. Under ordinary circumstances, an experienced shooter like Emma would have realized she was shooting blanks. But Emma had been tackled head-on in the same moment she fired the shot. She simply hadn't noticed.

"Easy, Edgar," I said. "Calm down. Having a stroke isn't going to do you or Olivia any good."

"Before that gun was found, Simon, I'd told the agents that I'd *personally* loaded it with live ammunition."

"There may still be another explanation," I said. "One of the intruders was already inside the house when Emma heard the other three enter. Did anyone besides you and Emma know the combination to the gun vault?"

He hesitated. "No, Simon."

"Not even Olivia? Olivia knew the security code to the alarm. Emma said she trusted her with everything."

"The police asked Emma. She told them she never gave Olivia the combination."

I remembered looking at the gun vault at the Trentons' estate. The combination was only three digits.

"What was the combination, Edgar? Did the numbers have any significance? Could the combination have been easily deduced?"

He hesitated again. "Eight, twenty-one," he said, a sound of relief burrowing its way into his voice. "It's our anniversary, Simon. *Of course*, someone could have figured it out."

Edgar was a smart guy. I wondered why he wouldn't have come to that conclusion himself. Could be that he was getting hit from all sides, that he simply wasn't thinking straight.

Or it could be something else.

"Well, there you go," I said tentatively. "What else did the feds recover from the bandola case?"

The question seemed to bring Edgar back down to reality. He said, "The so-called poison that Emma was injected with. It turns out it was made up mostly of a harmless blue dye used to make ink, mixed with a small amount of sedative."

That confirmed that the assailants had no intention of killing Emma, just as I'd thought.

"Anything else?"

"Yes." He paused and I thought I'd lost the call. Then he continued, "The worst of it, Simon, is the knife they recovered from the bandola case. It's a huge thing—the blade's a foot long. Two of them were made for me by this craftsman in Moldova during preproduction of this *Hostel* rip-off we released straight-to-DVD a couple years ago. One of the knives hangs in my den at the house. The other was apparently stolen from my office at the studio."

"You didn't notice it missing?"

"Simon, it was hanging in my office the day I left for Berlin. Now it's gone."

"Edgar—"

"I know, Simon. None of this is important. The only thing that matters now is finding Olivia. My fear is that if the feds think I'm involved, they're going to head off in the wrong direction and my daughter will never be found."

"We'll find Olivia," I said. "And finding her will clear your name."

If *you're clean*, I wanted to add.

In case he wasn't, I remained vague about what I was doing in Costa Rica. I promised I'd keep him posted on my progress, then stuffed the BlackBerry into my pocket and continued to wait.

I watched with envy as motor scooters blew by the Land Cruiser on both my left and my right.

It was another fifteen minutes before I reached my destination—CIMA, a Costa Rican hospital designed and organized specifically for Americans. I parked the Land Cruiser in the lot in front of the main wing and entered the hospital, where I was met by an American flag belonging to U.S. veterans, who maintained an office right there in the lobby.

I stepped up to the information desk and spoke in English. "I'm here to see Aubrey Lang. She's an emergency room nurse."

"Is she expecting you?"

"I don't think so, but I'm pretty sure she'll see me. I'm an old friend. My name's Simon Fisk."

"Please have a seat, *señor*."

"*Gracias.*"

I took a cushioned chair in the waiting room and made a mental note to stop by the cafeteria for some strong Costa Rican coffee. I didn't bother with a magazine, didn't think my eyes would be able to focus. So I looked up at one of the small television sets, which showed a female talking head jabbering in Spanish. The volume was set too low to hear, but it soon became clear what she was going on about, when a photograph of Carousel Pictures' studio head, Edgar Trenton, appeared in the upper left-hand corner of the screen.

Edgar had become the worldwide story—the Trentons' daughter, Olivia, all but forgotten.

Forgotten by all except me.

I filled my lungs with oxygen and opened my eyes wide, sat as straight as I did back in grammar school. I needed to feel young just now.

But the fatigued appearance two minutes later of Aubrey Lang in her tattered blue green scrubs didn't help in that respect. Not one bit.

"Simon," she said, clearly not thrilled to see me.

I pushed myself out of the chair. "It's been a long time, Aubrey."

She nodded. "Eleven years."

I choked back the emotion, said, "Since Tasha's funeral."

Chapter 26

While we were attending American University, the woman sitting across the table from me was Tasha's best friend. Aubrey Lang—a farmer's daughter from Ames, Iowa—always had dreams of seeing the world. But for her parents, Ames *was* the world, and if Aubrey wanted to live a life beyond the borders of the Hawkeye State, then she'd do so entirely without their financial or emotional support. And that's just what she did.

After obtaining her nursing degree in the States, Aubrey joined the Peace Corps, requesting placement in Costa Rica's Protected Areas Management program. In short, she wanted to save the rain forests. Since the Corps required a degree in an area such as wildlife management, she continued her education at the University of Wisconsin in Madison, where she took part in a variety of local conservation activities.

Once the Corps sent her to Costa Rica, Aubrey went to work providing technical training to park managers, guards, and guides; promoting community-based conservation; and aiding in the development of the country's ecotourism industry.

While she was working in Costa Rica, she fell in love with the country and its people. After two years, she requested and was granted an extension of service and went on to work with the children of San José's outlying slums—locally called *tugurios*—which year after year were becoming increasingly desperate and violent.

After her tours in the Peace Corps, Aubrey Lang still couldn't see herself leaving the country, so she became certified as a nurse in Costa Rica and went to work in the ERs of San José's busiest hospitals. She'd been here with CIMA in at least some capacity since the hospital's inception in 2000.

Now, as we sipped rich Costa Rican coffee in the cafeteria, Aubrey Lang and I discussed Life After Tasha. The two women had always shared a special bond I couldn't begin to understand, and long after we graduated from American University, Aubrey and Tasha continued to see more of each other than most people see siblings living abroad.

The day Hailey was abducted, Aubrey boarded a flight to D.C., took a room at the Georgetown Best Western, and remained there through the entire ordeal. When Tasha took her own life a few weeks after Hailey's disappearance, Aubrey blamed herself for not accepting our invitation to stay with us at our house.

"I'm a goddamn nurse," she'd said to me at Tasha's funeral. "I knew she shouldn't have been prescribed all those tranqs and sedatives and painkillers and muscle relaxers at the same time. But I never said a word. I should have been there in that house with her, Simon. I could have stopped her. I could have saved her."

Aubrey and I exchanged a few phone calls after she returned to Costa Rica, but they became too painful for both of us and ceased within six months.

"So, I'd better get to why I'm here," I said.

"You mean this cup of coffee with me isn't the purpose of your trip?"

"Afraid not, Aubrey. You've been watching the news?"

Her head fell to one side. "You mean the missing teenage girl in California?"

"Olivia Trenton, yes."

"You think she's here in San José?"

I explained why I'd flown to Grand Cayman and the steps I took to attempt to piece together Olivia's missing day, which followed her night at the Next Level. I told her what I'd learned from Jon Krusas, the Ritz-Carlton doorman. Then I showed her Kellen's picture.

Aubrey frowned. "You'd think he'd stand out here with that blond hair and those blue eyes, but this is a big city. We're going to have to look for him."

"We?" I said hopefully.

"Of course. Do you have any information besides his first name?"

"Just that his father likely works for some shady land developer."

Aubrey smirked. "A shady American land developer in Costa Rica? Well, that really narrows it down."

I smiled. "I've missed that sense of humor, Aubrey. Even though, as I recall, most of your jokes were at my expense."

She grinned. "You were always an easy target. Besides, that's what most made Tasha laugh. Gotta give the audience what they want."

I swallowed the remainder of my coffee. "I suppose that's true."

Aubrey turned serious again. "If this guy Kellen is what his roommate in Grand Cayman suggests he is, then he's connected to some very dangerous people."

"I've dealt with a few of those in my life."

"Well, be ready to deal with a few more."

"So, then, you have an idea where to start?"

Aubrey ran her hand through her short dirty-blond hair.

"Sure," she said. "In San José, when you need to buy fruit, you go to *el mercado*. When you need to buy information, you go to *los tugurios*."

Chapter 27

La Carpio is the type of slum you imagine exists only in the worst war-torn regions of Africa, like Sudan. To say I've seen worse would be an injustice to the residents of La Carpio barrio because there comes a point when a place is simply unlivable, and it can't be said to be a "better" place to exist than anywhere else.

The air here was thick with the smell of rotting garbage. In front of us stood a city constructed of corrugated tin and old automobile tires, surrounded on two sides by filthy rivers and another by an active landfill comprising thousands of tons of waste. Adobe shacks and wooden huts leaned on one another for support while tendrils of brown-green grass clung to the sides of rudimentary structures, reaching in through boarded windows as though seeking a shelter in which to break off and die.

The only signs of human life in La Carpio hung from laundry lines—hopelessly stained shirts and torn denim jeans long dried in the equatorial heat.

Then the sound of children at play. A glimpse of a soccer ball as it bounced off one of the tin walls with a *clang* that I felt in my chest.

"They'll always have soccer," Aubrey said. "Come on. We'll start with the kids."

There were six of them, all in their early teens or almost there, all dressed in shorts and T-shirts depicting Major League Baseball teams. The boys stopped their game and eyed us suspiciously as we approached. Two dipped their hands in their pockets, undoubtedly to feel the security provided by their weapons. Switchblades, I guessed. Another two pivoted to the right, readying themselves to run if need be.

"*Hola,*" Aubrey called out to them.

The nearest of them recognized her voice instantly and smiled. He began to run toward her, then slowed himself, apparently not wishing to appear too eager in front of his friends. When they met, Aubrey wrapped her arms around him and he hugged her back. He had dark skin, blemished by the beginnings of acne. He was tall and dangerously skinny; his eyes came up to Aubrey's chin.

She turned him ninety degrees and spoke softly in his ear. He then motioned to his friends, indicating that he would be back in a few minutes.

The other five children continued their game.

"Simon, this is Fernando."

I shook the boy's hand.

Aubrey asked me whether I spoke Spanish.

"Some," I conceded.

"Fernando doesn't speak English, so I'll interpret."

"Thanks, Aubrey." I reached into my pocket and pulled out Kellen's picture, though I didn't show it to the boy just yet. First, I said, "I'm looking for bad men."

The kid grinned, motioned to the barrio behind him, and said something in Spanish.

Aubrey translated. "He said, 'Then you came to the right place.'"

According to Aubrey, there were roughly forty thousand residents in La Carpio. About half those people were immigrants from Nicaragua, Costa Rica's neighbor to the north. Recent migration to the capital city of San José in search of jobs had led to the explosion of shantytowns such as La Carpio. Although the sentiment was not entirely unfamiliar, Costa Ricans—or Ticos as they predominantly called themselves—were quick to place the blame at the feet of the

Nicaraguans (or Nicas) who continued to cross the border in record numbers in search of a better future for their children.

Fernando was a Nica. His family had been drawn to San José by the city's growing economy and Costa Rica's superior education and health-care systems. Due to decades of civil war and a five-year U.S. embargo imposed by Ronald Reagan, Nicaragua was presently one of the poorest countries in the western hemisphere, second only to Haiti. Unfortunately, despite the fact that Ticos and Nicas shared much in common—including language and culture and history and tradition—the two peoples despised each other, and children like Fernando were the ones who most suffered from the prejudice and hatred.

"The criminals I'm searching for prey on women and children," I said, pausing to allow Aubrey to translate. "They kidnap mothers, sisters, and daughters, and force them to sell their bodies to men who visit from other countries."

Fernando spoke at length and Aubrey translated.

"He said, 'I know these men you speak of. When I lived in Nicaragua, these men came to our village and stole one of my cousins. I have never seen her again. Maybe she is dead.'"

I said, "Do you know where to find these men?"

The child shrugged, spoke softly.

Aubrey translated. "He's saying, 'What good does it do to find them? You are one man. They are many, and they are dangerous. They carry guns and they are protected by police because of money.'"

I unfolded the picture of Kellen and showed it to him.

"Then let's start with one man," I said. "This man, do you know him?"

The boy stared at the photograph for nearly a minute before he spoke.

Aubrey said, "He doesn't know him, but he's seen him in San José. At night this man talks to the visitors you spoke of, the ones who come here to pay for women's bodies."

"Where can I find him?" I said.

Aubrey listened to Fernando as he spoke animatedly, apparently giving directions.

Finally, she cut him off, turned to me, said, "He mentioned a bar in the university district. I know where it is."

Chapter 28

Aubrey and I spent that evening in Los Yoses and San Pedro, in the vicinity of Vyrus, the popular rock-and-roll bar that Fernando had once seen Kellen standing in front of. There were numerous bars in the area and we checked them all to no avail. When it became clear that we wouldn't spot Kellen ourselves, we began asking around, showing some university students and other partygoers his picture. We told them he was my nephew and I was supposed to meet up with him but had lost his mobile number. Everyone was friendly enough, but no one could tell us where to find him. My heart raced; my neck tensed. My thoughts continually returned to the fact that the more time passed, the more likely the trail would go cold, the more likely Olivia would be gone for good.

At two in the morning, I conceded that we'd hit a dead end.

"There's no such thing as a dead end," Aubrey said.

Before I could reply, she smacked her own forehead with the palm of her hand.

"How could I be so goddamn *stupid*?" she said.

"What are you talking about?"

She grabbed me by the wrist and pulled so hard, I thought my arm might rip out of its socket. She didn't speak again until we were in the Land Cruiser.

"He's an *American*," she said.

"So?"

"So if he's ever had so much as a stubborn head cold in the past decade and a half, he's been to CIMA. Take us to my hospital. Now."

I started the engine and pulled away from the curb.

"We don't have his last name," I said. "You'll be able to find him in your database?"

"How many Kellens you think live in Costa Rica?" she said.

End of discussion.

When we reached the hospital, I again parked in front of the main wing.

"Wait here," Aubrey said. "I'll be back in five minutes."

While I waited, I dialed the cell phone number I'd found in Jason Gutiérrez's e-mail account.

"The subscriber you have called is not able to receive calls at this time."

I considered calling Edgar, but if on the off chance he and Emma had been able to fall asleep, it'd be monstrous for me to wake them. I knew just how valuable those few hours of sleep were. When Tasha and I were waiting on news about Hailey, only once had we fallen asleep at the same time. And we were both woken by a well-meaning caller forty-five minutes later. As it happened, we never got the chance to sleep in the same bed at the same time again.

Tasha. Seeing Aubrey again after all these years made my wife's death feel fresh, made her absence sting like an open wound. After Tasha was gone, I was assured again and again that time heals all. Sure, time might eventually dull some of the pain. But those who tell you that time actually *heals* are feeding you a crock of shit.

Several minutes later, Aubrey Lang returned to the Land Cruiser with a beautiful and genuine smile. Without a word, she handed me a small piece of stationery with the Viagra logo at the top. Scribbled below was an apartment address in San José.

"He's listed under the name Kellen Adams," she said. "But there's a note in his chart that says he had no identification on him either time he showed up in the ER."

"You're wonderful, Aubrey."

Before I could enter the address into the Land Cruiser's nav system, she slapped my hand away and said, "Just drive, Simon. I know where it is."

Escazú, Aubrey told me, was an elite residential neighborhood known for attracting expatriates, from not only the United States but countries in South America and Europe as well.

We parked across the street from Kellen's condominium complex and gazed up at the dark windows on the sixth floor, where our subject apparently maintained a flat. I turned off my BlackBerry and started toward the building with Aubrey Lang at my heels. I'd tried to drop her off at her own apartment before coming here, but she wouldn't hear of it. She insisted I should have a lookout, which was technically true. But if anything were to happen to her, I'd never forgive myself. Aubrey was too extraordinary a person, too good.

No one was entering or exiting the building at two thirty in the morning, so we'd have to find another way in. Blocking the artificial outside light with my hands, I pressed my face up against the glass door, which led into a dark vestibule.

"No alarm," I said.

I pulled hard on the handle, and the door shook in its frame. I considered the diamond in my pocket but I didn't particularly care to look like a fool in front of Aubrey. So I took a step back, lowered my shoulder, and threw my weight at the area nearest the lock.

I was in, and not entirely able to suppress my smile.

I held the door open for Aubrey.

As she passed through, she said, "Don't they make tools for things like this?"

"I'm saving up for a set."

We took the stairwell, which was lit with flickering fluorescent lights that were hell on the eyes. Our feet were fast and light as we took two steps at a time up six flights.

At the entrance to the sixth floor, I asked Aubrey to wait at the door, to keep her eye on the hallway, and to alert me if anyone approached Kellen's apartment while I was inside.

"What's the signal?" she said.

"Just yell, 'Simon, someone is approaching the apartment you broke into. I think you should get out of there right now.'"

She grinned despite herself. "You've gotten a little funnier in the past several years."

"Just a little?"

She reached into her pocket and pulled out a tiny silver tube.

"What's that?" I said.

"It's a lady whistle. San José can be . . . not safe for single women at night."

"All right," I said, "you see someone coming, you blow that whistle until he goes deaf. Then give me the signal."

I took her smile with me as I crept down the length of the hall. When I reached Kellen's door, I gave a smile of my own. No dead bolt. Which meant a simple credit card would do.

I reached into my back pocket, pulled out my wallet, and swiped the lock with my AmEx Blue. Quietly I turned the knob and opened the door, very aware of the fact that I wasn't armed. I'd have to rectify that problem very soon.

I stepped inside the apartment and waited for my eyes to adjust to the darkness. Nicer than my studio in D.C. Bigger, too. No wonder the kid spent more time here than with Jon Krusas in their rinky-dink flat in Grand Cayman.

The furniture represented every color of the spectrum, but the sofas looked soft and comfortable. Even with the adrenaline pulsing through my veins, I was tempted to have a seat, maybe even take a brief nap. Each year, this job was wearing me down a bit more. Not just the traveling, but also the constant worry I'd screw something up, cost someone their child. Emotionally, these past eleven years had taken a hell of a toll.

I crossed the room, pressed my back up against the wall, and stole a glimpse down the foyer. Three more doors, two were open.

Of the two, one led to a bathroom, the other a closet. Which meant Kellen had to be behind Door Number 3.

I took two strides, turned and backed myself into the opposite wall, feeling along the Sheetrock with my fingers for the door. When I reached the door, I took a deep breath and twisted the knob.

I entered the room cautiously, crouched low in case Kellen had a weapon.

And he did.

A lightweight Spyderco Manix with a blue handle.

A blade of about three inches—thrust into his right eye up to the hilt.

"Christ," I said.

Looks like my asking around had gotten the kid killed.

Chapter 29

I cleared the closet, checked under the bed, then turned on a small lamp. Saw that the blood on the bed was still fresh. Still flowing freely from the steel-filled eye socket. Meant that I didn't just get Kellen killed; I'd arrived just in time for the frame.

I clenched my ungloved hands into fists and made a decision. Olivia didn't have time for me to get myself arrested. Hell, given the evidence—my presence in the room around the time of the murder, my prints all over the apartment, my asking around the university district for the victim's whereabouts—if I got picked up on this, I might never go free again.

So I ran.

I bolted out of the apartment and down the hallway, grabbing Aubrey at the stairwell.

"What's going on?" she said urgently, just loud enough for me to hear.

"Kellen's dead," I said between heavy breaths. "The blood's fresh. Which means we've got to get out of here, fast."

Together we bounded down the steps without looking back. My right ankle screamed out in pain, and on the second landing, I thought I'd broken it. But I grimaced and cursed under my breath, and kept moving.

Out of the stairwell and into the vestibule, I threw myself at the crash bar and Aubrey and I were outside running through the night in the direction of the Land Cruiser.

Aubrey stopped at the door to the passenger side and I kept going toward the driver's.

But as I rounded the rear of the vehicle, I heard Aubrey let out a panicked yelp, followed by a hushed command uttered by a man in Spanish.

I knew there was no time to freeze; I had to do something. So I threw my right foot onto the back bumper and heaved myself onto the roof of the Land Cruiser, making as little noise as possible. In my peripheral I spotted a second man, who'd been waiting for me on the driver's side. This second assailant turned his head to sneak a peek around the rear of the vehicle to determine whether I'd spun in the other direction to help Aubrey.

When he did, I turned and leapt from the roof of the SUV onto his back, dragging him down to the blacktop. A gun dropped from his hand and landed a few feet away. When he reached for it, I grabbed the fingers of his right hand and bent them all the way back till I heard them snap, and he screamed. I slammed his head hard against the pavement, saw the other man coming around the corner with Aubrey in front of him, so I twisted Broken Fingers' body on top of me to act as a shield, and sure enough, Broken Fingers took two bullets for me—one in the chest, one in the gut.

The man who had Aubrey spun himself around to take cover as I rolled over Broken Fingers' dead or dying body to get to the gun. When I saw Aubrey's shadow coming around the corner again, I rolled Broken Fingers' body back on top, and he took two more bullets for me—one in the leg and one in the head. The other guy was getting sloppy.

And nervous. I could see his feet shuffling under the SUV as he decided whether to run, now that Broken Fingers was dead and I had the gun.

Beneath the SUV, I had a clear shot at his legs, but he was still holding a gun to Aubrey's head. So I tossed Broken Fingers' broken body aside and leapt to my feet, crouching along the side of the Land Cruiser until I had the angle.

When I reached the front of the vehicle, I stole a glance. The gunman wasn't even facing in the right direction. I raised my weapon and sighted the back of his skull, but before I could squeeze the trigger, the screech of police sirens shattered the night silence.

The gunman threw Aubrey hard to the ground, pivoted, and ran toward the front of the Land Cruiser—and me.

Before he could pass the left front fender, I delivered a blow square to his jaw.

He dropped as though he'd been hit in the head with a sledge-hammer.

I looked up, saw Aubrey getting to her feet.

"Are you okay?" I shouted over the blare of the approaching sirens.

"I'm fine."

"Open the rear door," I said. "This one's coming with us."

She didn't hesitate.

I tossed the unconscious gunman inside and got behind the wheel, while Aubrey took the passenger seat. I turned the key over in the ignition and the engine roared.

I threw the transmission into drive and pressed down on the accelerator, the large tires spinning before gaining traction, then screeching as I peeled away from the curb.

In the rearview, red and blue lights were now visible.

To Aubrey, I said, "If they catch us, I took you as a hostage."

"They're not going to catch us," she said.

I grinned in the light of the dashboard.

There was something to be said for the optimists of the world.

Chapter 30

I turned right on Avenida 2, then jumped onto the 105 as per Aubrey's shouted instructions.

"Shouldn't I avoid the main roads?" I said.

"Not yet."

"What about roadblocks?"

"We need to get as far away from San José as we can before they have time to set them up. Don't worry; we have time. This isn't exactly the NYPD we're talking about."

"Fine," I said. "Where are we going?"

"Just keep driving north."

Costa Rica is only about the size of Vermont and New Hampshire combined, but it seemed much larger hours later as we drove farther away from the city, toward the Nicaraguan border. We'd begun our journey aimlessly but now had a destination, thanks to the gentleman currently hog-tied on the backseat of the Land Cruiser.

As soon as we stopped hearing sirens, we'd pulled off the road. Aubrey didn't have any smelling salts, but the gunman seemed to be coming around—thanks largely to a couple cupfuls of cold water procured at a nearby convenience store.

The assailant had not only seen his partner die, but put four bullets in him himself. So as soon as I leveled the gun on him, he started jabbering about his bosses and where they were located. Said if we were to spare his life, he could take us to them.

We were headed to Los Chiles, a border town four klicks south of Nicaragua. During the '80s, Aubrey explained, the area became a vital supply route for the Contras, who were fighting to overthrow the Sandinista government in Nicaragua—with a bit of clandestine help from Oliver North.

From there, we'd be heading to Caño Negro, a wetlands site and refuge to numerous endangered species, including cougars, jaguars, and capuchin and spider monkeys.

We were destined for the untouched Costa Rican rain forest.

It was there our captive said we'd find the men we were looking for—and the young women they held against their will.

"This is the refuge I fought to save when I first joined the Peace Corps," Aubrey said solemnly as we neared the reserve.

As a result of illegal poaching and logging operations, the stability of the area was now in great danger, she said. The rain forest was dwindling due to deforestation, and the wildlife was suffering. Bird counts were at an all-time low. Fewer migratory birds returned to the park each year, and the macaws had completely vanished.

"The water levels of the once mighty Río Frío are falling rapidly," she said. "Manatees and sharks used to call the park home. But no more. The caiman and tarpon populations are petering out. The lake is drying up. Used to be that this marsh resembled the Florida Everglades." She sighed. "Unless we step up our conservation efforts, someday it will look more like the Arizona desert."

In her voice was a desperation I'd only ever heard from the parents of missing children. It moved me that such a love could be expressed for the earth, even after two millennia of being told that the planet was put here for us to rape and plunder as we saw fit.

As we cruised up a paved road with fields of sugarcane on either side, Aubrey informed us that we were nearing Los Chiles.

I couldn't help but feel excited. I was dead certain Olivia was with these men. Why else kill Kellen and come after Aubrey and me?

"We have two options," she said. "There's no bridge to cross over the Frío River, so we either have to find a boat or turn west off the main road and drive about six miles south to the nearest bridge at San Emilio."

"I opt for the drive."

"I was hoping you'd say that." Aubrey turned to face me, and I could see the exhaustion in her eyes.

"You okay?" I said.

"Yeah. I was just thinking it's a good thing you splurged for the four-wheel drive."

As I soon discovered, that was an understatement. Once we turned off the main road, it felt as though we were navigating the surface of the moon, only with tremendous trees standing guard on either side, their canopies all but blacking out the starlight.

I turned off our headlights and checked the clock. Since running from the cops in Escazú, we'd been driving for over three hours. The sun would be rising soon.

Our captive had confirmed for us that Kellen acted as a lure when he was out of the country, attracting young girls on vacation in the Caribbean, then passing on information about them to his confederates, who'd later abduct them. The gunman, however, claimed not to recognize Olivia Trenton or her three friends and balked at the idea that four men had flown from Costa Rica to Los Angeles to invade a home and kidnap a single teenage girl.

"Where would be the profit?" he said in Costa Rican Spanish.

I didn't mention the eight and a half million dollars they'd extorted from the girl's father.

The assailant certainly didn't know anything about the money.

And to some extent, that worried me.

After a slow, dark, and bumpy drive, we eventually ran out of dirt road. Through the high trees we could see the early light of dawn. Given what I'd learned about the rain forest's other wildlife during the drive, I was comforted by the chirping and squawking of rare birds coming from all around us.

"They have us surrounded," Aubrey deadpanned.

I reached under the seat and grabbed our captive's Glock 20, which had a magazine capacity of fifteen rounds. Our friend had an additional two magazines on him. Ten-millimeter, auto.

I stepped out of the Land Cruiser, opened the rear door, and pulled our attacker out by the hair. I untied him but left him gagged, kept his hands bound. Lifted him off the dirt.

"Stay here," I told Aubrey, gathering up the rope I'd stolen from the stockroom of the convenience store. "Turn the vehicle around so we can leave quickly. If I'm not back in thirty minutes, drive."

I pushed the gunman forward into the forest. According to him, the camp wasn't far from here. Maybe a five-minute walk. I could hear the Frío River in the distance and recalled Aubrey's warning about alligators.

As though cougars and jaguars aren't enough to worry about.

A few minutes later we reached the clearing.

There were four huts constructed in a semicircle with the leavings of a fire in the dead center of the clearing. According to my hostage, two men slept in each of the two outer huts, the women and teenage girls in the inner two.

The men were armed with guns and machetes.

Here's where my Marshals training would come in handy.

I'd gathered as much intelligence as I could from my hostage. My greatest concern wasn't the four men guarding this clearing or even the cougars and jaguars. My captive had claimed there was another clearing not far away, one with no hostages but far more men. He may well have been lying, but I didn't want to take that chance. If he was telling the truth, this rescue could turn into a massacre.

So instead of rushing into the clearing and firing, I'd use close-quarters combat techniques and try to keep the noise to a minimum so as not to disturb the other camp.

First thing I did was tie my captive to a tree and make sure his gag was securely in place. Last thing I needed was for him to alert the others to my presence.

Second, I surveyed the scene, estimated the distance between each hut, determined the maximum number of people who could be in each. Four comfortably, eight if cramped.

Third, I decided on my diversion. I wasn't carrying a flashbang, smoke, or gas grenade, and I didn't want to explode any of my ammunition. That left something a bit less conventional. I set the alarm on my BlackBerry; in sixty seconds, we'd be listening to a nice calypso.

The element of surprise was essential. In that respect, my timing couldn't have been better. I watched as one man stepped out of the hut nearest to me and stretched his arms as high as he could. He yawned, cracked his back. Clearly he'd just woken up.

I placed the BlackBerry in the grass and moved behind a tree off to the side. I held my gun ready, just in case.

I counted down in my head.

Six . . . five . . . four . . . three . . . two . . . one . . . calypso.

The alarm was just loud enough for our friend Sleepy to hear but not loud enough to wake the others. He looked around, not necessarily concerned but irritated. He started toward the noise. His own gun remained in his waistband, so that was where I placed mine as well.

He stepped into the woods and I followed silently. He stopped just short of the BlackBerry, looked down, but didn't see the device, because it was hidden in the tall grass. He went to his haunches and felt around, finally found it. He pushed himself to his feet.

Standing directly behind him, I said, "That's mine, pal."

When he spun around, I snatched him by the front of his shirt and whiplashed him toward me, lowering my chin to my chest so that the crown of my head would strike him flush in the face.

He went down, instantly unconscious.

The trick had been not to grab him by the back of his neck to allow him time to tense his shoulders. An effective headbutt catches its target completely off guard, just as mine had. During my training, we'd called it by its Scottish name—the Glasgow kiss.

I left him facedown in the grass, then turned back toward the clearing.

One down, at least three to go.

Chapter 31

I skirted the edge of the clearing and cautiously moved toward the hut I'd seen the first man exit. The hut was well built but not perfect; I could see through the bound pieces of wood in some places. Inside there were two bunks, one occupied. The sleeper was snoring, which would of course make things easier for me. What I wasn't thrilled to see was how much firepower they actually had. Not just handguns, but high-powered automatic assault rifles too. There were tools as well, not just hammers and screwdrivers but also chain saws and one big, nasty axe.

The only way in was the front door.

First I checked the other three huts. From what I could see, six young women were sleeping in one, seven in another. Two more guards slept in the third, one of whom was stirring. I had to act fast. Best thing to do, I thought, would be to silence the one in the first hut and gain access to the weapons. At that point, I'd be able to walk right into the last hut and demand their surrender. I'd give them the option: give themselves up and let the girls go, or die by their own guns. Should be a simple decision for anyone.

Quietly I pushed open the door to the first hut. In my right hand I held the Glock. Light seeped in through the walls and the ceiling; the interior reeked badly of sawdust, and it was all I could do to keep from sneezing and giving away my location to the other two guards. Not to mention the men possibly stationed at the other clearing.

I stepped slowly across the wood planks, trying to make as little noise as possible.

I'd want to reach out and cover his mouth with my hand so that he couldn't shout.

To my left, I could see my shadow creeping across the space with me. To my immediate right hung the axe.

I was within a few feet of the sleeping man when I suddenly felt a cool breeze from behind me.

I glanced to my left and saw a second shadow overlapping mine.

Someone was standing behind me.

I still had a chance to keep things quiet.

In one fluid move, I snatched the Glock from my right hand with my left, and with my right arm I reached for the axe on the wall.

As I gripped the axe, I ducked and spun around.

The man standing behind me aimed his gun.

But I buried the business end of the axe deep into his gut before he could fire.

The cut was so deep, I half expected his torso to separate from the lower half of his body like in a *Tom and Jerry* cartoon.

Instead his corpse simply slumped forward and dropped to the ground with an ugly *splat*.

Before the body hit, I'd already turned back around and locked on to the sleeper with my Glock. He'd been reaching under the bed—presumably for his own weapon—but instantly stopped once he found himself staring into my barrel.

With both arms, he slowly reached for the ceiling instead.

"*Gracias,*" I said.

Keeping one eye on him and the other on the open door, I approached him. When I was close enough, I twisted the Glock and hit him square in the face with the butt.

His body instantly crumpled, rolled off the bed, hit the floor with a *thunk*.

I made sure he was unconscious, swiped his gun from under the bed, then turned to walk out of the hut so I could finish the job.

That was when the screaming began.

Chapter 32

I pressed my face up against the wall inside the hut and watched the fourth man run into the jungle, shouting "*¡Socorro!*"

I had to assume that was the Tico term for "I need some fucking backup."

I leapt over the body of the man who caught the axe in his stomach and ran out of the hut, turned left, and kicked in the chained door of the first inner structure.

Sleeping women shot up in their beds and sleeping bags in surprise, all of them staring directly at the Glock. I lowered it, said, "Hurry, ladies. You're free."

The ones who spoke English translated it to the others, and as I ran out the door, I heard a stampede of bare feet following me.

I pointed. "Follow the path just beyond those trees. There's a woman waiting with an SUV."

I turned toward the next hut, kicked in the door, and shouted the same instructions.

Some of the women appeared drugged, all were bruised, but none of the girls seemed critical. The uninjured women assisted the others.

I waited for the last one to exit the huts; then I followed.

Behind me I heard male voices yelling in Costa Rican Spanish. The voices were followed by footfalls through the jungle, then gunshots.

I spun and saw them coming, at least a half dozen of them. I needed to buy the girls some time.

So, I stopped.

Removed the second Glock from my waistband.

Aimed both weapons.

And fired.

Our pursuers jumped to the jungle floor, ceasing their fire.

I turned, ran to gain cover just as they began shooting again.

I ducked behind the first tree I reached and returned fire.

Then I paused, waiting until the first men were up and pursuing again before dropping to the grass and taking aim.

I struck the first two men to enter the clearing. Both went down spraying blood, and that slowed down the others.

I stood and fired again, then turned and followed the women. I sourced their screams and knew I wasn't all that far behind them.

Bullets continued to fly in our direction, ricocheting off the trunks of thick trees, kicking up grass and dirt and fallen branches at my feet.

Every time a new barrage came forth, I turned and fired back.

Short of breath, my right ankle aching worse than ever since the accident on Mulholland, I stopped behind a tree to switch magazines and nearly took a shot to the head.

I waited for a break in the fire, then leapt out from behind the tree with both guns blazing.

The onslaught of bullets coming from their direction instantly stopped, and I took off again, unsure how much farther I could run on this ankle.

After a minute or so, the silver Land Cruiser was within my line of vision.

I turned one last time and unloaded both clips before hopping onto the rear bumper and screaming, *"Drive, Aubrey! Drive!"*

And drive she did.

Chapter 33

When we reached the small town of Upala, nine klicks south of the Nicaraguan border, we released our collective breath. In a large dirt lot from which we could see the main road, we emptied out of the Land Cruiser and stretched our limbs, took in the full light of morning.

I had plenty of questions for these young women, but the one thing I was able to discern with certainty during our drive was that Olivia Trenton was not among them.

After a few minutes, Aubrey gathered them around, spoke to them in Spanish. I remained in the background, out of earshot. Whatever hell these girls had endured, it would be a woman who first heard their story.

As I waited, I dialed the number from Jason Gutiérrez's e-mail again.

"*The subscriber you have called is not able to receive calls at this time.*"

Then I called Edgar Trenton.

"Simon," he answered, "tell me you have good news."

"I'm afraid not, Ed."

I remained vague but apprised him of the events in the jungle and how we managed to escape the clearing with thirteen survivors stuffed into an eight-seater Land Cruiser.

"But none of them are Olivia," I said. "Aubrey is with them now. She's getting what information she can."

Meanwhile, the FBI had continued its focus on Edgar, and showed little progress in finding his daughter.

"They're going to arrest me," Edgar said. "My lawyer, Lepavsky, tells me maybe tomorrow, perhaps the day after. But now it's just a matter of time."

I didn't know what to say to that. It was the one common aspect of a missing-child case I'd been spared—I'd never been considered a suspect. Neither had Tasha.

"What does Emma think of all this?" I said. "Is she supporting you?"

When he didn't respond, I knew that Emma too was beginning to suspect him.

"Will you come back here, Simon? Continue to help us look?"

"Of course," I said. "There's an airport here in Upala. Charters only, unfortunately."

"I'll call the airport now and make arrangements."

"All right," I said. "I'll see you in a few hours."

Whether it was from lack of sleep or lack of food or both, I felt ill, my head buzzing, my thinking unclear. My gut felt as though I'd just stepped off a roller coaster after a dozen rides in a row. My legs were unsteady, my right ankle threatening to fold in the damp grass, and I needed something to grab on to. I stumbled, then felt someone supporting me from under my arms.

Slowly, I turned.

"Are you okay?" Aubrey said.

I wasn't sure how to answer her. I was covered in blood but it wasn't mine, so I supposed I couldn't complain much.

My eyes fell on the young women as Aubrey began to tell me more about them. Most of the girls were from Central America— Guatemala, Nicaragua, Panama. Two were from the Dominican Republic. One was from Colombia.

Aubrey said, "They were taken all over Costa Rica to turn tricks. Not just San José, but Guanacaste, Limón, Puntarenas. They'd get picked up at that clearing—two or three girls at a time—and get taken to a certain province for the night."

My gaze remained locked on the girls, a single thought circling: *One of them could have been Hailey.*

"How old are they?" I managed.

"About half are in their early twenties. The rest are teenagers. The youngest is sixteen."

The field around me seemed to be spinning, and I couldn't for the life of me remember why I hadn't killed those men.

"They'll be okay now?" I said.

Aubrey bowed her head. "I'll take them to my hospital, then we'll need to get them out of the country as soon as possible. It won't be safe for them here."

I reached into my back pocket, pulled out my wallet, removed the AmEx I'd used to break into Kellen's apartment. "Here," I said. "Take this. Make sure each girl gets home safely. Hire bodyguards if you need to."

"Thank you, Simon." She placed the palm of her hand gently on the scruff of the left side of my face. "I'm sorry you didn't find Olivia."

"It's not over," I said.

"Where to next?"

"Back to California."

"Why don't you wait until tomorrow, Simon? You're exhausted. Come with us to the hospital and get that ankle X-rayed. Tonight, stay with me in San José, then fly out fresh in the morning."

I stared into her eyes and it was like staring into the past. A place where it was warm and comfortable and familiar and our cares were much simpler.

"I'd love to," I said. "But I can't."

"Excuse me?" came a small voice from behind us. "I am sorry if I am to interrupt."

She was tall, clearly one of the older girls. Her accent was thick and South American.

"My name is Mariana Silva."

She was from Colombia. Big brown eyes; long, straight, jet black hair. Even gaunt, she was beyond beautiful.

"I did not speak up before," she said. "Because I was afraid. But after the courage you have shown to us, how is it possible I can remain silent?"

I took a painful step toward her, the fog in my head lifting. "Remain silent about what, Mariana?"

She hesitated. But she'd already made this decision.

She looked back to be sure none of the other girls was listening and struggled to relate her thoughts in English. "I possess information that may help you to find this girl, Olivia Trenton."

Chapter 34

Mariana Silva led me farther away from the others so that she could speak freely.

"I can tell you nothing with absolute certainty," she said quietly, holding her narrow arms tightly as though to protect herself against some chill only she felt. "But the men who held us, they spoke just yesterday about a *mara*—from Honduras, I think— that sent some men to the United States and made a great sum of money."

"*Mara*?" I said. "A gang?"

"Yes. The reason I listened so intently is that I heard them speak of my country. This *mara*, it is known for kidnapping women and selling them to the cartels in Colombia to work as mules."

"Drug mules."

"Yes. Since the 9/11, it has become more and more difficult to hire mules even from the poorest parts of my country. Security increases and more and more young women from South America are caught and imprisoned in the United States."

"So the cartels kidnap women to smuggle drugs."

"It has become a very, very dangerous job. Because it is so difficult to succeed, they make the women carry more and more drugs. Sometimes one hundred, maybe one hundred fifty balloons inside their bodies. If just one balloon bursts or leaks, the mule, she will—"

"She will die," I finished.

"These *maras,* they threaten to kill the family and friends of the mule if they are to say anything once they reach the States. Once they are a mule, they are a mule for life. There is no escape. Except suicide." She pointed to the group of women standing around the Land Cruiser, all of them still visibly shaken. "We are the lucky ones. The Caucasian women, they are not so lucky, because they are much easier to get past customs."

"Do you know the name of this *mara* these men were talking about?"

Mariana shook her head. "There are so many. They did not even know for sure this *mara* was from Honduras. Only they think this. Could be they are from Guatemala or El Salvador."

"Do they have anything in common, these gangs? Any tattoos or markings?"

"Yes, this is true. They wear tattoos, almost all of them. They read, *La vida por las maras.*"

" 'The life for the gangs.' "

"Yes. The life for the gangs."

I held up a finger. "Excuse me one moment, Mariana."

I hobbled toward the other side of the lot, my heart racing. I dialed Edgar's number on my BlackBerry.

"Simon," he answered, "your flight back to the States is booked. You're going to be flying directly into Van Nuys Airport. It's used only for private, chartered aircraft. Nicholas will be there to pick you up. Your flight—"

"Change of plans," I said. "I need to fly into Bogotá instead."

I considered the fact that Olivia's U.S. passport was in my pocket. It made sense. She couldn't use it, of course. They'd have to create for her an entirely new identity.

"Bogotá? Tell me, what's happening, Simon? Do you have a lead?"

"Maybe," I said. "Maybe not. One of the women here overheard something her captors were saying about a Central American gang making a big score in the United States. If that's the case, it's possible that they then sold Olivia to the Colombians to work as a drug mule."

Edgar remained silent for nearly a minute. I twice checked the connection to be sure I hadn't lost him.

"But why, Simon?" he said. "Why? They got their money. Why didn't they just release her?"

"I don't know the answer to that," I admitted. "Maybe they knew Olivia could identify them. Maybe there were other parties involved from the beginning. Maybe they're just greedy. There's no telling until we get our hands on them."

"All right," he said, his voice cracking. "I'll arrange a flight for you from Upala to Bogotá, Colombia."

I looked in the direction of Mariana Silva, called out to her. "Do you need a lift home?"

Mariana nodded hopefully.

Into the phone I said, "Make it for two."

Since Mariana had no identification, I tried to provide Edgar with instructions on how to take care of customs and immigration agents in Colombia, but he assured me that he and his people were well-versed "in the law."

After hanging up, I joined Aubrey out of earshot of the women. I passed on what Mariana had told me.

"The cartels?" she said, her lower lip suddenly trembling. "Simon, we're not talking now about a few men with guns holed up in huts in the Costa Rican rain forest. These cartels, they're like armies."

"I know, Aubrey." As beautiful a country as it is, if there was one place in the world I could have lived without ever returning to, it was Colombia.

"But then—"

"This is different, Aubrey. I'm one man, not a platoon. I'll be able to use stealth. If Olivia's in Colombia, I *will* find her and bring her home."

"I'm going with you," she said.

I smiled. Touched her face. "No. You're going to stay here. You're

going to help these women get treatment at CIMA, then you're going to make sure each and every one of them gets home safely."

She sighed heavily, wrapped her arms around me, and I held her
as closely as I had held anyone in a long while.

"Good-bye, Simon."

"*Adiós,* Aubrey. I'll be seeing you again when this is over."

She smiled despite the tears in her eyes. Said, "I guess that means
I'd better not abuse your American Express too badly."

I winked. "Just be sure to leave enough for the two of us to sit
down and enjoy a good strong cup of Costa Rica's finest coffee when
all this is over."

Part
Three

THE LORDS
OF BOGOTÁ

Chapter 35

Everything I knew about Colombia I'd learned while I was a U.S. Marshal.

The South American country was in a state of perpetual conflict. Since the mid-'60s, guerrilla insurgents calling themselves the Revolutionary Armed Forces of Colombia (FARC) and the National Liberation Army (ELN) had sustained attacks on the Colombian government. Just what the bloody civil war was being fought over was a matter of perspective. The peasant revolutionaries claimed to be fighting for the rights of the poor and to protect all citizens from government violence, while the government claimed to be fighting to preserve order and stability. Meanwhile, far-right paramilitary groups such as the United Self-Defense Forces of Colombia (AUC) had joined the fight against the guerrillas; their specialty: slaughtering peasants, labor union leaders, and anyone else suspected of having ties to the left. Other powerful neo-paramilitary groups, such as Los Urabeños and Los Rastrojos, specialized in killing each other in an attempt to gain complete control of Colombia's multibillion-dollar drug trade.

Tens of thousands had died; millions had been displaced. And the country remained the world's largest producer of cocaine.

When Mariana and I touched down at El Dorado International Airport in Bogotá and exited the plane, I was surprised to find it cold and rainy. It was Colombia's warm season, its dry season. Yet everything I could see from the tarmac was colored gray with fog and frost.

So much for Tommy Bahama. In Colombia's capital city, I would need to dress a bit warmer, preferably head to toe in black attire so as not to stand out.

I'd slept through the entire flight, as had Mariana, so it was only now on the tarmac that I was able to ask her about her family, whether she had a place to stay.

"I do not," she said, but didn't elaborate. And there was really no time for questions.

"All right," I said. "Let's take a taxi. My client booked me a room at Casa Medina; I'm sure he'll pay for a second room for as long as necessary."

"Thank you, Señor Fisk."

"Call me Simon."

Once we reached the hotel, I went straight to my room and laid out a map of Colombia. Kidnappings in the country were very common. FARC, ELN, the M-19, and other guerrilla groups regularly used the hideous tactic to demand ransom in order to raise funds to sustain their war. Paramilitary groups kidnapped in order to intimidate their adversaries, while the cartels used the practice in order to coerce politicians and judges who might otherwise deign to legislate and enforce harsh drug laws.

Colombia continued to boast one of the highest numbers of kidnap victims in the world.

Since the guerrillas and the paramilitary groups also financed their endeavors through the trafficking of illegal drugs, if Olivia was indeed sold by a Central American gang to a Colombian syndicate in order to act as a smuggler, the field was wide open. No organization could be counted out. So I'd need to determine which part of the country each group was based out of, then attend to them one by one.

Problem was, Colombia's a large nation, roughly the size of Portugal, Spain, and France combined. The country has a population of over 45 million, and its land is ecologically diverse. Between Colombia's Atlantic and Pacific coastlines lay not only the thick Amazon jungle, but also vast flatlands and burning deserts and high mountain peaks capped with snow.

I moved the map from the desk to the table to the bed, but the country appeared no less imposing. I knew then that I couldn't tackle this alone.

The U.S. Marshals had recently opened a foreign field office in Colombia, but I didn't know anyone there. I did, however, have a contact at the DEA's Bogotá Country Office.

All incoming calls to the office were recorded, so unfortunately, I couldn't just pick up the phone and dial. I'd have to stake out the U.S. Embassy and wait for my contact to come out. Of course, if someone recognized me and saw us together, there would be questions, and I certainly wouldn't be able to count on his assistance. So I'd have to get a message to him to meet me at a location where we could talk. For that, my new friend Mariana Silva would come in handy, and I knew she'd be more than happy to help.

But first, I needed a shower. Then I had to head downstairs to buy some clothes befitting an American in Bogotá. And most of all, I needed an espresso. Because if there *is* one thing Colombia is known for—besides its cocaine, cartels, kidnappings, and killings—it's high-quality, rich, delicious, full-bodied coffee.

Chapter 36

Two hours later, Mariana and I sat at a table at an outdoor café down the street from the U.S. Embassy. I was on my third espresso of the day and feeling recharged. The sun had replaced the rain, but the air remained chilled. I wore a black suit over a black shirt and tie and felt wired yet comfortable as I watched the entrance to the embassy, hoping to catch a glimpse of Special Agent Samuel Greyson.

"How does he look, this man?" Mariana said.

"African American. Around my age, maybe a few years older. Good-looking guy."

I'd met Greyson—or Grey, as he preferred to be called—shortly after I finished Basic Training at FLETC, when we were both assigned to the nation's capital. We'd hit it off right away, and I'd never forget one of our first conversations.

We'd been mocking interagency squabbles, which we thought were worse in D.C. than in any other part of the country. FBI versus DEA versus Secret Service versus ATF versus the U.S. Marshals—it was all nonsense, as far as we were concerned. After a few too many beers, we decided that we, the new generation, would be the ones to put an end to it; we'd be the pair to unite all the federal law enforcement agencies to boost morale, communication, and above all, cooperation, to make America a safer and better place.

Toward the end of the night, Grey set his beer down and said,

"You know, Simon, dismiss everything I told you tonight. Forget interagency cooperation."

"Forget it?" I said, still smiling, waiting for the punch line.

"Forget it. Maybe we at the DEA can hash things out with ATF, maybe even the FBI. But the U.S. Marshals, no way."

"No way, huh?" I tried to set the joke up for him. "Why's that, Grey?"

He looked me in the eyes, his mouth a single flat line, and said, "Because y'all are a bunch of goddamn racists."

The music in the bar was low, and he'd said it loud enough for other patrons to hear. We were still fairly new to D.C., and we didn't know who was there—there could've been some up-and-coming congressman, a cabinet member, even a director, sitting right behind us.

Aside from being a new friend, back then Grey was also the perfect male specimen. I didn't want to tangle with him; that much I knew. And I still couldn't tell if he was serious.

"What?" he said, reading my face. "You going to deny it, Simon?"

"The Marshals Service was on the front line of the civil rights movement in the '60s," I argued. "We provided protection to civil rights volunteers, accompanied that kid James Meredith when he registered at the segregated University of Mississippi. We protected black schoolchildren during the integration of the public schools in the South. Hell, we're even depicted in that Norman Rockwell painting, for Christ's sake."

"You also recovered fugitive slaves in the nineteenth century."

There was nothing I could say to that. The Marshals were the oldest federal law enforcement agency in the United States, around since 1789. When Wyatt Earp was sworn in as a Deputy U.S. Marshal in Tombstone, the agency was already nearly a century old. The Marshals had a history, for better or worse. Often we'd like to think of history as something detestable that happened to other people. But when you join a law enforcement organization like the U.S. Marshals, in at least some capacity, you adopt its history, the good right along with the bad.

Grey added, "Then there's this lawsuit pending against Janet Reno and the Justice Department. How do you feel about that?"

"I don't know enough of the facts," I admitted.

Once the facts did come to light, the jury found the Marshals Service to be a racially hostile environment and to have demonstrated a pattern of discriminatory behavior against blacks in its promotion practices. Chief Deputy U.S. Marshal Matthew Fogg won $4 million as a result of the Marshals' Title VII race discrimination and retaliation violations. And for months, I hung my head low when I walked the streets of D.C.

As for Grey, when I brought the conversation up to him over beers at the same bar a year later, he confessed that he had forgotten the entire discussion. "Must've been drunk," he readily admitted. "*Blacked* out, no pun intended." He laughed. "But I'll tell you, Simon, there isn't anything in this world that I hate more than racists." He threw back the rest of his beer, added, "Except maybe for Hispanics."

That time, Grey had made it abundantly clear he was joking, and he went on to talk about how great it was that we could finally openly discuss race in this country (at least here in D.C.), and he predicted that the American people would elect the first black president in his lifetime. I admit, I wasn't so sure at the time. Then, lo and behold, ten years later I shook the hand of a young presidential candidate named Barack Obama during a campaign stop in Orlando, Florida, where I'd been voluntarily searching for a missing two-year-old girl named Caylee Anthony. Obama, of course, went on to win the presidency, and little Caylee Anthony was found dead in a wooded area near her home six months after her disappearance. Her mother, Casey, was tried and acquitted of her daughter's murder three years later despite a mountain of evidence against her.

Hell of a world, I suppose. You take the good with the bad, the bad with the downright ugly. Like the large tattoo Casey Anthony had placed on her shoulder in the weeks after little Caylee supposedly went missing.

Bella Vita. "Good Life."

Brought me back to the gang from Honduras, or some other Central American country: *La vida por las maras.* "The life for the gangs."

I took a sip of espresso and turned to Mariana. "Which part of Colombia are you originally from?"

"The southwest part of the country, near the Pacific coast." Her voice was soft and warm. "Outside Cali."

I nodded my head in sympathy. Much of the southwest region was controlled by the leftist guerrillas or right-wing paramilitaries and remained extremely dangerous.

"You have no family in Colombia?"

Slowly she shook her head. "My father, he died when I was an infant. He worked for the Cali Cartel. He was really just a boy when he first impregnated my mother, and still just a boy when he was killed by the Medellín Cartel. It is said that he is one of the last men killed personally by Pablo Escobar."

"And your mother?"

"She died when I was older, maybe sixteen. My mother, she was sick all the time after my father died. But she would never go to hospital. She feared they would kill her if she went. Escobar had promised to kill my father's whole family. Even after Escobar himself was killed, my mother continued to think he would find her. She was—how you say?—paranoia."

"You have any siblings?"

She bowed her head. "Two brothers. They took care of me for a few years after our mother died. Then they took a job as smugglers. It is a truly awful story. They were best friends, my brothers, only a year apart. They'd been together their entire lives. Then they went to the States. . . ."

Their names were Mateo and Hernán, she told me. Mateo was the older brother; he was the one who convinced Hernán to quit his job at the flower plantation to go to work for a man named Leandro.

The job was easy.

The job paid well.

The job involved traveling.

On their first trip, they would fly to Newark, New Jersey, where they would be met by a man who would give them money in exchange for the cocaine they were carrying. Each brother had swallowed more than a hundred balloons before boarding a flight from Bogotá to the United States.

When they arrived at Newark Liberty International, the man they were told to expect was not waiting for them. They didn't know what to do. They each had a stomachful of cocaine balloons but little cash. They decided to take a room at the Howard Johnson Hotel near the airport and try to contact Leandro for further instructions.

Only when they called, Leandro's number had been disconnected.

They would later learn through their lawyer that the man who was supposed to meet them—a guy known only as Paco—had spotted a tail and called Leandro to tell him he couldn't meet the Silvas at the airport. Leandro, coked up and paranoid himself, got scared and made for Venezuela, cutting off all contact with Colombia.

The brothers were left on their own.

Bellies stuffed with balloons of cocaine.

Nothing to do but wait.

The morning after they arrived in Newark, the younger brother, Hernán, began complaining of chest pains.

Mateo told him he'd be fine. "Just hang on while we figure something out."

But by late afternoon, Hernán was convinced he couldn't wait anymore.

His chest felt as though someone had parked a car on top of it.

He was sweating profusely.

He felt pain down his left arm.

Hernán begged his brother to take him to the hospital, but Mateo refused. "Are you *loco*? They'll take X-rays and we'll be busted for sure. We'll each spend twenty-five, thirty years in federal prison. No way."

As Hernán became more desperate, he told Mateo that he'd go to the hospital alone.

But Mateo wouldn't budge: "If they catch you," Mateo told his brother, "they will catch me. And I'm not taking that chance. Just man up and wait."

But Hernán couldn't wait. He was sure he was dying. So he rolled himself off the bed and went for the door.

When he did, Mateo tackled him, struck him, dragged him back to the bed.

Hernán screamed and Mateo struck him again.

Then Hernán struck back.

The two brothers engaged in a long and bloody brawl that resulted in broken bones and broken mirrors and broken lamps—and a hell of a lot of noise.

Enough noise for other residents to call the front desk.

Enough noise for the front desk to notify the police.

Enough noise for the police to break down the door.

As soon as the police stepped into the hotel room, Hernán confessed. He pleaded to the uniformed officers for medical attention. Cried out that he was going to die.

The police placed both brothers under arrest. They took Hernán to Newark Beth Israel Medical Center, Mateo to the Essex County Jail.

From there, the DEA took over the investigation. The U.S. Attorney's Office brought the matter to a federal grand jury and obtained a multiple-count felony indictment. Six months later, the Silva brothers pleaded guilty and were sentenced to two decades each.

They were now serving out their sentences at the Federal Correctional Institution in Otisville, New York.

As for Hernán, turns out it was a false alarm. No balloons had broken in his stomach.

He'd just suffered a bad case of indigestion.

Doctors suggested that the airplane food was to blame.

Chapter 37

There he is," I said with no small measure of relief.

Mariana craned her neck to view the embassy, then stood and started across the street.

Grey headed in the other direction, and I witnessed Mariana catching up with him just as he turned the corner and vanished from sight.

I leaned back in my chair and scanned the narrow street. A stray dog, a dog more ribs than meat, scurried unnoticed along the sidewalk past a group of skinny young men with mustaches and backward baseball caps loitering in front of a liquor store. Before the dog reached the corner, it sniffed around some overstuffed black garbage bags piled at the curb, clearly searching for something to eat. When it didn't find anything, the stray silently moved on up the street until it was out of sight.

When Mariana returned a few minutes later, she said, "The café at El Museo del Oro in half an hour."

Twenty minutes after that, I spotted Grey at a table in the far corner of the restaurant at Colombia's famous Gold Museum, which was located downtown in the historic hamlet of La Candelaria—Bogotá's "Old City"—a neighborhood of museums, universities, and churches.

The building itself was awe-inspiring, a state-of-the-art facility housing the world's largest collection of pre-Hispanic gold relics. As

I took a seat across from Grey, I thought of the old treasure hunter on Seven Mile Beach in Grand Cayman. What he wouldn't do to see this place, to spend a few precious minutes on the top floor in the museum's eight-thousand-piece "gold room."

Grey slid a menu across the table to me, opened with, "I recommend the chicken soup and red bean stew."

"It's awfully good to see you too," I said.

He still hadn't so much as smiled, yet it was all I could do to suppress my own grin. A hell of a thing, old friends. Sometimes you don't realize you've missed them until they're right there in front of you again.

"What are you doing in Bogotá, Simon?"

"I need a—" *Here comes that damn word again.* "—I need a *favor*, Grey."

"Well, I figured that. The question is, what kind of favor? And what kind of trouble is it going to get me into?"

I tried to read him, but if Grey's face were a book, it'd be scribbled in Ancient Greek. Physically, he was the same man he'd been a decade ago. Still fit and handsome, the only difference a smattering of gray hair that only made him look more distinguished. But for all I knew, in other ways he could have changed immeasurably over all those years.

"You've been watching the news?" I said. "The home invasion in L.A.? The abduction of that teenage girl, Olivia Trenton?"

He nodded. "The Bureau likes the father for it."

"Yeah, well. I don't."

I told Grey about Grand Cayman and Costa Rica and what Mariana Silva had overheard, how her captors had been talking about a *mara* that came into a lot of money in connection with a job in California.

When I finished he said, "These Central American gangs, they don't actually travel to the United States to kidnap women for the cartels. You know that."

"Of course I do."

"They take girls traveling abroad. If they wanted Olivia, they would have taken her while she was in the Caribbean. They wouldn't have waited two months, then executed a home invasion in Southern California."

I held up a hand. "Look, I realize there has to be more to it. And I admit that I don't know what that is. But I intend to find out. This is too much of a coincidence."

He sighed. "This has been all over the news for something like seventy-two hours. The talking heads have been doing nothing but speculating. They *do* have televisions up there in San José these days, don't they? Mariana's captors could have heard about the home invasion themselves from Wolf Blitzer or Soledad O'Brien on CNN."

"Don't you think I've thought of that?"

He leaned back in his chair. "If you thought of it, what are you doing here?"

A waiter came by and Grey ordered something off the menu.

I said, "Just coffee, *por favor.*" Then I turned back to Grey, told him something I thought he of all people would understand. "I have a gut feeling about this."

Grey flashed his teeth, though it was more of a smirk than a smile. "The old law enforcement fallback, huh? Didn't you have to turn in that gut when you turned in your gun and your badge?"

"I haven't exactly been sitting on my ass for the past decade," I said, maybe a tad too defensively.

"No, I know that. But you also haven't worked on a *team* in that time. When you decide to follow your gut instincts as a private dick, you don't necessarily put others in danger. When you involve, say, the DEA, and ask for help going up against the Colombian cartels, you don't do it based on a 'gut feeling.' You go on cold, hard facts."

"That's all I'm asking for, Grey. I'm not here to request suppressive fire. I'm here in the hopes that you can provide me some information that might just lead me to Olivia."

"You mean, you want me to give you just enough information so that you can go out and get yourself killed. Just enough rope to hang yourself, right? *That's* what you're asking for." When I didn't respond, he added, "I thought you didn't deal with these types of cases anyway. I thought you only handled parental abductions."

I tried to hide my anger but I'd discovered long ago I'm no good at it. In a gruff tone I hadn't intended, I said, "I'm expanding my business."

He took a sip of his soft drink. "That's the entrepreneurial American spirit I know and love."

"Will you help me?"

"Have I ever said no to you, Simon?"

"Only when I've asked you to pay for the drinks."

This time Grey's smile was genuine. "Before we get into the nitty-gritty, let me be completely honest with you." He leaned forward and lowered his voice. "Aside from spraying the coca fields with herbicides every once in a while, we don't deal a whole hell of a lot with the farmers or the workers who cut and package the stuff. And we certainly don't concern ourselves down here with the small-time couriers. We go after the big boys and we hit them where it hurts—in their wallets."

"You focus on the money laundering."

He touched his finger to his nose. "It's all about the pesos down here. That said, it would help if we knew which group we were dealing with."

"Mariana specifically used the word 'cartel,' but I'm not sure she understands the distinction between the cartels and the insurgents and the paramilitaries."

"I'm not sure there *is* a distinction to understand anymore," Grey said. "Narco-trafficking is how *every* group in Colombia makes its money. If we had Girl Scouts down here, they'd be farming the coca fields instead of selling Thin Mints and Do-si-dos." He paused. "But if we were to begin with the most active area, I'd suggest starting in the Valle del Cauca."

"All right, then. We'll begin there."

The waiter arrived and set two bowls down in front of Grey, and Grey said, "If you don't mind—first I'm going to enjoy my chicken soup and red bean stew."

I told him to have at it, then ordered another cup of joe.

Chapter 38

When we returned to my hotel room, Grey went to the window and drew the curtains closed. He said, "You really are out of practice, aren't you?"

"The maids must have opened them," I said, though I wasn't sure. Maybe I wasn't as cautious as I used to be. If that were the case, Grey was right; I had no right asking for anyone's help. My slipups could easily get someone killed.

Grey went to the map of Colombia, which I'd finally tacked to the wall. "All right," he said. "I'm going to try to do this without giving you an unnecessary history lesson." He pointed to an area abutting the Pacific coast. "This here is the Valle del Cauca. As you can see, it stretches inland and includes the city of Cali. You probably remember the Cali Cartel, a seven-billion-dollar-a-year operation."

"Of course."

"Then you know it doesn't exist anymore. But when it and Pablo Escobar's Medellín Cartel began fragmenting in the '90s, that made room for the Norte del Valle Cartel, which has recently breathed its last breaths, due at least in part to our arrests of its leaders and seizures of billions of dollars. Essentially, we cut off its head—*and* its neck, just to be sure it couldn't grow another one."

"Which leaves . . . ?"

"Micro-cartels, which are nearly impossible to keep track of. So here on the Pacific coast, we have a valley just west of the Andes that remains the epicenter of the country's armed conflict. We have the left-wing guerrillas and the right-wing paramilitaries and the Colombian army and a countless number of drug traffickers all fighting one another over the territory. It's the ultimate hellscape, Simon. If Olivia was sold to be a smuggler, that's where she'd be, somewhere in this region. But you go in there, I guarantee you'll never come out again."

"I thought you were going to help me."

"I *am* helping you, Simon. I'm saving your life by explaining to you that once Colombia has someone in its mouth, it either chews them up or swallows them whole. But it does not spit them back out, not unless you're dealing with a kidnap-for-ransom, which this may have been at the start but isn't anymore."

"What if we contact a professional negotiator and put out the word that we're willing to pay more?"

"They'll smell a trap. Olivia will become too hot a potato, and they will slice her up and feed her to the peasants."

"*Christ,*" I said, slapping a lamp off the desk. "I'd read in the *Times* that the homicide rates here in Colombia are at an all-time low."

"They are, Simon. Which *still* leaves Colombia as one of the most dangerous and violent countries in the world. The only country in South America with more murders per capita is Venezuela—and it only recently attained that honor. And it's doubtful they'll keep it for very long."

Grey stepped past me and picked the lamp up off the floor, set it back on the desk.

"Look," he said, "this country has received a lot of support from the States under Plan Colombia. The Department of Justice has been assisting Colombia's efforts to strengthen its justice system, and we've been crucial to its recent progress in combating terrorist groups from both the left and the right. But this is a nation in transition, Simon. Fewer murders are being committed for political reasons, but *more* murders are now being committed for control of the drug trade. Dismantling the cartels may have resulted in slightly less cocaine reaching the States, but one major consequence of that is more cocaine remaining *inside* Colombia. Rural violence is down, but urban violence is on the rise."

"What does that have to do with finding Olivia?"

"Everything, Simon. It has *everything* to do with finding Olivia. Five or ten years ago, we could go to one cartel and ask them for information on another and they'd gladly give it to us, if not for a free pass, then to put their competitors out of business. Same with the rebels. Today, we don't know who the hell's who anymore. The drug trade's being operated by goddamn street gangs, two-bit organizations that were more than happy to pick up the scraps left behind by the major cartels. How many groups right now do you think are trying to find ways to get drugs into the United States? How many men right now do you think are competing to be the next Pablo Escobar? If Olivia's in Colombia, then one of *those* men has her—and those men are amateurs, and they will cut off her head the minute they begin feeling the heat."

I felt dizzy. Too much caffeine and nothing to eat.

I looked into Grey's eyes and instead of my friend, I saw the FBI agent in charge of Hailey's investigation all those years ago. He seemed small and weak and cowardly. I heard his voice as clear as though he were here now, standing right in front of me just as he did in our living room in Georgetown. He was telling me he had no leads.

But you do, I thought. *You're just too goddamn scared to see where they might take you.*

". . . leave you some equipment?" Grey was saying. "Simon? Simon?"

How could I leave my daughter's fate in your hands?

I turned my back to Grey, stepped over to the window, slightly parted the curtains, and gazed at the dim horizon.

"Grey, you've said all you need to say. I'd appreciate it if you just left now, so I can try to get some sleep."

"Simon—"

"Please, Grey." I held up a hand, lowered it when I noticed it trembling. "Please, Grey. For Christ's sake, just leave."

Chapter 39

There are plenty of advantages to not flying commercial. But by far the best thing about the private flight from Costa Rica to Bogotá was that, thanks to Edgar's people, I was able to bring the Glocks I'd recovered from the Ticos.

I'd showered and dressed in a black outfit that skirted the edge between dressy and casual. In the room, I double- and triple-checked the magazines I'd purchased from a teenage boy on the street near the hotel. I'd also picked up a Glock 27. The .40-caliber subcompact was small and light, yet accurate and powerful—the perfect backup weapon.

I placed all three weapons and the extra magazines into my duffel, along with a small case that contained a listening device Grey had left at the front desk for me. I zippered everything up, and just as I was about to leave my hotel room, I heard a knock at my door.

Cautiously, I checked the peephole.

"Mariana," I said as I opened the door.

She looked past me at the duffel sitting on the bed. "You are leaving?" she said.

"Just for the night. I'll likely be back in the morning."

"Where are you going?" she asked, moving past me into the room.

I closed the door. There was no use lying, I decided. What was I going to tell her? That I was going sightseeing? That I felt like taking in a movie this evening?

"I'm heading to Cali."

She frowned even though she seemed to know what was coming. "To find the girl, Olivia? But you cannot go to Cali alone."

"This is what I was hired to do, Mariana. This is my job."

She grabbed my forearm, dragged me in front of the mirror atop the dresser. "Look at you," she said in her smoldering accent. "You are Caucasian. Worse, you are an American. I have not heard you speak one complete sentence of Spanish. You look, you sound, you *walk* like a U.S. federal agent. You will not receive a single word of information in Cali unless that word is written on the bullet they put into your skull."

She smacked me in the back of the head as though to demonstrate where the bullet would enter. Those frail arms were a hell of a lot stronger than they looked.

"I can manage," I told her.

"Do not be so stupid. I will go with you. The men who have this Olivia, they paid or bartered for her because they cannot find volunteers. But I can act as a volunteer, and they will be happy to have me. I can get inside and find the girl so that you can take her home to her family."

"It's too dangerous," I said.

She gripped me by the shoulders this time, looked deep into my eyes. "You saved my life, Simon. I can pay you back in different ways, but I think you most like this one. You want most to save this girl from these killers, and I can help you to do that."

Amped though I was on caffeine, I felt her warm breath on my chin and it worked to relax me. The tension flowed out from my shoulders, down along my biceps and triceps, into my forearms, and finally seemed to fall from my fingers as she held me.

I placed my hands on her hips. I'd meant to gently push her off, but instead I pulled her closer. There was such a ferocious courage in her eyes, it was all I could do not to touch her lips with mine.

Too frequently, naiveté was mistaken for goodness. But the damaged, I'd found, were often the most righteous. When I first met

Tasha in college, what I'd most loved about her was her innocence. But the world wasn't innocent; it was full of pain. Tasha and I had learned that together the hard way. And she didn't survive it.

To become fully human, you had to know you were dispensable—and accept it, not want it any other way. Then, if you were still willing to sacrifice for the sake of others, you'd be more alive than most men and women on the planet. Because it wasn't your ability to avoid the fire that made you special; it was your willingness to walk through it; it was how resilient you were when you came out the other side.

As I held Mariana, I thought again of Ana, of being alone with her in our hotel room in Ukraine. Days before, in Poland, she had unquestionably withstood the flames, sacrificed more for a child she'd never met than most people would for their own blood. There in Odessa, she too balked at the idea of remaining behind; she'd insisted on helping me infiltrate a violent organization despite the further risk to her own life.

That night Ana and I went to a nightclub, where Ana allowed herself to be picked up by a dangerous man. For a time, I lost track of her whereabouts. And I'd felt utterly shattered for giving in and accepting her help. I couldn't allow that to happen again, not to Mariana.

"I can't put you in danger, Mariana."

"Then don't. Just don't stray too far, and I will always be safe."

I thought about it. Truth was, I would never have had a chance at finding Lindsay Sorkin in time without Ana's help. She'd handled herself as well as anyone I'd ever worked with, and she was only a lawyer. Mariana had already lived through hell. She knew this world, and I needed her.

I could do it; I could protect her.

I'd stay on her, make sure I could see her or hear her at all times.

"All right," I said, tearing myself away from her while beating back a desire I hadn't felt in a long time. "Let's go find our girl."

* * *

I rented a black Toyota Hilux pickup truck, which was essentially a 4Runner given a different name to attract South American consumers. The drive from Bogotá to Cali would take roughly eight hours. Of course, with the clock constantly ticking and a young girl's life on the line, I would have preferred to take a plane—but then the Glocks couldn't have come along.

Two hours into the drive, I pulled over near a roadside fruit stand and purchased some fresh mangoes, guavas, and a few varieties of bananas. We pulled back onto the road and ate on the way.

During the drive, Mariana asked me about my childhood, as I had asked about hers at the café. Although I rarely shared that with anyone, I figured it was only fair I open up to her just as she'd opened up to me.

"I was born in London," I told her. "My father, Alden, was a doctor; my mother, I'm not sure. When I was five years old, my father took me to the United States for reasons that were never made clear. All I really know is that we left my mother and my slightly older sister, Tuesday, behind. I never saw either of them again."

"You were stolen by your father," she said.

I felt her eyes on me. "I can't say anything for sure. I just don't know."

"You never asked your father?"

"Oh, I asked him. Especially as a child. In the early years, after we arrived in Rhode Island, my father became a master at changing the subject. Whenever I asked about my mother and sister, we just happened to be near an ice cream shop or a toy store. If I asked him at bedtime, he'd suggest I get up and have some late-night cookies with him while we watched one of my favorite movies on the VCR."

"And as you grew older?"

"He turned to emotional blackmail, made me feel as though asking about my mother and sister hurt him in some deep, irreparable way. He'd say, 'Why, son? Am I not enough? Have I failed you in some way?' How does a seven-year-old answer questions like those?

'Of course you're enough,' I'd tell him. 'You haven't failed me in any way.' 'Then, let it be,' he'd say."

"And you would let it be?"

"Not always. As I got a little older, I caught on to the emotional manipulation. I persisted. As soon as I did, he became defiant. He reacted with this extraordinary rage—which I suspected was really guilt, but I could never be sure. 'What the hell business is it of yours?' he'd say. 'I raised you, I sacrificed for you, I paid for your education.' He'd escalate it into such an argument that he could justify giving me the silent treatment or walking away."

"And?"

"And it just further eroded my relationship with my father. Eventually, I went away to college and saw less and less of him. Then I met Tasha and rarely saw him at all, only talked once in a while over the phone about nothing. Finally, Tasha and I became engaged and I waited six months to tell him. Then when the time came to send out wedding invitations, instead of stuffing his into an envelope, I decided to take a match to it. I watched it burn away and knew that was the end of our relationship. Tasha and I wanted to start a family. I knew I'd never allow my father near our kids, so what sense did it make stringing him along."

"And you never went looking for your mother and sister?"

"Not until last year."

"And?" Some hope had found its way into her voice. "You found them?"

"Just my mother. She'd been buried at Streatham Cemetery nearly a decade ago. The headstone was small and simple, engraved with her maiden name, Tatum Fuller, and her dates of birth and death. Below her name, in small letters, it read 'Beloved Mother.'"

"I am sorry," Mariana said. "And what of your sister?"

"After finding Mum like that, I didn't think I could handle a reunion with my sister. At least not right away. So, from London I went on to Berlin to see an old friend. I intended to return to London to search for my sister, Tuesday, just afterwards. But then from

Berlin, I drove west to Warsaw to see a woman I'd fallen in love with."

Mariana smiled. "A woman?"

"Anastazja Staszak."

For a moment I became lost in my own thoughts. I suddenly remembered how badly Ana had wanted to see Hollywood. I'd assured her I'd take her there at some point. I'd been in L.A. at the Trentons' estate just a few days ago and never once even gave it a thought.

I said to Mariana, "I left things badly with Ana. She wanted me to remain in Warsaw, where she practiced law. She'd recently been hired as a prosecutor. I explained that I couldn't stay in Warsaw, that my work was in the United States. We ultimately reached an impasse, and although it was left unspoken, I think we both decided after I left that it would be too painful to ever see each other again."

The corners of her lips fell into a frown. "How sad that is."

I felt Mariana's eyes on me again as I drove. I said, "I made a few more stops in Eastern Europe—paid a visit to some troubled kids in Kiev, then to a number of struggling clinics caring for very sick children in Minsk—and by the time I was finished, I was emotionally drained. I couldn't bear going back to London to search for Tuesday."

"So you didn't."

"So I didn't. And for some reason I can't quite get my mind around, I still haven't."

As I watched the road disappear underneath our vehicle, I pictured Tuesday as a child. I remembered looking at my daughter on her fifth birthday and seeing Tuesday's face. Hailey hadn't been the spitting image of my sister, of course. But there were certainly similarities. Part of me wondered if that was why I was so reluctant to seek out Tuesday as an adult. Was I afraid to see the woman that Hailey would never have the chance to become?

"So your parents," Mariana said minutes later, "they are why you search for the missing?"

"No." I said it so softly that my voice was drowned out by the pickup's engine. "I do this because of my wife and daughter."

I went on to tell her the terrible story of Hailey's abduction eleven years ago. Of the long and fruitless investigation. Of Tasha's nervous breakdown and subsequent suicide.

I felt her eyes on me once more; this time she was looking at me through tears. "I am so sorry, Simon."

For the remainder of the drive, we stayed silent.

Chapter 40

When we reached Cali, it was dark and there were decisions to be made. Afraid that time might be running out on Olivia, we were both eager to begin as soon as possible. But I worried that for Mariana, the night would be more dangerous than the day.

"The people I must talk to," she said, "they will be harder to find once the sun rises. I should seek them out now, in the bars and nightclubs."

We parked on Avenida Sexta, better known as Av Sexta, which Mariana assured me was the nucleus of seedy nightlife in Cali.

Av Sexta. Sounded about right.

She entered a few bars on her own, looking for people she recognized, but each time she came up empty.

She wore a tight black dress that made her look even more striking than usual, *so* striking that it was difficult to concentrate on her words when she finally reentered the vehicle.

"We should leave the car parked here and take a taxi to the clubs," she said. "It is not like the old days. The men with money to afford mules, they will not be hanging out at these shitty bars."

"All right. Which club?"

She brightened. "That depends. Shall we start at the most famous, the most expensive, or the one that attracts the best dancers?"

"Let's start at famous and work our way down from there," I suggested.

After I wired her for sound, we took a twenty-minute taxi ride to the Changó nightclub on Via Cavasa in Juanchito. The listening device Grey left us consisted of two simple earbuds—one for her ear, the other for mine. The buds were tiny and invisible to the naked eye; the audio was crisp and clear.

We had the taxi drop us at a corner a couple blocks away from our destination.

"We'll need a code word," I said before she walked toward the club, "in case there's any trouble. Keep in mind, my Spanish is a little rusty."

Mariana gazed skyward in thought. "In a sentence I will say the name Gabriel García Márquez."

The world-famous Colombian novelist was the author of *One Hundred Years of Solitude* and *Love in the Time of Cholera*. In the early '80s, Gabriel García Márquez—or Gabo, as he's affectionately known throughout Latin America—was the recipient of the Nobel Prize in Literature.

"Perfect," I said.

Mariana continued to find new ways to impress me; under any other circumstances, I would have asked her to save the last dance for me.

We could hear the music from more than a block away. Undeniably salsa.

Mariana must have noticed me grinning as we walked toward the club. "You know Cali-style salsa?" she asked. "No? Cali is known as 'El Capital de la Salsa'—the salsa capital of the world. Perhaps, when all this is over, I can teach to you this dance."

"I'd like that," I said, stopping her at the corner across from the club. "Be careful in there. Say the word, and I'll be inside within sixty seconds."

Mariana turned and started toward the entrance, which was

blocked off by red velvet rope. She sidestepped the long line outside, went straight up to one of the two large bouncers, said something in his ear, and was immediately allowed inside.

I removed my BlackBerry and dialed what was by now a familiar number.

"The subscriber you have called is not able to receive calls at this time."

I considered calling Edgar but then thought better of it. If there were any news on his end, I would have heard about it by now—if not from him, then from Don Lemon or Anderson Cooper on television back at the hotel.

I turned to the street, which was quiet with the exception of the pounding bass from the club. Parked on the opposite side of the road, about a block up, stood a dark SUV, which looked similar to an SUV I'd seen several times on the road to Cali but had thought nothing of.

Now its presence disturbed me.

I placed the BlackBerry against my ear and pretended to make a call as I crept up the street toward the vehicle. The SUV appeared to be an older-model Chevy, maybe a Trooper. I wouldn't know until I got a good look at the rear, and the vehicle was currently facing forward. There appeared to be someone at the wheel, though I couldn't make out a face in the darkness.

As I neared the vehicle, its headlights suddenly flashed on, momentarily blinding me. I threw my arm up in front of my face. The SUV backed out of its space, but instead of moving forward, it continued in reverse until it entered the previous intersection. Then the vehicle swiftly performed a partial K-turn and sped down the avenue and out of sight.

I cursed under my breath. I hadn't been able to catch the plates.

Meanwhile, in my left ear, Mariana chatted away in Spanish. The salsa music caused my eardrum to pulse, but I felt that if I spoke decent Spanish, I could have made out every word she was saying.

This was state-of-the-art U.S. equipment we were using. And for that, I had to be grateful. Grey didn't need to leave me anything after the way I'd tossed him out of my hotel room.

In my ear I heard Mariana repeating the word *"permiso,"* and I assumed she was trying to weave her way through the crowd.

A few long minutes later, Mariana's voice came clearly over the wire. She'd started a conversation with someone. A male with a deep baritone.

"Perdón," she said. *"¿De dónde eres?"*

"Soy de Medellín. Cómo te llamas?"

"Me llamo Mariana."

"Mucho gusto, Mariana."

"El gusto es mío."

I vaguely understood the introductions but was completely lost after that initial exchange.

She's from here, I told myself again and again. *This is her world. She knows what she's doing.*

I paced outside the nightclub, using my phone as a prop, thinking all the while about Ana and how I'd thought I lost her for good in Ukraine. I thought I'd put it firmly behind me, but my conversation with Mariana brought it all back.

The longer Mariana was gone, the more anxious I became.

Whenever there was silence on the wire, I'd consider storming inside.

Then I'd hear Mariana's voice and it would soothe me.

At least for a few precious minutes. Then I'd become a wreck all over again.

Chapter 41

I maneuvered farther from the nightclub so that I wouldn't give myself away. The listening device had excellent range, so it was really just a matter of remaining within a short enough distance to the entrance so that I could reach Mariana quickly if I heard her utter the name Gabriel García Márquez.

I rounded the corner and slunk into the shadows of the side street. I stayed just close enough to the main road so that I could catch sight of the Trooper if it returned. As far as I knew, no one but Edgar and Grey were even privy to the fact I was here. Yet I couldn't shake the feeling that I was being watched. Paranoia can be paralyzing. Or it can prove to be a vital instinct. You simply didn't know until you knew.

The side street I was on was empty. It was almost as though the nightclub existed in another dimension. From my vantage point, the only evidence of the club was the salsa music and Mariana's warming voice in my ear. She'd broken off the conversation with the first man, presumably because she wasn't getting anywhere. As I listened, she ordered an aguardiente, which if I remembered correctly was an anise-flavored liqueur made from sugarcane, its name derived from *agua* and *ardiente*, the Spanish equivalent of "fiery water."

I'd never been a big drinker. But just now I could've used something to take the edge off. Something strong and good, like an aged single malt scotch on the rocks.

I was trying to remember whether I'd ever tasted aguardiente when in my ear a man opened a conversation with Mariana. I was struggling to understand the Spanish, but it sounded as though he'd offered to pay for her drink and she had accepted. Then he asked her to dance.

I turned into a dark and narrow alley to better avoid the noise from the main road.

After a few moments of welcome silence, a soft voice emanated from the shadows. A female voice asking me a question in Spanish.

"No," I replied, *"entiendo."* I don't understand.

I kept moving but the voice followed. I could tell that the alley came to an end a couple hundred feet ahead of me.

"¿Hablas inglés?" she said.

I ignored her, tried to focus on Mariana, who was apparently speaking as she was dancing, which made it that much more difficult to understand her words.

"You looking for a date, honey?" the woman in the alley said. Good English despite the strong Hispanic accent. And, unfortunately, tenacious as all hell. No wonder the ladies had gotten to the Secret Service agents in Cartagena.

I shook my head, said, "No, thank you," as I continued walking.

"What, you don't even want to take a look?"

I stopped, turned to her, and smiled. "I'm just not interested tonight," I said, surprised to be meeting her at eye level. I figured her heels had added a few inches. But still.

"Oh, no?" she said. "Why not, sweetie?"

"My girlfriend is in the club. She just went in to get her brothers. They'll be out any second now."

"Then we better act fast, baby," she said, inching toward me as she let her purse fall from her shoulder.

She inserted her long middle finger into her mouth, then slowly pulled it out between her bright red lips. It was pitch black farther back in the alley, and for a second I tried to tune out Mariana to listen for the footfalls of this woman's confederates. If you were going to get yourself attacked in a South American city, wandering alone down a dark alley was a damn good way to go about it.

I tried to reason with her. "Look, I appreciate the invitation, but I'm really not interested tonight."

I needed to get back to the side street, but as I attempted to move past her, she stretched those long legs and slid in front of me, blocking my path. Her tight black dress crept up, revealing her thighs.

Just then, a small amount of light fell on her.

Not much.

Just enough for me to discern that she was a man. A convincing transsexual. Surgically altered—at least in the northern region. But a man, all the same.

Not a *puta* but a *puto*, as they'd say here in Colombia. A male prostitute.

"How about it, honey?" he said. "A quick blow job and you're off. Your girl will never know it happened."

"I'm flattered," I said. "Really. But I can't take the chance."

That's when the *puto* reached for his crotch and came up with a knife. Told me to hand over my wallet.

If you're faced with a knife when you're unarmed, your survival depends on establishing and maintaining an offensive mind-set. You can't afford to think about getting cut or hurt.

Unfortunately, it's difficult to disarm your opponent until you're affirmatively attacked, so all I had in my arsenal right now were insults. I needed to provoke him.

"Fuck you, *puto*," I told him calmly. "You might as well have pulled your dick out, for all the good that blade's going to do you."

He hesitated, but luckily, my words were enough to cause him to strike.

As the knife came at me, I stepped forward at a forty-five-degree angle, moving out of the line of attack. With my hands up, I thrust my forearms at his right arm to block the knife. I then wrapped my left arm tightly around his right, trapping his arm between the biceps and torso. In the same moment, I placed my right arm on his shoulder and executed an armbar, applying pressure until I heard a bone snap followed by the *clang* of the blade hitting the pavement.

The transvestite may have possessed boy parts—but he sure as hell screamed like a lady.

When I finally let go, he went to the ground, curled up like a fetus, shrieking and yelling for help.

I kicked the knife handle and watched the blade spin its way under a Dumpster.

I leaned over and picked up his purse, unzipped it, and found a cell phone. I dialed 112, the national emergency number for Colombia.

Slowly, I set the phone down next to his face and told him to ask for an ambulance.

He continued screaming something in Spanish.

I covered one ear, listened for Mariana's voice in my other, then turned and walked out of the alley.

I moved to the next block.

It was twenty minutes before I saw the ambulance park at the curb, the paramedics dashing out of the vehicle in the direction of the alley.

The transvestite was carted away. While I continued to wait.

And wait.

Over an hour after she entered the club, Mariana stepped outside. As planned, I flagged down a taxi without acknowledging her. She boarded one just behind me, and I directed the driver back to the Hilux on Av Sexta.

By the time we arrived, Av Sexta was a flurry of activity.

Once we were both safely inside the pickup and out of sight, I said, "So, how did it go?"

She smiled at me. "It went perfectly, Simon. I got a job. I am to show up tomorrow afternoon at a pool hall in Bogotá."

"That's terrific," I said.

"And you? Anything interesting happen while I was inside the club?"

I turned the key in the ignition as an older couple clad completely in black leather strolled past us.

"Same old, same old," I said.

Chapter 42

Mariana and I had shared the driving duties back to Bogotá so that when we arrived late the next morning, we'd each had roughly four hours of sleep. Doctors vehemently disagree, but I had always felt four hours of sleep were sufficient. Anything more and you were encroaching on real life. And you sure as hell never knew how much of that you had left.

The pool hall was located in a grisly barrio in the southwest section of the capital city. It was the type of neighborhood where even early in the day, you wouldn't walk a block without looking over your shoulder.

I stepped into the pool hall two hours earlier than the scheduled meet. The place was empty but for a pair of old drunks. I bellied up to the bar and ordered a bottle of Aguila, a popular beer brewed here in Colombia.

I was dressed in tattered clothes I'd purchased this morning in a Bogotá thrift store. I hadn't shaved in two days. I didn't smell like the bar's other patrons, but I was confident that no one would come close enough to notice so long as I got the look right.

If anyone asked, I was a fugitive from the States. Running to avoid the electric chair in Laredo, Texas. Killed a man just to watch him die, or something like that.

I was strapped. Two Glock 20s and the backup stashed down

around my ankle. I wouldn't hesitate if it meant Mariana's life. Wouldn't hesitate if it meant Olivia's.

The listening device was neatly tucked away in my right ear.

I took down the first beer and ordered another to make it look good. Even though I'd never been much of a drinker, I could put them away when I had to. It's the luck of the draw when it comes to livers and lungs. So far, I'd been fortunate enough on both counts.

We might also have hit a bit of luck with our target, but I wouldn't know until the meeting started. Early in the conversation at Changó last night, the man had spilled a little English—and Mariana complimented him on it, told him it was incredibly sexy. He'd switched back to Spanish because of the noise in the club but gave her another taste of the Queen's when they stepped outside for a smoke.

I dropped some pesos onto the bar and took my second bottle to one of the three decrepit pool tables. Each of the tables was lopsided, with badly worn green felt. I set the beer down, picked up a cue, and racked the balls with a cracked triangle.

I glanced over at the bartender just before I broke. He had his arms folded over his chest and he was staring right at me. I wondered just where behind the bar he stored the shotgun. Decided it would be a good day if I never found out.

Mariana arrived right on time. The man, whose name was Estefan, was already present, tucked in a booth in the corner of the café area with his back to the wall so that he could watch the door. It was a small place, but I would still have been well out of earshot were it not for Grey's listening device.

I continued shooting pool and drinking beer, one of five daydrinkers now patronizing the place, as Mariana walked back to the booth.

In my ear, I heard, "It is good to look at you, Mariana. You are as beautiful in the sunlight as you are in the moonlight."

I breathed a small sigh of relief. Our friend in the corner was going to continue to try to impress Mariana with his English.

"Thank you," Mariana said.

I caught a glimpse of her as she sat. She looked stunning in a black cotton dress that reminded me of a spring Tasha and I had spent in New York. Her long straight black hair was clean and neat. She wore no makeup and needed none; she was a natural beauty with dark eyes, very feminine features, a thin gold chain around her neck, a small gold crucifix resting on smooth sunned skin just above small breasts.

"So," Estefan said, "I am to understand that you are looking for the employment, yes?"

I could almost hear her smile through the earpiece. "Yes, yes."

I took a shot, banked the eight ball. Stood up straight and peered out the window at a motorcycle flying by. On the other side of the street was an aqua blue minivan parked in front of an old Catholic church. Catholic churches were everywhere in this country. Until the early '90s, Catholicism was the only religion recognized by the Colombian government. Today, very few people attended Mass regularly, though the vast majority of the population still considered itself Catholic for the purpose of filling out questionnaires.

"I can help you," Estefan said to Mariana. "You understand, this work will require traveling. But the work is easy—and the pay, it will make it worth your time."

I stole a glance in their direction. Estefan was an older man—probably in his mid-fifties, with the graying hair and beer gut to prove it. He wore a groomed mustache and was dressed well. It was obvious we didn't shop at the same Bogotá thrift store.

Estefan said, "You cannot tell anyone about this job, you understand? Not your parents, not your siblings, not your friends." He paused, uttered the next words as though they were a question. "Not your boyfriend?"

"I do not have a boyfriend."

Again, I could hear that smile in her voice. She was a master at flirtation. For some, seduction is a powerful weapon; for Mariana, I suspected, it was more powerful than the Glock 20 I had stuffed in my waistband.

"Okay, that is good, very good. You are a little bit skinnier than most girls who do this job. But that may work in your favor."

"What do you mean?"

"You will probably appear to be pregnant, and pregnant women are extended courtesies not granted to most women—especially at places such as airports. At security, if they request a full-body scan, you will tell them you are with child. They are required then to pat you down manually instead."

"All right," she said tentatively.

I'd told her not to appear too eager to get the job, to express the proper concerns. Acknowledge that she was about to be placed in danger and that she was a bit nervous, if not downright scared. Ask questions of the sort one would normally ask under these circumstances: *Who besides you will I be dealing with? What if I get caught? Where will I be going? How will I get my money? When?*

"Do not worry about your figure," Estefan said. "You will look only like you are in your first trimester. When the job is finished, you will be slender again. And you will have enough money to shop on New York's Fifth Avenue."

"Is that where I will be going, then? To New York?"

"You will be traveling to Philadelphia. It is not so sexy a city as New York, but you will be in the U.S. for a week. If you would like to see the Big Apple, you can take either a bus or a train."

The way that Estefan pronounced it, New York was the *Beeeg Opple.*

"I will certainly do that," Mariana said. "If you do not mind me being—how you say?—presumptuous, when can I start?"

I took a pull off my beer and waited to hear his answer. Unless it was the reply we wanted, I'd have to follow Estefan out of the pool hall and snatch him off the street. I'd have to find someplace private to interrogate him in the hopes he could lead me to one of the larger cartels.

But Estefan saved us all a lot of trouble by saying, "You can start tomorrow, Mariana. Now, let me buy you a nice sandwich. Because after your sandwich, I am afraid that for the next twenty-four hours, you will not be permitted to eat."

Chapter 43

I don't like this," I said, pacing the length of Mariana's room at Casa Medina. I repeatedly reached for the curtains to bring in light, then abruptly stopped myself.

"We do not have the choice," Mariana said.

Of course, she was right. Estefan wouldn't give her the address at which she was to show up later today. Which meant they'd be watching for trails and it would be tough for me to follow their vehicle through the streets of Bogotá.

I made up my mind. Reached for the phone and called the concierge. "I need to rent a motorcycle," I said.

"Excellent, sir. What type of bike?"

"Something small but fast. A bike with off-road capabilities, if possible."

"Hold while I check."

Salsa music came over the line and I waited. The bike wouldn't be any less conspicuous than the Hilux, but at least I'd be able to maneuver if necessary.

The concierge returned. "Sir, I can have a Kawasaki KLX450 downstairs in half an hour."

"*Gracias,*" I said. "That will do nicely."

*　*　*

Mariana was picked up from Carrera Séptima in a large white van, a sparkling new Chevy N300. I started the motorbike and drove on a parallel street. I caught another break; traffic was just heavy enough to ensure that I wouldn't lose them.

Shortly after the pickup, it seemed clear where they were headed—La Candelaria, in the hills of downtown Bogotá. The destination surprised me, though it shouldn't have. In my years as a Marshal, I'd discovered that criminals often hide in plain sight. Bogotá's "Old City" was a colonial town of tourist and cultural attractions, including the Museo del Oro, where I'd met Grey when I first arrived in Colombia.

Had Grey been trying to tell me something by selecting that location?

No. Couldn't have been more than a minor coincidence. After all, he hadn't even known what I was there to see him about at the time.

The van pulled over. Four men got out before opening the door for Mariana. They assisted her out of the van. Only then did I notice she was wearing a strip of silver duct tape over her eyes.

They led her down a narrow pedestrian-only cobblestone alley.

They left one man at the entrance to the alley so that no one could follow.

The others vanished in the direction of the Monasterio de la Candelaria, a sixteenth-century monastery founded by Augustine monks. Only part of the monastery was open to the public.

I imagined they were headed for the part that was not.

The monastery was made up of several beautiful white buildings with bright red doors and shutters. Without an aerial view, I couldn't be sure—but I suspected the property transformed into a maze somewhere past the main gate. I couldn't allow the men to get too far ahead of me, or I'd be placing Mariana in peril.

Slowly I walked toward the entrance to the alley. There were very few people visible on the street, probably none who'd be willing to act as witnesses if something went down right in front of them. In

Latin America, you constantly had to remind yourself that gun-fights could take place in broad daylight without anyone ever being arrested. Lawlessness remained as common in some places in South America as it was in the Wild West.

The man stationed at the entrance to the alley wore a black leather jacket. Casually, he smoked a cigarette while taking notice of every-one and every*thing* in the area. He held his cigarette in his right hand, but switched it to his left when he noticed me approaching.

That told me all I needed to know.

I didn't even bother slowing down. As I neared him, he drew a pistol, aimed it at my chest. I placed my hands up, palms out, so that they were about level with my shoulders.

He spit out something threatening in Spanish, then cocked the hammer.

With my left hand I swiftly grabbed his right forearm, pushed it away from his body so that the barrel was no longer facing me. At the same time I rotated my right shoulder back and spun around so that I was almost standing beside him. Maintaining control of his arm with my left, I grasped the pistol with my right. With my right hand wrapped tightly around the muzzle, I rotated the pistol in his hand so that he was holding the gun on himself.

I dared him to fire.

When he didn't fire, I ripped the pistol out of his hand, heard the crack of his index finger as it caught in the trigger guard.

As he screamed, I swung around behind him, turning the weapon in my hand. Then with the butt of the gun, I struck him hard on the back of his head, and he crumpled.

I pocketed his pistol, looked around. Just as I'd suspected, no one even turned toward his scream. Not their problem.

I rolled his unconscious body under the van, out of sight.

Then I started up the broken cobblestone alleyway after the men who had Mariana.

Chapter 44

I caught sight of the crew just as they were leading Mariana down a steep set of cement stairs. One of the men looked back but I ducked behind a wall just in time. I waited a moment, then stole a glance. The man was apparently tasked with guarding the stairwell.

I could hear Mariana's voice in my ear but it faded the farther she descended. I couldn't very well wait here. I'd have to deal with this second sentinel, and fast.

Behind the tall reddish pillars across the courtyard, I glimpsed movement. There was my ticket, and he was crossing this way. A man of the cloth. I didn't need the man so much, but the cloth would come in pretty damn handy.

I stood flat against the wall and waited. There was no way to know whether the monks were involved in any way with this criminal organization, but I decided I wasn't going to afford them the benefit of the doubt. Anyway, it wasn't as though I were going to kill the clergyman. At worst, he'd wake with a rotten headache.

Now I had a decision to make. I could use an air choke, which would temporarily cut off the air to the monk's lungs and heart. Problem was, rendering him unconscious could take as long as three minutes. The clock was ticking. So I decided to go with the riskier but quicker blood choke, temporarily cutting off the blood to the brain by applying pressure to his carotid artery.

I grabbed him soon as he stepped past me.

Within eight seconds he was out cold and as silent as, well, a Byzantine monk.

I removed his hooded black robe and threw it on over my clothes. The robe fell down to my ankles. I slipped the hood over my head and stepped out into the sunny courtyard.

I folded my hands and kept them in front of me, waist-high. I hung my head as though in deep thought, perhaps praying.

As I approached the man at the top of the stairs, he hardly gave notice. When he finally did turn in my direction, I delivered a single blow to his nose. His head snapped back, struck the wall; then his body leaned to the right and went over the stairs. He tumbled down a baker's dozen before coming to a stop, his face all bloody, his left arm bent back in the wrong direction.

I grimaced. I hadn't intended for him to pull a Father Damien.

I started down the steps. Checked his pulse. Fortunately, unlike Damien Karras, this guy was going to make it. No broken neck, just a badly fractured arm.

I left him there and continued down the stairs.

Mariana's voice slowly returned to my ear, and I breathed a sigh of relief.

Head down, the black hood pulled low, I crept along the wall of a tunnel that seemed to be leading me closer to the signal.

I reached a small wooden door and propped myself against the wall just next to it.

I was further relieved to hear that Estefan was still trying to impress Mariana with his English.

"We have clothes for you to wear this first time," he was telling her. "In the future, you are to purchase your own. Dress neither like a pauper nor a princess. You want to remain as unnoticeable as possible." He paused. "Of course, your natural beauty, nothing can be done about."

"What are those for?" Mariana said.

"Relax, dear. They are just scissors."

My right hand instinctively moved toward my gun.

"What for?" she said.

"Javier here will cut the fingers off latex gloves and use the fingers to wrap the merchandise in." He uttered something to Javier in Spanish, then said, "See, Mariana?"

"That looks rather large."

"We will dip it in milk. That will make the pellet easier to swallow."

"How many pellets will I have to carry?"

"The first time, only fifty or so. Once you arrive in the States, you will be provided laxatives so that the pellets pass swiftly."

"What are those?"

"These? They are only grapes. Before we make our first attempt with a pellet, we shall practice with these grapes. Now, dear, lean your head back, open your mouth wide, and relax the throat."

We hadn't anticipated any practice. We'd agreed that Mariana would try to extract the information before she was asked to swallow anything—but we assumed she'd be swallowing the balloons only.

"I can do this," she said.

I didn't know whether she was speaking to him or trying to get the message to me. She may have been telling me not to come in, to wait: *I can handle a couple grapes.*

It was a difficult decision but I waited. There was always the code—Gabriel García Márquez.

I heard her gag reflex kick in and I nearly kicked in the door.

But then Mariana seemed to recover. "I am all right," she said between coughs. "Just give me a minute or two."

The room was silent for a few moments; then she asked, "Do the other girls have so much trouble swallowing these in the beginning?"

"It depends," Estefan said.

"On what exactly?"

Javier muttered something crude in Spanish, and he and Estefan laughed heartily.

"Yes," Estefan said, still cracking up. "It depends mostly on their *level of experience.*"

Mariana feigned a bit of laughter herself, then said, "When will I get to meet these other girls?"

There was a lengthy hesitation and I readied myself. There were at least two men inside. Two, if one of the men who'd exited the van was Javier. At least three, if Javier was already here when they arrived.

"Darío," Estefan said, "get me some water."

That cleared things up somewhat. Now I knew there were at least three.

I had to assume all of them would be armed. I didn't know the layout of the place, which created a terrible disadvantage for me. I'd told Mariana to duck for cover but I couldn't rule out Estefan or one of the others using her as a human shield.

"Why do you wish to meet the girls?" Estefan said to Mariana.

"I would like to ask them what to expect when I reach Philadelphia."

"Relax. We will tell you everything you need to know."

"Do all the girls receive the same amount of pay?"

She was trying to find out if any of the girls worked against their will, but I highly doubted Estefan would provide the relevant answers.

"Do you think I am not paying you enough?" he said.

"I am just—how you say?—curious."

"Well, you would do well to remember, Mariana, that curiosity killed the pussycat."

The men in the room became hysterical again, and I tried to distinguish their laughter. I was pretty sure now that there were only three and that Estefan was closest to Mariana. The others were considerably farther away. Which meant I'd have to take Estefan out first.

"What you should be concerned with, Mariana, is only these pellets. Watch Javier. Make sure he wraps them well. If one were to open in your stomach, terrible things would happen. You would die. And if you died, I would lose a lot of money."

It seemed clear that Estefan intended to evade any questions about the other girls, so I'd have to go in, neutralize the threats, and keep at least one man alive.

"Open your mouth," Estefan said. "I am just going to spray this mixture of analgesic and water. It will lubricate and numb your throat so that you do not gag. Then I will give you pills to slow your digestion. After you take those pills, we will practice some more with the grapes before we begin with the pellets."

"And after the pellets?"

"Once you swallow the pellets, you will lie down and Javier will manipulate their positioning in your stomach so that it looks as though your uterus has expanded, as opposed to just your belly."

Estefan would be holding the spray bottle in his hand, but he'd be standing too close to her for me to get a safe shot off. I'd told Mariana that if she couldn't get the information to wait until everyone was far enough away from her so that she could gain cover, then signal me with the code.

I listened to the mist.

Removed the Glock 20.

Felt my heart pounding hard in my chest under the heavy black robe.

"Tell to me," Mariana said. "What should I do if I get stopped at the airport?"

"You will not get stopped. Just act natural and do not tremble and you will be fine."

"But if I am not fine?"

"There will be several girls boarding your flight at the same time. If one gets stopped, then the others pass through." Estefan's voice was filling with impatience. "Now, are you ready to practice with the grapes?"

"Just one more question."

He sighed, reined himself in. "What is this last question?"

"Will I be able to bring a book with me on the plane?"

Estefan chuckled. "Don't be silly. Of course you may have a book on the plane."

I moved directly in front of the door and lifted my leg. Aimed for the spot just below the knob.

"Good," she said. "Because I would very much like to read *One Hundred Years of Solitude* by Gabriel García Márq—"

Chapter 45

By all rights, kicking in that door should have been my final act in life.

Cut to black.

Wait sixty seconds.

Roll the credits.

I stood about as much of a chance as Tony Soprano getting out of that diner alive, with his onion rings intact.

Javier reacted as fast as any federal agent I'd ever known. Standing only a few feet from the door—a major miscalculation on my part—he raised a sawed-off shotgun. With his arm fully extended, the shotgun's barrel was less than six inches from my right temple.

I had no chance to defend against it. My Glock was aimed at Estefan, who was already reaching for his own gun. I knew then that I had fucked up. Badly. Once I was dead, they would kill Mariana, and Olivia Trenton would be gone for good.

But for Darío.

When I entered, his own weapon was already raised. In fact, he had already fired. It was as though he'd moved on the phrase "Gabriel García Márquez," same as I had. Maybe even at *One Hundred Years of Solitude.*

Darío's bullet nearly sliced Javier's head in half. It was so fast, Javier hadn't even managed to slip his finger around the trigger of his sawed-off shotgun.

I fired the Glock at Estefan, aiming for his right shoulder. The bullet spun him around and caused him to drop his weapon.

From the corner of my eye, I'd seen Mariana dive for cover. So it was just Darío and me, mano a mano.

Had Darío simply missed his target? Javier had been standing so close to me, it was impossible to tell.

Nevertheless, I swung the Glock in Darío's direction and hesitated for half a second.

That half second was enough time for Darío to shout, "D-E-A."

Slowly and simultaneously, we lowered our weapons. I kicked Estefan's gun clear, then asked Mariana whether she was all right.

"I am fine," she said breathlessly.

Meanwhile, Darío was moving like a dart toward the front of the room. He checked his handiwork, then stepped over Javier and closed the door.

"The other two men," Darío said. "Where are they?"

My heart raced. Had I just knocked one DEA agent unconscious and sent another tumbling down a dozen concrete stairs?

"Out cold," I said.

"Good," Darío said. "Then we have some time."

I released a sigh of relief. "Time for what?"

He stared down at Estefan, who was holding his left hand tightly to the gunshot wound on his right shoulder, breathing heavily.

"To get the information you need," Darío said to me.

He held out his hand. He had a mop of dark hair atop his head, a prominent scar trailing from his left ear to his jaw. "Emanuel Vega," he said. "Bogotá Country Office."

I took his hand in mine. "Simon," I said. "Simon Fisk."

With Estefan seated on the floor, back against the wall, suffering, I thought of Emma Trenton and the hell she'd gone through the night of the home invasion, and it strengthened my resolve.

Before we began our interrogation, I turned to Vega and asked, "Any chance more of Estefan's confederates are on the way?"

"I don't think so, but Grey has set up a perimeter around the monastery nonetheless."

"This is an official operation, then?"

Vega smiled conspiratorially. "This is Colombia. There is a very fine line between official and unofficial. Let's just say, we will get creative when it comes time to prepare our reports."

I placed my hand firmly on his shoulder. "Thank you," I told him. "You saved my life."

Almost imperceptibly, Vega shook his head. "Thank Grey," he said as he turned away from me.

It was only then that I realized why Grey had left me the listening devices. Only then did I determine who was in the dark Chevy Trooper outside the Changó nightclub in Cali, who was in the aqua blue minivan parked in front of the church across from the pool hall here in Bogotá. Mariana and I had never once truly been alone. Grey had been watching and listening like a guardian angel the entire time. I owed him a great deal of thanks, not to mention an apology.

I turned to Vega. "How long have you been undercover with Estefan?"

"Less than twenty-four hours, Simon. Estefan tried to throw all this together in a single day. He's small-time. As far as I know, he's never attempted to smuggle so much as a gram outside Colombia before today."

"I don't understand. Why didn't Grey call me off?"

Vega pointed at the body near the door. "Estefan led us to Javier. He was the one we thought might have information on the girl you're looking for. I didn't want to kill him. But he was fast. I couldn't risk anything less than a headshot, or you'd be dead." He paused. "Then Grey would never have let me hear the end of it."

"So Estefan won't be able to help us at all?"

"Maybe yes, maybe no. He has connections. He supplies a number of young dealers in Bogotá. As we dismantled the major cartels and improved interdiction, more and more cocaine began circulating in Colombia's major cities. It became cheaper and even more accessible, so more Colombians tried it, especially teens and pre-teens. They became hooked, and domestic demand rose to absurd levels. Small-time criminals like Estefan replaced the big-time drug lords."

It was essentially what Grey had told me. By trying to prevent cocaine from reaching the States, we'd inadvertently turned Colombia into one giant crack den.

"So we are dealing with a new business model," Vega said. "I suspect Javier over there got his product directly from the factories."

"And Estefan?"

He turned and looked at the man sitting on the floor against the wall. The man I'd shot in the shoulder.

Vega said, "We won't know until we ask him."

I nodded. Said, "All right. Let's get to it, then."

Chapter 46

Estefan did indeed have intelligence on the whereabouts of Olivia Trenton. In fact, as Vega pressed his thumb into the gunshot wound on Estefan's right shoulder, the Colombian drug pusher fed us more details about Olivia's abduction than any of us ever expected.

He didn't know who had actually executed the home invasion and kidnapping in Calabasas, but Estefan did learn from Javier that it was a Panamanian *mara* that had passed Olivia onto the Colombians. In return, the Panamanians received a significant amount of product, which they would then ship through Mexico into the United States. Without having to pay wholesale, their profit margin would be 100 percent. Estefan estimated the Panamanian gang would make a few million dollars off the deal.

Estefan didn't know who had taken the eight and a half million dollars, but he had heard plenty of rumblings about it. The Colombians had threatened not to provide the cocaine to the Panamanians unless they explained exactly where the $8.5 million had gone. The Panamanians insisted they had nothing to do with the ransom. Whatever transpired, the Panamanians said, it had transpired in Los Angeles, not in Panama City.

At first Estefan flat-out refused to tell us just who was involved here in Colombia.

"They will *kill* me if I tell you," he said.

"*I* will kill you if you don't," I replied, removing the Glock from my waistband again.

"You *cannot*," Estefan insisted even as his face turned pale. "You are men of the law and not Colombian law. You are cowardly Americans. You will taunt me, you will torture me, but you will *not* kill me. You will turn me over to Colombian authorities or you will lose your cozy jobs."

Vega pressed his thumb deeper into Estefan's wound. He waited for the Colombian's screams to die out before saying, "Haven't you heard *anything* about the United States over the past twelve years? Or have you been living under a fucking rock?"

I placed the muzzle of the Glock under Estefan's chin and applied pressure, pushing his skull into the wall.

I said, "And in case you didn't get the memo, Estefan—I'm retired."

Oddly enough, Estefan looked to Vega for help, but the agent simply stood and turned his back.

"Now, who has the girl?" I said.

I had to relieve some of the pressure so that Estefan could move his jaw.

"Los Rastrojos," he said. "They are the group that supplied Javier. Los Rastrojos."

An hour later, Grey, Vega, Mariana, and I were in my rented Hilux, heading west in the direction of Colombia's Pacific coast. Three SUVs filled with agents followed us. Another four would be meeting us there—as well as members of the Third Division of Colombia's National Army and Marine Infantry. Grey had not contacted anyone in Colombia's National Police force. Too much corruption, he said. One leak and we'd all be killed.

"Is *this* operation official?" I asked.

Grey, sitting next to me in the passenger seat, furrowed his brow. "It's a very fine line, Simon."

"So I keep hearing."

Our destination was the area known as Valle del Cauca. This was the main region out of which Los Rastrojos were known to operate. Los Rastrojos were a neo-paramilitary group funded primarily by cocaine and heroin trafficking, as well as illegal gold mining. They were also heavily involved in money laundering, arms trafficking, extortion, and of course, kidnapping and murder.

According to Grey, the group had a membership of nearly fifteen hundred, all armed. Some of their soldiers and assassins were tied up in a constant conflict with Los Urabeños, a rival group operating mainly in the north.

The Rostrojos maintained laboratories in the jungles along the Pacific coast and moved their product north to Central America and Mexico, where they sold it to Mexican traffickers who smuggled it into the United States.

Rostrojos also controlled one of the most crucial smuggling routes into Venezuela, which served as a bridge for cocaine marked for Europe and certain parts of the U.S. that remained accessible by boats.

As we drove west, the distant sky looked like dark smoke, and rain began splattering the windshield. The smell of precipitation filled the air.

"Los Rastrojos are the heirs of the Norte del Valle Cartel," Grey said, "which had picked up the pieces of the thoroughly dismantled Cali Cartel. Some of the players remain the same. In fact, a few of our informants have claimed that the Rastrojos *are* the Norte del Valle Cartel, just operating under a different name. Regardless, we do know that the group inherited the cartel's network of assassins and distributors in the international markets."

"They're a private army," Vega added from the backseat. "Well funded and commanded by one of the most ruthless warlords in South America's history."

I watched Vega in the rearview. "What's his name?"

"Óscar Luis Toro de Villa."

"Known to all of Colombia as *el hombre malo*," Grey added.

"'The bad man,'" I said. "Not very original down here, are they?"

"The reason that nickname stuck is because his mother gave it to him."

I shrugged. "Still."

Grey added, "His mother branded him with the nickname when he was only six months old."

Chapter 47

When we reached our destination deep in the Colombian jungle, Grey directed me to pull into a small clearing. His instructions were unnecessary since we'd run out of road. The rain was now pounding the windshield, beating the roof of the Hilux like fists. In the distance, I could just barely make out a brown-green river, its waters rushing south.

"Stay here," Grey said as he and Vega exited the Hilux in order to conference with the other agents.

Mariana climbed up front. Once again, she'd insisted on joining us. But this time, when Grey pushed back, telling her she was just a civilian, I couldn't help but remind him that, technically, I was too.

Now Mariana appeared nervous.

"Are you all right?" I said.

"I do not like the involvement of the military. They are not to be trusted."

I understood her concern. Much of the Colombian population was wary of the military, and of the United States' presence in their country, for that matter. Roughly fifteen years ago, the U.S. adopted legislation known as Plan Colombia. Ostensibly, the plan was meant to aid the Colombian government in reducing coca production and trafficking as part of the U.S. government's so-called War on Drugs. But a decade and a half later, it wasn't difficult to determine who had reaped the benefits—and who had suffered the most egregious injuries and damage.

One winner in Plan Colombia was the U.S. military industrial complex. Billions of dollars went toward building planes and helicopters, all at U.S. taxpayer expense. It was a rare bipartisan effort; the only issue U.S. politicians seemed to be arguing over was which companies would receive the contracts.

Another winner was a multinational American biotech giant called Monsanto. Monsanto was the corporation that initially patented and sold glyphosate, a broad-spectrum systemic herbicide used to kill weeds. The U.S. government contracted with Monsanto to create a version of the herbicide with enhanced toxicity, then put crop dusters in the air over Colombia's fields.

The poisonous chemicals were dropped onto farms large and small, farms that grew coca but also farms that were growing only legal crops like coffee, tobacco, and fruit. The fumigation succeeded only in pushing coca growers up and down the Andes. In fact, production of cocaine in Colombia had doubled since Plan Colombia went into effect. Yet still the reckless fumigation continued.

The toxic chemicals fell not only on crops but also on poor villages, killing and injuring men, women, children, and infants. The poison had entered the country's water supply. It was known to cause tumors in the thyroid, liver, and pancreas. People continued to get sick and die.

Meanwhile, small farmers in Colombia were expected to exist on the pittance of aid they received to grow legitimate crops. It had become a choice each farmer was forced to make: grow coca or allow your family to starve to death.

The other groups to benefit were the deadly paramilitary groups such as the United Self-Defense Forces of Colombia, or AUC. Far worse than any left-wing guerrilla group, the AUC allegedly received training, intelligence, and other aid from the Colombian military, who were receiving the same training, intelligence, and other aid from the United States. Meanwhile, the AUC and other paramilitary groups were massacring not only members of FARC and the ELN, but sympathizers and human rights activists as well. They considered any area controlled by guerrillas as the enemy, and they targeted all residents of such areas, including civilians.

"People in the U.S., they have no idea what is happening here," Mariana said. "Your government privatized this war because it would not have public support."

She was right, of course. The U.S. continued to shell out taxpayer money, but rather than use the U.S. military, Washington hired private contractors and mercenaries who were subject to little or no oversight.

"The U.S. government," Mariana said, "they created these monsters who are slaughtering my people. When their War on Drugs became unpopular, they dubbed the FARC and ELN as terrorists. Then justified their actions by claiming it was part of their more popular War on Terror."

There was a tap on my window and I turned to see Grey standing in the downpour.

I lowered my window.

"We've confirmed the location of a laboratory about twenty klicks west of the river. Our sources say that the Rastrojos have about two dozen men guarding the place and another two dozen inside the factory, most of which is belowground."

"And Olivia?" I said.

"Unlikely that mules would be on-site, but Don Óscar's younger brother is believed to be in charge of this laboratory."

"Don Óscar's brother?"

"José Andrés. If we can capture him alive, he can lead us to *el hombre malo*."

I felt a surge of excitement. "Does this José Andrés have a nickname?"

"Yeah," Grey said, placing his hand over his eyes to keep the rain out. "*Hermano pequeño del hombre malo*—the bad man's little brother."

Chapter 48

Minutes later, marines in full camouflage arrived and set up a shelter made of green tarps and wooden poles in the clearing. An agent extracted a large map from one of the SUVs and spread it out on a folding table under the tarps.

I stepped out of the Hilux and joined them.

Grey was speaking to another agent and two commanders, briefing them on the layout apparently provided by a confidential informant inside the lab.

"... but our CI tells us the money may be booby-trapped. If that's the case, we're going to need—"

"Wait a minute," I said. "Money? What money?"

Grey shot me a look of annoyance. He asked the others to excuse us, then pulled me aside. "This isn't the Trentons' money, Simon. This is dirty money, narco-money."

"But this raid," I said, "it's to apprehend José Andrés, not to seize money or drugs, right?"

"The objective of this mission is twofold, Simon."

"But which objective takes priority?"

"Look, Simon, how do you think I got all these men down here? By telling them a teenage girl's life is at stake? It doesn't work that way, and you know it. Some of these Colombian soldiers have seen more dead teens than they have days. You think a little rich white girl is going to melt their hearts and get them to risk their own lives? You're in Colombia, Simon, not the U.S. of A."

I felt heat crawl up my neck and advance on my cheeks despite the icy rain.

"What did I tell you when you first arrived in Bogotá, Simon? It's all about the pesos down here."

"The problem is, Grey, that if these men have their sights set on the money, then everyone in that laboratory is going to end up dead today, *including* Don Óscar's little brother José Andrés."

"It's a chance we're going to have to take, Simon. Unless you think that you and I and your girlfriend Mariana over there can raid this goddamn lab guarded by twenty-four men with M16s on our own."

Something strong grabbed at my chest but I had no response. Grey had a point. We needed these men. But I wasn't going to remain behind as I'd promised. I was the only one who needed José Andrés alive, and I was going to be damned sure I got to him before anyone else did.

"I'm going in," I told Grey.

"You go in, Simon, and you're not coming out alive."

I shrugged. "Like you said, Grey. It's a chance we're going to have to take."

Following the strategy session, I returned to the Hilux. I couldn't call Edgar, because we needed to maintain cell phone silence. Until the raid began in earnest, all our communications would be made using hand signals.

I handed Mariana my BlackBerry.

"Make me a promise," I said. "If something goes wrong, if I don't make it back, call Edgar Trenton as soon as you return to Bogotá. His number's in my phone. Tell him what happened. Tell him where we left off. Tell him everything we heard from Estefan, including everything we know about Óscar Luis Toro de Villa."

"Of course, Simon."

"There's another number in my phone, a number I'd like you to give him. It's listed under the name Gustavo Z. Tell Edgar to call him. Gustavo is a good friend of mine. He essentially does what I do. He works out of Tampa. Tell Edgar that Gustavo may be able to help him."

"Gustavo," she repeated.

"When Edgar calls, he should tell Gustavo I referred him. Gustavo will ask for a word—a name, actually. The name is Nadya with a *y*."

"Simon, why do you not stay back with me? There are so many men. Why must you go too?"

I explained to her about the money.

"I learned a long time ago, Mariana, that you can't rely solely on authorities to get you through the dark times. Sometimes it's incumbent on you to lead the way. Most of the governments of the world, they consider me a vigilante. And maybe I am a vigilante, I don't know. What I do know is that if I don't accompany these men into that laboratory and they kill José Andrés and destroy our only hope of getting to his brother Óscar Luis, I won't be able to live with myself. So what good would I be doing myself by playing it safe?"

Mariana leaned over and wrapped her arms around me and I held her back, burying my face in her dark hair, devouring her scent. I realized then how much my body needed rest. But there wasn't time. The longer Olivia Trenton remained missing, the less chance we had of ever finding her alive.

I listened to the patter on the roof. The rain wasn't coming down so hard. I looked out the windshield through the canopy of trees. The sky wasn't so dark.

There was a rap on my window and I turned to see Grey standing at my door. I lowered the window, and the Hilux instantly filled with the smell of wet earth.

"Still insist on coming with us, Simon?"

I bowed my head.

"All right, then we have some camo fatigues for you, some weapons, and a vest."

"Thank you, Grey."

"Don't thank me, Simon. At least not until this is over. As much as we may know about our target, we never truly know what to expect."

"Did the CI give you a probable location on José Andrés?"

"He did. The CI also gave us José's most likely route of escape. I think the best course of action would be for you and me to station ourselves nearest that possible exit and hang back, allow Vega's team and the Colombian military to flush him out. That will give us our best chance to take him alive."

"Sounds about right."

"Then let's go, Simon. The boys are ready to roll."

I turned to say good-bye to Mariana but before I could speak, her lips were on mine and her hands were grasping the back of my neck. "Be careful, Simon," she said, her teeth gently tugging at my lower lip. "I understand why you must go in. But please understand that you must also come back."

I pulled my lip free, took her in as best I could. "I intend to," I said.

Chapter 49

Uniformed Colombian soldiers set up a perimeter. Grey and I were part of the cover unit, tasked with sealing in those guards or factory workers attempting escape. Of course, I had only one face in mind—that of José Andrés Toro de Villa.

I stuffed the photo Grey gave me into the pocket of my fatigues and checked my Glock. We were well hidden on a hill covered by jungle. I was ordered by the other agents to exercise great restraint. They didn't want me mistakenly firing upon them. Of course, I didn't care to fire on anyone. The one man I needed, I needed alive.

The entry unit was composed of Grey's men, with Vega leading the team. It was the smallest unit, only a few men. Too many go in, and it would create complete chaos—and chaos gave advantage to the enemy.

A support unit would follow the entry unit in once the facility was secured. They would be responsible for taking custody of the prisoners and conducting a thorough systematic search of the laboratory. They would search for hidden targets, explosives, weapons, cocaine, and of course, the money.

Preparation for the raid was limited to one hour of reconnaissance and whatever information was previously obtained from Grey's confidential informant. We knew the construction and layout of the facility—the placement of all lights, switches, hatches, and closets.

The surrounding area was all jungle, and though the soldiers seemed fairly familiar with it, I certainly was not. If José Andrés got past me, he would have the upper hand.

"Be ready for anything," Grey cautioned me. "These guys don't like to be taken alive."

Grey and I sat silently on our haunches, hidden in the tall grass, watching the raid team wordlessly swarm down the hill toward its target. I readied my Glock, a fierce pounding in my chest reminding me that I was alive—and that I may not be for long.

In my ear, I suddenly heard the phrase "trip wire," and radio silence was immediately no more. In the distance, I watched a small explosion. Then clandestine trapdoors blew open, and men with M16s started popping out of the ground and spraying the jungle in all directions.

"*Down,*" Grey shouted to me, and we both fell flat on our stomachs as bullets buzzed overhead.

Our men were firing back while ducking for cover. In my ear, I heard the word "abort," and suddenly, all our men were moving backwards.

"What the hell's going on?" I shouted to Grey.

"No good," he shouted back. "Vega's team just spotted another two dozen armed men running up through the gorge."

"Soldiers?"

"Mercenaries."

Grey jumped to his feet and grabbed the back of my camouflage jacket. He pulled me to my knees but I broke away, headed in the direction of the machine gun fire.

"*Simon,*" he screamed at the top of his lungs.

Breaking through the dense jungle, I spotted a gunman hunched low, facing in the opposite direction of my approach. His body lay half in, half out of the trapdoor and I instantly decided that the trapdoor would be my way in.

I didn't go unnoticed.

Someone alerted him and he turned just as I entered the small clearing. I fired my Glock as I ran, the bullets ripping away at the wooden trapdoor, causing him to duck for cover. It was just enough time to close the ground between us, and I sprinted, leapt in the air, and collided with him as soon as he showed himself to fire.

Our bodies rolled together down a flight of makeshift stairs into a dusty rough-and-ready laboratory where we fell into a heap onto the hard dirt floor. The remnants of flash grenades made the area thick with smoke, which blinded me but also made for excellent cover.

I tensed myself for a struggle, but the gunman I'd rode down seemed to be unconscious. I lifted myself on my haunches. I rolled him over, found a wide gash on his forehead, but he seemed to be breathing. I collected his M16, replaced the magazine, and tucked the Glock into my waistband.

Slowly I got to my feet. I scanned the room. Through the smoke, I could see long wooden tables upon which sat piles of bags containing an off-white powder and buckets of paste. There were a few men scrambling at the far end of the lab, collecting money and weapons. Each wore a white face mask covering nose and mouth. Particles of cocaine could be seen floating in the air like dust.

I lifted myself up.

Soon as I did, a bullet struck the table in front of me, then another, striking a bag of product. A cloud of white fog suddenly enveloped me, and I breathed deeply and choked, a drip instantly forming in the back of my throat.

My eyes bulged as I hacked. But when I finally recovered, every part of the room before me seemed as clear as though I were seeing it through a high-definition flat screen, and I raised the M16, yelled at the top of my lungs, and returned fire in an unexpected rage, causing the few men still in the lab to scatter.

Hyperalert from the cocaine I'd inadvertently inhaled, I again surveyed the lab, trying to orient myself according to the layout I'd seen aboveground. I turned right, operating with laserlike focus, and ran in the direction I was most likely to find José Andrés.

Behind me I heard shouting. I turned to see men in face masks returning belowground. The assault was evidently over as soon as it had started.

I kept running.

Ten feet ahead of me another gunman deftly lowered himself down a ladder. I stopped, took aim with the M16, and waited for him to turn.

"*Grey*," I shouted when he spun around.

He didn't waste a moment. "This way," he yelled, motioning for me to follow.

We ran down a long damp corridor that led to what looked like a dead end.

Grey stopped in front of the wooden wall blocking our path, lifted his boot, and kicked, breaking one of the larger planks in half.

I followed his lead.

We kicked at a few more planks, then began tearing them away with our hands, splinters piercing our palms, nails slicing our fingers.

When there was enough of a hole for us to crawl through, Grey motioned for me to stop, then took the lead himself.

Once we were through, we moved slowly down a dark corridor. Quietly, at Grey's instruction.

I no longer felt any fear, only a fierce determination to take José Andrés alive and have him lead us to his brother and, with any luck, ultimately to Olivia Trenton.

As we approached, the corridor lit up with gunfire, and Grey and I went to our stomachs, firing back. My M16 took out at least one of the two gunmen; the other man seemed to vanish into thin air.

"*Forward*," Grey shouted at me. "Let's *move*."

We reached the end of the corridor and turned the corner.

Twenty feet away stood the second gunman, his hands in the air, his firearm on the floor in front of him.

Grey shouted something in Spanish. The man bowed his head and Grey cautiously moved forward, his gun raised.

As he advanced, Grey said, "This guy says that José Andrés is behind that door."

I felt my teeth grinding inside my mouth. "We take him alive," I growled.

Grey gave a slight nod, motioned for me to get into position with my back flush against the wall next to the door.

I exhaled.

"On three," he said, lifting his right leg. "One . . . two . . . *three.*"

Grey kicked the door in and I took point, ready to drop anyone who might fire at us.

Only one man stood in the room, however, and he was unarmed, his hands out at his sides. His grungy gray flannel shirt hung open, revealing a narrow brown torso heavily inked and scarred. His face wore no expression. Like a department store mannequin, there was no light or movement in his eyes.

The room was surreally silent following all the explosions, and for a moment I fully expected a sudden blast would take all three of us apart.

I waited, then finally turned to Grey, who smiled.

"Simon," he said, "I'd like to introduce you to *el hermano pequeño del hombre malo.*"

The bad man's little brother.

Chapter 50

Don Óscar's hacienda rested just above a breathtaking gorge several miles outside of Cali. As I drove the Hilux up the dirt road, I thought of the Trentons' house in Calabasas and how it paled in comparison. Don Óscar's country estate was larger than most shopping malls, with enough land to make all of Rhode Island envious.

At the towering gate stood a half dozen men with M16s slung over their shoulders. As I approached, one man stepped forward and held out his palm like a traffic cop. The Hilux rolled to a stop, and the man moved toward the driver's side.

I lowered my window.

"Are you the valet?" I said.

He motioned for me to step out of the vehicle. When I did, two of the others approached while the first one frisked me. Thoroughly.

"Ever think of applying for a job with the TSA?" I said as he worked his way down my left leg. "They can always use a guy like you."

All he found was my BlackBerry. I'd left my weapons with Grey and Mariana back in the city.

"I'm going to need that," I told him, pointing to my phone.

He handed my BlackBerry to one of the other two men, who indicated they were the ones about to lead me inside.

I'd changed out of the camo fatigues and into a black T-shirt and blue jeans so that I wouldn't look quite so imposing. The men walking me inside were all wearing dark suits, so I felt a bit underdressed. But then, my attire was really the least of my worries.

My life—and maybe Olivia Trenton's—depended solely on a brotherly affection that I wasn't sure existed between two low men. Could be that Don Óscar had invited me into his hacienda just to blow my goddamn head off face-to-face, either for killing Javier or destroying his lab and kidnapping José Andrés.

The walk through Don Óscar's courtyard seemed to take longer than the drive. The blistering sun had replaced the black clouds and hard rain we'd found in the jungle. It was hot and hazy, and sweat was continuously dripping down into my eyes.

When we entered the house, I felt thankful for the cool breeze blowing in from all sides. The place itself looked like something straight out of a '70s crime movie. Although the décor was light and unimposing, I half expected to find a fountain with a globe wrapped in the words THE WORLD IS MINE.

After stopping several times for no reason I could discern, I was led to an enormous room on the third floor. There, Don Óscar's wide body sat on an oversize sofa, his thick legs casually crossed, an unlit cigar hanging loosely from the corner of his mouth.

Roughly, the men sat me on a wooden chair placed several feet in front of him.

"Where is my brother?" He said the words so matter-of-factly, you'd think his brother was downstairs mixing our drinks.

"He's safe," I told him. "I left him with my associate. As long as you cooperate, he'll be dropped off somewhere in Bogotá, unharmed, later today."

Don Óscar was unmoved. "I need to see him. Proof that he is alive."

I turned to the man who held my BlackBerry and stretched out my bloodied hand.

Once I had the phone, I pulled up a picture of José Andrés in a pitch black room. He was on his knees, bound and gagged, but otherwise okay.

I passed the BlackBerry over to Don Óscar.

When he looked up from the phone, I could see in his eyes that he wanted to kill me. Calmly, he said, "You realize, do you not, that once my brother is safe, I will have you hunted down and killed like a dog in the street?"

"That's a chance I'll have to take."

Don Óscar tossed the BlackBerry back to me, then rose out of his seat and nodded to his men, who promptly stepped outside the room, shutting the door behind them.

"All this for a teenage girl," he said as he picked up a gold lighter and thumbed the flint wheel. His English was fluent and Americanized; clearly he'd been educated in the States. From the sound of it, probably the East Coast.

I waited as he took several pulls from the cigar until it was securely lit. He turned his head just slightly, blowing smoke in my direction.

He stared at me through the smoke, his face a mask of cruelty and indifference. "First I require another promise from you," he said. "I can tell you up front that you will not like what I have to say. Regardless, I want your word that if I tell you the truth, you will release my brother."

I leaned forward, a fresh wave of anxiety flooding my system. "You have it," I said. "Now get to it. Where is she?"

He lugged his girth a few steps around the sofa, then returned. He was letting me know we were going to do this at his pace, not mine.

"Several days ago," he said, "I received a phone call. It was from someone who for years had been an ally, and when our conversation began, I'd expected a simple request. A request was eventually made, but it was not so simple. It wasn't a request for money or *cocaína* or weapons or even women. It was a request for a *particular* woman." He lifted his heavy left shoulder. "Not even a woman, but a girl. A child my own daughter's age. I flatly refused before I heard even the first detail.

"But this man, he persisted. He called it a simple kidnapping. But this was *not* a simple kidnapping. The girl he wanted lived with her parents in the United States. 'The *United States*?' I said to him. '*Are you mad?* I can do *nothing* in the United States.' He said, 'Your product makes it to the United States every day.' Before I could argue that this was apples and oranges, this man—this old friend, this *ally*—turned his request into a threat."

Don Óscar puffed his cigar, blew out a cloud of smoke that reminded me of the flash grenades going off in the underground laboratory in the jungle.

"This man, he demanded I use the routes that I use to send my product to the United States to extract this girl and bring her here to South America. '*Impossible,*' I said. 'I do not deal directly with *anyone* in the United States. I deal with *maras* in Central America and Mexico. It is *their* responsibility to get the product to the United States.' I said, 'If you wish, I will put you in touch with these men.' But he refused. He said, 'Have any of these *maras* ever crossed you?' I said, 'Of course not.' He said, 'Why?' I said, 'Because they know I will kill them.' He said, 'Exactly. Because they fear you. That is why *you* will continue to deal with them directly while I continue to deal with you.'"

"And this threat?" I said, trying to steady my left knee, which had begun trembling during Don Óscar's speech.

Don Óscar hesitated as he debated how much he should tell me. He said, "Los Rastrojos move their product—*my* product—primarily up the Pacific coast to Central America and Mexico, where we sell it to traffickers who bring it into the United States. But a large part of our business involves moving product toward Europe and to major *northern* U.S. cities on aircraft and go-fast boats. We are able to do this because of one major smuggling route. A bridge, if you will. Without this bridge, our business would be cut nearly in half and we'd become vulnerable, not only to law enforcement but to our competitors as well."

In my head I conjured a map of the Americas. There was only one route he could have been speaking of, and it immediately caused me to shudder.

"I had no choice," Don Óscar said. "The moment I got off the phone with this man, I contacted my largest buyer in Central America. I told him I needed a job done. Before I even quoted a figure, he balked. He said, 'No way. Too much risk.' I had no choice but to do to him what my old friend had done to me."

"You threatened him."

"I threatened him. First with cutting off shipments. When that didn't work, I told him he and his family had seventy-two hours to live. I hung up the telephone on him. Forty minutes later, he called me back and told me I'd have the girl. In exchange, he wanted several million dollars in product. We negotiated."

"Who's this buyer in Central America? I need a name."

He took another pull off his cigar. "A name will do you no good. I do not even know who did this job in California. My buyer, he evidently outsourced. It is none of my business. But the girl, I can assure you, is no longer in my buyer's hands."

"How can you be so sure?"

"Because she was already delivered here to Colombia. Four of my best men picked her up in Sapzurro, an isolated resort town minutes from the Panamanian border."

"Where did they take her from there?"

"I do not know exactly. My *old friend*, he would not tell me. He demanded to speak to my men directly. *He* instructed my men where to go. That was yesterday. I have not heard from them since."

I pushed myself off the painful wooden seat. "Why? Why did your old friend want this girl so badly? For what purpose? Why her, particularly?"

Don Óscar shrugged. "I do not have answers to these questions. I know only what I have told you." He took a long drag off his cigar, breathed the smoke out his nose. "Now," he said softly, "if you will call your associate, I would like for us to make our trade. Your life for my brother's."

I slowly removed the BlackBerry from my pocket. I had one more question, but I was afraid to ask. And Don Óscar knew it. This was the answer he'd promised I wouldn't want to hear.

Whoever it was, I suspected, would make going up against Los Rastrojos seem like child's play.

"The call you received," I said, my thumb hovering over the BlackBerry's keyboard, "who was it from?"

Don Óscar bowed his head, bore his eyes into mine. "It does not so much matter whom the call came from as whose behalf the caller was acting upon."

"All right, then. On whose behalf was the caller acting upon?"

When Don Óscar spoke again, he did so with the cigar in his mouth and in a voice so small, it seemed to come from a frail and frightened child locked away in a dark basement. *"El presidente de Venezuela."*

Part
Four

THE CARDINALS
OF CARACAS

Chapter 51

As we touched down at Venezuela's Simón Bolívar Aeropuerto Internacional in Maiquetía, I thought again of the old treasure hunter and the first words he spoke to me on Seven Mile Beach in Grand Cayman: *If it wasn't for bad luck, I'd have no luck at all.*

It was a cliché that might well end up carved into my tombstone if I didn't survive the next forty-eight hours. Because as fate would have it, Mariana and I were arriving in Caracas on the third day of Carnaval—arguably the loudest, wildest, most crowded festival on earth.

As though Caracas weren't "exciting" enough with its daily gun violence, kidnappings, and political unrest, we'd now have to contend with thousands of alcohol- and drug-fueled partygoers dressed up in animal, alien, and monster costumes surging through the city's streets.

At the airport, I rented a black BMW R1200GS. The people at the rental agency seemed so certain I'd get the motorcycle into a fatal or near-fatal collision that they flatly refused to rent me the bike until Mariana and I had both provided them with our blood types. Maybe they'd already heard from Edgar's neighbor Freddy back in Calabasas.

Dressed in thrift-store clothes we'd purchased before leaving Bogotá, we headed toward the heart of the city. With no real clues as to Olivia's specific whereabouts, I'd decided to begin at the U.S. Embassy. Although I didn't expect this ordeal to end with diplomacy, I figured that the U.S. chargé d'affaires had to have at least *some* ties inside the Venezuelan government, connections who could narrow down the search area within the vast country.

From the air, I'd spoken briefly with Emma Trenton, and now as we crawled through traffic toward the U.S. Embassy, I spoke to her again through my Bluetooth, this time at length. She sounded as though she were on the verge of a nervous breakdown, and it made me think of my late wife and wonder for the umpteenth time what else I could have done to prevent the downward spiral that ended with Tasha's suicide.

An arrest warrant had been issued for her husband, Emma told me, and he was in the process of surrendering with his celebrity defense lawyer, Seymour Lepavsky. Ultimately, it was an affidavit from an FBI forensic accountant that convinced the U.S. Attorney to take the case before a grand jury.

"I have no idea what the forensic accountant said, Simon, but whatever it was, it was evidently enough. According to Seymour, after a few hours of testimony, the grand jury handed down an indictment on multiple felony counts. I'm not even sure what Edgar's charged with yet."

"The initial arraignment will take place within forty-eight hours of his turning himself in," I told her over the hum of the BMW's engine. "You'll know then. In the meantime, you might want to talk to Lepavsky about Edgar's plans to make bail."

"I already have. Artie Baglin is flying in from New York. He's going to meet with Seymour and arrange to pay Edgar's bail, whatever it is."

Artie Baglin, I mused. Arthur Baglin had been the film director attached to *Unfathomable,* the movie based on Will Collins's book about my daughter's disappearance. Had events gone differently, Baglin would have been the man directing Jason Statham on how to properly portray Simon Fisk. Edgar and the director were lifelong friends who'd already worked on more than a dozen movies together, including three films nominated by the Academy for Best Picture.

Arthur Baglin was also one of Hollywood's most controversial activists. The subjects of his films ranged from historical conspiracies to assassinate world leaders to a highly inflammatory biopic of a sitting U.S. president. He'd recently filmed a documentary called *The Pink Tide,* in which he glorified the leftward revolutions in South America. Baglin spent weeks interviewing left-leaning Latin leaders, including the presidents of Bolivia, Argentina, Ecuador, Paraguay, Brazil, and Venezuela, all of whom had been consistently demonized by the mainstream media in the United States.

The centerpiece of Baglin's documentary was his extensive interview with Venezuela's president, who—though democratically elected—had been repeatedly vilified as a dictator by scores of U.S. politicians from both sides of the aisle. Critics of the film charged the polarizing director with offering only one side of the Venezuelan story, to which Baglin infamously replied, "It's a fucking documentary. Of course the film's going to be sympathetic to one side."

The Pink Tide had premiered at the Venice Film Festival, where its reception was largely split along political and geopolitical lines.

"And there's been no progress whatsoever in the search for Olivia," Emma said breathlessly. "They're not even *looking*, Simon. Even though they're not saying it outright, it's clear that they think *Edgar* has her stashed away somewhere, or that she's *in hiding*."

I offered my sympathies, then followed with a condensed version of the events that had transpired in Colombia, ending with the words supplied to me by Don Óscar, specifically that the order to take Olivia had come directly from a government official supposedly acting on behalf of the president of Venezuela.

"My *God*. Should I tell the FBI?" she said. "Maybe they can send some agents down there, I don't know. Maybe the CIA?"

Trust me, they're already listening, I wanted to tell her. But the fact was, it didn't matter. Once the feds liked a suspect enough to bring charges, they stopped looking for leads and only continued searching for evidence that fit neatly into their theory of the case.

"Forget the feds, Emma. They can't do anything in this country anyway. Venezuela isn't exactly an ally. Besides, if our government intervenes, Olivia's as good as gone. Once the U.S. is involved, whoever has taken her will have no choice but to cut ties and run."

"*Jesus*," she said, breaking down.

Sure enough, as I drove up a street parallel to the parade route, there he was—Jesus Christ carrying what looked to be a long, heavy wooden plank. Surrounded by Roman soldiers in plastic helmets, the bearded, loin-clothed messiah was gently being whipped with modern-day cotton belts from Banana Republic. Atop his head sat a plastic crown of thorns.

"Christ," I said.

Emma instantly became alarmed. "What is it, Simon?"

"Nothing. Listen, Emma. I'll call you as soon as I have some news. I don't want my BlackBerry's battery to lose too much juice; I don't know when I'll be able to charge it again. On account of Carnaval, there's not a single vacancy in all of Venezuela."

Once Mariana and I reached the end of the next city block, I had no choice but to pull over and double-park. A frustrating number of roads had been blocked off for the festival, so we'd have to hoof it the rest of the way to the embassy.

"Beware of the pickpockets," Mariana said as we walked toward the main road. "They will be everywhere today."

Ironically, Carnaval was a religious festival leading into the Christian period of Lent. In reality, what it amounted to was one final gust of hedonism before the traditional forty days and forty nights of self-denial. In Europe and South America—even as far north as New Orleans—hundreds of thousands of people dressed up in odd and provocative costumes, shook their bare asses and breasts, and customarily imbibed until they collapsed. This, of course, also resulted in a fair amount of both petty and violent crime.

"I don't have much cash on me anyway," I said. "Maybe enough for a bite. Remind me; I'll have to stop at an ATM before we can grab a decent meal."

On the next street, we had to wade through a sea of people wearing elaborate papier-mâché masks and little else. Men and women alike bared enough flesh to make you feel as though you were walking through a coed strip club without having to flash any dollar bills. Everyone in sight was gyrating to Latin music blasting from speakers hidden in high windows and aboard mammoth floats. No matter how conservative the country, Carnaval was the one annual party unlikely to be broken up by cops.

I gripped Mariana's hand as we shoved through the crowd. When I glanced back at her, I noticed tears in her eyes. "Are you all right?"

"I am fine," she said.

But clearly she wasn't fine. Behind the tears I could see anger in her eyes as she watched hordes of highly intoxicated young men groping women of all sizes and ethnicities, shouting at them to pull up their shirts and skirts, hurling beads at their heads as though they were throwing food at feral animals.

I thought I could read her. I tried to imagine what she'd gone through a year ago, during Mardi Gras in Costa Rica. I had no doubt that throughout the four-day festival, she and the other girls had been used like throwaway paper plates and plastic utensils.

The walk was slow going, and it became worse the deeper we penetrated the city. For ten minutes straight we stood idle as a colossal float exhibiting no less than two dozen dancing women made up like seed-eating birds froze everyone in their place.

"They are cardinals," Mariana said as she gazed up at the spectacle. "There are more than forty species of cardinals around the world. Nearly twenty of them exist in this part of South America."

"You're a bird enthusiast?" I said, intrigued but anxious to move forward.

"When I was young," she said loudly in my ear so that I could hear her over the music, "I would watch birds with my mother. All kinds of birds—pelicans, herons and egrets, hawks, doves, plovers, woodpeckers, ravens, jays, sparrows, larks, even hummingbirds. But the cardinals, for some reason, they were always my favorite. When the winter approached, I would wait for the rose-breasted grosbeaks. The male of the species has a black head and wings, a black tail and back, and a white underside with a bright rose-red patch on his breast. They are beautiful, these birds. They are songbirds. I used to pray for them to fly me and my mother away with them at the end of the winter when they returned north to the States."

I placed my arm around her and held her tight.

"Look," she said. "That woman there, she is a redbreast."

For some reason I couldn't quite put a finger on, inside I ached. It was the kind of ache that would bring me to my knees if I were sitting alone in my D.C. apartment. Here all I could do was fight off the pain and do my damndest to stand up straight.

That, and continue to wait.

Chapter 52

The U.S. Embassy was guarded like the gate at the White House. Understandably, U.S. officials weren't taking any chances during Carnaval. The United States wasn't exactly popular in Latin America, particularly here in Venezuela. For eight years, the previous administration and nearly all U.S. media outlets had accused the Bolivarian Republic of Venezuela of being a rogue nation, and dubbed the country's leader a buffoon.

To the first American guard I came across, I flashed my U.S. passport.

"What's your business here today, sir?"

To get inside I'd have to lie or risk being told to contact the FBI back in the States. The best lies, of course, are short and simple. So I simply pointed to Mariana and said, "My wife had her U.S. passport stolen last night."

The guard held up a clipboard. "Do you have an appointment?"

"No, we don't have an appointment."

"I'm sorry, sir. You'll have to go online and make an appointment, then come back at the scheduled time."

"I'm afraid this is an emergency," I said. "It can't wait."

"Passport Services isn't open today, sir. It's a Venezuelan holiday. The passport section will be closed until Wednesday morning."

"We don't have until Wednesday morning," I said. "This is urgent. I need to speak to the chargé d'affaires right away."

The United States didn't currently have an ambassador in Caracas. The last one appointed by the White House was sent home because the Venezuelan president hadn't liked him. Said the ambassador had spoken ill of Venezuela some twenty years ago. Instead of trying to come to terms, the White House tossed the Venezuelan ambassador to the United States out of Miami in retaliation. It's hardly a secret that it's often politically expedient for U.S. leaders to appear hostile to other nations.

The guard wasn't sure what to do, but I remained patient. Because I was sure that he possessed a certain amount of discretion—and that he was the only chance I had of seeing an American official today. Maybe Jason Bourne could break his way into a closed and heavily guarded U.S. Embassy, but I wasn't likely to get past the front door. Chances were I'd end up dead—maybe in custody, if I was lucky.

No, sometimes you just have to kill them with kindness.

"Please," I said. "I'm a retired U.S. Marshal. I'm just trying to get home."

He nodded, but his face remained noncommittal. "Let me see what I can do, sir."

After more than an hour's wait and several varying explanations (that became more truthful the deeper I made it inside the embassy), I was finally led into the office of the chargé d'affaires, Walter Brewer. Brewer was a slight man, closer to sixty than fifty, with thinning blond hair and large red spectacles. His navy blue suit didn't contain a single wrinkle; the same couldn't be said for his skin. There are men who age well and men who age badly; Walter Brewer was unmistakably one of the latter.

As I took a seat in front of his desk, he fell into his chair with a heavy sigh.

"Now," he said, straightening his muted red bow tie, "I'm not sure what it is you think I can do for you, Mr. Fisk. You told my assistant you lost someone down here? Your teenage daughter, was it?"

I did my best to conceal my frustration. "Let me cut to the chase, Mr. Brewer. I need a face-to-face with Venezuela's Minister of Foreign Affairs."

He smirked. "Oh, you do?"

"I do, Mr. Brewer. An American girl's life hangs in the balance."

"Who are we talking about here?"

It was a catch-22. I wanted to tell Brewer as little as possible until I received his assurances that he would do whatever he could to help. But it seemed fairly clear that I wouldn't receive any such assurances until he knew precisely what was going on—*if then*.

"Olivia Trenton," I said. "The girl who was recently snatched from her home in Los Angeles during a violent home invasion."

Brewer frowned. When he did, his entire face seemed on the brink of caving in. "I read something about the kidnapping online yesterday." He shrugged his narrow shoulders and checked his watch. "What in the world makes you think she's here?"

"Whoever took her ultimately received their instructions from the Minister of Foreign Affairs down here."

"And you know this how?"

"Because I had a long conversation with the man who passed those instructions along. A drug lord operating out of Cali, Colombia."

Brewer chuckled. "Who exactly are you working for, Mr. Fisk?"

"I was hired by Edgar and Emma Trenton."

"Ah, I see. And by Edgar Trenton, you mean the suspect."

"I mean the girl's father."

"Who, if I'm not mistaken, is also the FBI's prime suspect. In fact, hasn't he already been indicted?"

I leaned forward. "Look, Mr. Brewer. I don't know exactly what's happening back in the States. But I believe Edgar Trenton was indicted on charges relating to the eight and a half million dollars he paid in ransom."

"And by 'paid' you mean *hid*, don't you, Mr. Fisk?"

"No, I mean paid. I was there. I witnessed the phone call demanding the ransom, I watched Edgar Trenton step inside the bank where the transfers were made. And I confirmed in person that the money was received by a financial institution in Grand Cayman by a teller who was working there that evening."

Brewer shook his head. "Sounds to me like Mr. Trenton's lawyer is sending you off on a wild goose chase, Mr. Fisk." He folded his hands on his desk. "Who is his lawyer anyway? One of those Hollywood hotshots, right?" His index fingers turned up to form a steeple. "You know, this sounds an awful lot like Johnnie Cochran's argument in the O. J. Simpson trial twenty years ago. 'It wasn't *my* client; *my* client's innocent,'" Brewer said in a voice that sounded like a cross between George Jefferson and Muhammad Ali. "'It was South American *drug lords* that slaughtered Ron Goldman and Nicole Brown Simpson in Brentwood.' Do you even realize how ridiculous you sound right now, Mr. Fisk?"

I leaned back in my chair, kept myself from jumping over Brewer's desk and simply beating the information I needed out of him. After all, sometimes Jason Bourne's way does work best.

"This isn't a ploy, Mr. Brewer. I was hired long before Edgar's lawyer even came into play. I'm telling you—the trail leads here to Venezuela. It leads directly to the Minister of Foreign Affairs, if not the Venezuelan president himself."

"And you expect *me* to do what about this?"

Finally we were getting somewhere. "Either arrange an emergency meeting with the minister and bring me along as an attaché, or simply tell me where I might be able to find him today."

"It's a holiday, Mr. Fisk. I don't suspect you'll find him anywhere today."

"Surely you have an address or an emergency contact number for him."

"Contact number? Mr. Fisk, I don't even know his *name*."

I leaned forward. "Excuse me?"

"The president down here changes ministers like he changes socks. I don't know who the current Minister of Foreign Affairs is, let alone where you could find him."

I could hardly believe what I was hearing. "What the hell kind of embassy is this?"

"This is an embassy in the middle of a capital city in a country in which the president hates us. Not only that, but he's paranoid and delusional. He thinks there's an infestation of CIA agents in his country just waiting for the right moment to assassinate him. That we're here at all is something of a miracle."

I stood. I couldn't afford to waste any more time with this imbecile. "The real miracle," I said as I turned to leave, "is that eight percent of the population in the States is out of work, and yet an asshole like you somehow manages to remain gainfully employed."

Chapter 53

Ten minutes after leaving the U.S. Embassy, I felt as though I'd taken a kick to the gut. In the past year I'd gone up against the Polish Mafia, Ukrainian gangsters, former Russian KGB, Costa Rican sex traffickers, and the Colombian cartels, but how the hell do you take the fight to the Venezuelan government, particularly during a worldwide celebration that has taken over the capital city's streets?

Mariana and I moved slowly through the chaos: men with their heads wrapped like Islamic terrorists firing massive black water guns and throwing water balloon grenades into the crowds; women wearing hardly anything at all shaking their goods atop floats that looked as though they had just broken free of a Hunter S. Thompson acid flashback.

We needed help.

But there was no one to turn to.

No one who could lead me to the Minister of Foreign Affairs.

I scanned the masses. So many colors, my head was beginning to spin. We paused as a dozen shirtless child devils marched past us, holding pitchforks, displaying horns atop their tiny heads, their entire bodies painted blood red.

I'd never felt so helpless in my life.

That's a lie, I reminded myself. At least an exaggeration. Eleven years ago I'd felt every bit as helpless as this, sitting alone in our home in Georgetown, trying to come to grips with Tasha's suicide only weeks after Hailey's disappearance.

In those days, I felt as though my heart had been ripped from my chest and was being held in front of my eyes as I ran on a forever treadmill without a moment's rest.

"We must find someone who opposes the regime," Mariana said, bringing me back amongst the living.

She was right. But I knew too little about the politics of Venezuela to make the call. Or did I? I knew that wealthy businessmen opposed the socialist regime, including those businessmen who used to run the petroleum industry. I also knew that nearly all the Venezuelan media had supported the president's opponents in the past several elections.

"The church," Mariana said.

I turned to her. "What?"

"The Catholic Church." She must have read the reluctance in my eyes. "The bishops of Venezuela for years have criticized the president, accused him of trying to install a Marxist regime that was not in line with Catholic teachings."

I surveyed the crowded street. As in Bogotá, Catholic churches were everywhere in Caracas. Although only a quarter of the population actively practiced Catholicism, nearly all Venezuelans considered themselves Catholic. For that reason, the president had had to walk a fine line during his tenure. But he couldn't fully close the rift. Because of his lax social stances, the more power the president attempted to amass, the greater the pushback from the Catholic Church and its representatives from the Vatican.

"All right," I said. "Who do we go to?"

"The Archbishop of Caracas," she said without hesitation.

"Where do we find him?"

She grabbed my waist, went under my shirt, and pulled me toward her by my belt loops. She stared into my eyes as she dipped her hands into my front pockets and fished my BlackBerry out of the left.

She handed it to me with a smile that I felt in my chest. "Must I think of everything, Simon?"

A brief while later, after getting directions and brushing up on the clash between religion and politics in Venezuela, we were standing on the corner of Plaza Bolívar, outside the Caracas Cathedral, staring up at its bright white Romanesque façade.

"It is so beautiful," Mariana said.

I didn't reply, though an image of the dilapidated buildings and shantytowns on the edge of the city flashed through my mind as we crossed the street and made for the entrance.

The interior of the cathedral, of course, resembled that of a palace—all tall pillars and high arches and tremendous chandeliers, the pews carved meticulously out of a fine dark wood. Natural light gave the immense space the feeling of being outside, the vaulted ceiling rising at least two or three stories into the sky.

"Is something wrong?" Mariana said.

"Nothing," I told her. "I'm fine."

There was only one old woman sitting in the pews. She sat on the right side, near the aisle, about halfway between us and the altar. She was mumbling to herself, fondling a set of dark red rosary beads.

Just beyond the altar hung a giant gold Christ.

As we moved toward the altar, a man of maybe seventy stepped out from behind the marble back wall. He was light-skinned, dressed in a long, flowing red robe, and wore a crimson skullcap atop a headful of thick white hair.

His dark eyes fell on us immediately, though he didn't say anything at first, just watched as we approached the altar.

"*Permiso,*" I said to him. "*¿Hablas inglés?*"

He bowed his head. "*Sí.*"

I held out my hand. "My name is Simon Fisk. This is my friend Mariana Silva."

Tentatively, he took my hand and smiled at Mariana, exposing a set of sparkling white dentures.

"*Me llamo* Cardinal César Zumbado," he said. "Archbishop of Caracas. How can I be of service, Señor Fisk?"

My eyes were drawn to his white collar. I'd been educated in Catholic schools in the States, from kindergarten through the twelfth grade. Despite my fervent protests, my father had always insisted on a private and religious education.

"I need a . . . favor," I told him.

"What kind of favor?" he said.

"I have an issue with someone high up in the Venezuelan government, and I need an audience with him—*today*."

I was ready for the archbishop to dismiss me there and then, but it was apparent that his curiosity had gotten the best of him.

"Who?" he said with a slight tilt of his head.

"The Minister of Foreign Affairs."

"Vicente Delgado?" A sharp look of surprise crossed his face. "What is your business with him?"

I nearly asked for his word that he keep our discussion confidential. But I was sure he'd be offended. Besides, what was the use of his word without a threat of reprisal? In my experience, a holy man's word was only as good as anyone else's.

"You've seen the news about the teenage girl abducted from her home in California?" I said.

"I read something about it in this morning's *El Universal*."

"I just arrived here from Colombia," I told him, "where I had an intense conversation with Óscar Luis Toro de Villa."

His razor-thin white brows rode up his forehead. "The drug lord?"

"The same."

Zumbado spoke in a monotone; it was almost as though he were reciting something he intoned every day at Mass. "And what, may I ask, was this discussion about?"

"The girl," I said. "Don Óscar was told to take her and hand her over to individuals near Colombia's border with Venezuela."

Zumbado half smiled, but it came off as more of a smirk. "Or so this criminal told you."

"I have little reason to doubt his veracity, Your Eminence."

"And why is that?"

"Because my associate was holding a gun to the head of Don Óscar's younger brother when Don Óscar confessed."

Zumbado breathed in and out audibly as he considered what I'd just said. "You are suggesting Venezuela's Minister of Foreign Affairs ordered the kidnapping of an American teenager?"

"I'm doing more than suggesting it, Your Eminence. I'm telling you precisely what happened."

"And why would Vicente Delgado do that?"

"According to Delgado, he was instructed to."

"By whom?"

"By the president of Venezuela."

A flicker of light shone in Zumbado's eyes for the first time. "I see." He glanced over my shoulder, presumably to make certain no one else had entered the cathedral. "And this Don Óscar simply acquiesced?"

"Don Óscar was threatened."

"Was he?" A great deal of skepticism remained in the archbishop's voice, which I found excruciatingly ironic. "Threatened with violence?"

"Worse," I told him. "Threatened with the shutting down of his smuggling route through Venezuela."

He paused. "And what makes you think I can help you?"

"The rift between you and the regime is well documented, Your Eminence."

"Of course. I have spoken out against the anti-Catholic rhetoric of our current president. He levels attacks at me and my Church, and I fire right back. It is part of my role as the archbishop."

"With due respect, Your Eminence, you've done more than simply fire back. You've called the president's actions unconstitutional and illegal. You've accused him of being a liar and a criminal."

"Because that is what he is, Señor Fisk. He is a tyrant. However, I have also led my flock in praying for the president during his recent health crisis. This, despite the fact that he travels to Havana for treatment and treats the Castros as though they are royalty. Meanwhile, he calls me a Neanderthal." He shrugged. "But I could not care less. It is his attacks on the Holy See that he will have to atone for if his present affliction finally takes him."

"He's attacked the pope?" I said. "Didn't the pope visit with the president recently?"

"Not recently. Years ago, and only because I asked him to, in order to get the president's assurances that Venezuela will keep in place our strong laws against the murder of the unborn."

Mariana sniffled. I turned to her and thought her eyes had become moist.

"You have enough insight to help me, Your Eminence. Tell me where I can find the Minister of Foreign Affairs, or at least point me in the direction of someone who can."

"You presume that the president's ministers side with him rather than the Church with respect to our disagreements. It's a dangerous presumption. You have seen how the president treats the members of his cabinet?"

"Then you'd be in an even better position to assist me."

Zumbado shook his head slowly from side to side as he considered his response. "Unfortunately, Señor Fisk, I am not. I do sympathize with your plight. However, my best and only advice is to wait until the end of Carnaval. On Wednesday morning, after Mardi Gras, Caracas will begin returning to normal. You will undoubtedly have better luck locating Vicente Delgado then."

"Your Eminence—"

"I *am* sorry," he said with a raised palm. "But you will have to excuse me. I must return to work. I have to make preparations for an important wedding ceremony that's taking place in my church tomorrow afternoon. I wish you good luck. The girl will remain in our prayers."

Chapter 54

As we stepped out of the cathedral, back into the jam-packed streets, I turned to Mariana and said, "You seemed to get a little misty-eyed back there when we were speaking to the archbishop."

"It was nothing."

Clearly, it wasn't nothing. A wall of water was forming in front of her eyes even now as we stood in the falling sunlight. I couldn't decide whether to pursue it or let it go. As someone who'd lost his wife and daughter, I knew that pain could sneak up on you, that sometimes you didn't want your best friend to raise the subject of that pain yet other times you'd happily fall into the arms of a complete stranger. Not only are we all different when it comes to grief, we desire different actions and reactions at different times.

She said, "You are hungry, yes? Shall we get something to eat?"

"Sure."

A few blocks later we found ourselves in front of Restaurant Beirut. From the outside, the place didn't look like much, and it certainly didn't seem appealing. At least not to me. Mariana, however, said she loved Lebanese cuisine, so I told her, "Let's give it a shot."

We were seated in the far corner of the small eatery, my attention half-commanded by the menu I couldn't read, and half-distracted by the small television I couldn't hear and wouldn't be able to understand if I did.

I asked Mariana if she would choose something for me.

She asked, "What do you like?"

"Pizza."

I'd been joking, but after the waitress came by and took our order, I asked Mariana what she had ordered for me.

"Pizza, like you say."

"Really."

"In Lebanon, it is called manakish. It is like a pizza: dough and toppings. Yours will be topped with za'atar, mixed with olive oil. It is delicious; I am sure you will love it."

I watched the door as a party of four entered, two drunk middle-aged men with two drunker middle-aged women attached to their sides.

"You did not like the archbishop," Mariana said.

I gazed at her across the table. "Not particularly, no."

"I noticed this."

I tried to smile. "You're very perceptive."

She nodded. "As are you."

I was relieved she'd created an opening. "You're going to tell me what upset you back there?"

Mariana ran her hands through her shimmering black hair. At their thickest, her arms were so slight that I could hold both of them in a single hand. As alert and energetic as she was, I had to keep reminding myself that for the past sixteen months, she'd been held captive under unthinkable circumstances.

"Last year," she said quietly, "one of our keepers drove me into San José to work for the weekend. Usually, it was always two of them who accompanied each girl, but this was also the time of Carnaval, so they wanted to bring as many girls as possible into the capital. As soon as we arrived in San José, he brought me to this terrible apartment. It was in shambles, no furniture but for a filth-covered mattress. I asked him, 'What are we doing here? We should be outside; that is where the business is.' He said nothing, this big man. Just struck me with a closed fist, then threw me onto the mattress and dropped his tremendous body on top of me. He . . ."

She trailed off.

"You don't have to tell me any more," I said, reaching across the table and taking her hand.

"No," she sobbed. "I finish these things I start." She breathed in, and again it struck me how resilient this woman was. "Over forty-eight hours, he repeatedly raped me."

"Mariana—"

"It is okay." She continued, "Always, when they forced me to work, I insisted that the johns wear protection. But this man, he did not. I begged over and over again, but he refused. A few weeks later I realized I missed my period and I asked that I be allowed to take a pregnancy test. The men, all of them, said no. But one of the men, he was younger and kinder than the others. A few days later, he brought me a test when I was alone."

I bit down on my lower lip, a mixture of sadness and rage swelling in my chest.

"I was pregnant, yes. But I could not have this baby, this product of a rape." She touched her fingers to the small gold crucifix hanging around her throat. "But I am Catholic, and the Church says that you cannot end a pregnancy, no matter what. Even with a rape, they say it is a gift from God."

I felt my eyes welling up.

"The young man, the one that was kinder than the others, he brought me pills. They were regular contraceptive pills, but he told me if I swallowed enough of them . . ."

Gently, I pulled her chair closer to mine and held her to me. "It's okay, Mariana."

She pulled away, her head down, hair falling over her wet face. "But it is *not* okay, Simon. I took the life. Every night I have to think about it before I go to sleep. I have to beg of God forgiveness for this. I have to pray. . . ."

I knew that nothing I said would change the way she felt, nothing I said would alter what she believed. All I could do was listen and offer my sympathies. Anything else and I risked igniting her rage.

Before she could say another word, the waitress arrived with our plates of food. Mariana wiped her eyes as mine fell on the small television screen again. The local news was covering the Carnaval festivities in the coastal city of Puerto La Cruz. I squinted so that I could see better, make out whom they were focusing the camera on: a hulk of a man in a bright red polo shirt driving a golf cart in the middle of the mobbed parade.

I'd known he wasn't camera-shy. In fact, the president had been a master of the media for over two decades, ever since he'd led an unsuccessful military coup d'état against the Venezuelan government, then gone on television conceding that the coup had failed ("for now") and accepting full responsibility, for which he ultimately did two years in prison. As president he even had his own weekly television show that often went on for hours. In short, he *loved* the camera. Nearly as much as he loved the sound of his own voice.

"Can I do anything else for you?" the waitress said in English.

"Yeah," I said softly, my eyes still glued to the screen. "I'm afraid we're going to have to take this entire order to go."

Chapter 55

The drive from Caracas to Puerto La Cruz took us just under four hours. By the time we arrived it was full dark, but the festivities were still in full swing. The only question was whether *el presidente* had remained on the Caribbean Sea's south shore or moved on to another venue to continue the party.

The obvious place to start was where I'd seen the president's entourage on television. They'd been passing a city landmark, an enormous sea green crucifix situated on the Paseo Colón, a wide promenade just to the north of the city.

I parked the motorcycle down a side street and we headed toward the main road, locked hand in hand so that we wouldn't be separated by the human current.

I was still hungry. I had been able to pay for the food at Restaurant Beirut, but that wiped me out of cash. I'd given Aubrey Lang my AmEx Blue, so all I had on me was my debit card, which wasn't associated with any of the major banks. I'd need to stop at an ATM soon. And not only for food; in this job, you never knew when you might need cash to bargain for some vital intelligence.

At night, it seemed, the revelers were holding nothing back. The music was louder, the drunks drunker, the prostitutes selling hummers in just about every back alley and side street we passed.

"He must be gone by now," Mariana said, speaking of the president. I searched the crowd for a swarm of red shirts. When I didn't find any, I looked for news cameras, someone holding a microphone, yelling into a lens over the riot.

Nothing.

"Simon?"

Even though it was a popular name in South America, thanks to Simón Bolívar, the Venezuelan revolutionary who had led Latin America's successful struggle for independence from the Spanish Empire, I instinctively turned my head.

"Simon Fisk," the man said.

It took me a moment to recognize him. The man standing in front of me was Clifford Shermer, one of the wealthiest men to ever hire me, second only to Edgar Trenton. I'd last seen Shermer about six years ago, but age-wise he seemed to have lost a couple of decades since. He was tanner, thinner; the deep wrinkles he'd had when I worked for him were no longer carved into his skin. Botox, I supposed. Not bad, though he seemed to have sacrificed his ability to blink.

"Cliff," I said, shaking his hand. "Good to see you."

He smiled, ran his fingers through his thinning gray hair, possibly the only thing on him he hadn't had touched up. "What brings you down here, Simon?"

When Cliff Shermer came to me six years ago, he was frantic. He'd been given my name by a U.S. Coast Guard officer who formerly worked on his yacht. Shermer had had an even wealthier wife named Jackie, and when the couple split, she'd decided to split with the kid. Just tore up the court's custody order and took off for the south of France. There she hired private security, the best she could find, paid former French intelligence officers to hide her and her son in Monaco. It took me nearly three months to locate her. Another two to successfully retrieve the kid.

"On the job," I said.

Cliff's son, Kenny, was eight when he was taken, nine when I brought him back to the States. Which meant he'd be in high school now, back in Minneapolis, Minnesota.

"Not the girl from L.A.?" Shermer said.

"That's the one. Her last known position was Colombia, near the Venezuelan border."

He glanced at Mariana and smiled. "Is there anything I can do to help?"

"Is your boat here?"

"Of course." He motioned to the Caribbean. "Docked over by the pier."

I nodded, looked around to make sure no one was listening in. "You still prepared for the threat of piracy?" I said.

"Oh, you bet. It's worse than ever down here, Simon."

"Think you can spare a piece?"

Shermer laid his thick hand on my shoulder and squeezed. "For the man who rescued Kenny from my ex? I can probably scare up a cannon."

Shermer's luxury yacht *Rafalca* bore the Cayman Islands flag. He welcomed us aboard and I immediately turned starboard to gaze out over the dark Caribbean Sea.

"Couple years ago," Shermer said, "we were boarded by three young men wearing masks and wielding machetes. One of my crew lost his hand trying to be a hero."

"Sorry to hear it," I said as I moved back toward him and Mariana.

"Come downstairs." He motioned for us to follow. "I have a friend who was boarded off the coast of Guatemala by a couple of pirates. Know what they did? They put a gun to his three-year-old son's head."

Mariana crossed herself.

"Another guy I know," Shermer said, "he was boarded by four men in rubber masks. They raped his wife and kidnapped his twelve-year-old daughter."

"Where was that?" I asked.

"Somewhere near Panama. They took seven grand in cash off the boat. This guy ignored the ransom demand. Instead, he and his wife immediately flagged down the Coast Guard. Coast Guard conducted a wide search and came up empty. They've never seen their daughter again."

We walked through one stately room into another. In the second room, Shermer went to the far corner, knelt down, and carefully lifted a false floor.

"Christ," I said, staring into his armory.

"What are you looking for, Simon? A handgun? A rifle? A shotgun, maybe?"

"Handgun, Cliff."

"Sure, I've got Ruger, Beretta, Smith and Wesson, Springfield, Browning—"

"A Smith and Wesson will do."

"Revolver? Automat—"

"Auto. Nine-millimeter." I pointed at a gunmetal Chief's Special. "She'll do."

He set it in my hand.

It was lightweight, compact. Had a rubber grip. I turned, extended my right arm away from Shermer and Mariana. "Yeah," I said. "She'll do nicely."

Shermer asked Mariana if she wanted a weapon but thankfully, she declined.

I stuffed the handgun into the waist of my jeans and we started back toward the stairs.

"You know," I said to Shermer when we reached the deck, "I don't mean to sound ungrateful, but with the gun laws down here—"

He waved me off. "I know. Should've turned them in to customs. But I've got enough money stashed down there that if I got found out by *la guardia,* they'd look the other way. Rather give it to crooked cops than the goddamn pirates, ya know?"

I savored the cool breeze blowing in from the sea. "Sure, I guess." As he led us off the boat, I said, "Say, Cliff, how's your boy doing? Gotta be what, fifteen now, right?"

"Sixteen," Shermer said with a sigh. "To tell you the truth, he's back in Monaco with Jackie." He motioned back toward his yacht. "The kind of lifestyle I wanted to live, I couldn't do it with a kid anchored to my neck. Even with the child support I was receiving from the ex, it wasn't worth the hassle. I realized it less than four months after you returned him to me. Our next stop was the French Riviera with six dozen roses and a handwritten apology. I had to beg Jackie to take him back."

I stared past him into the blackness of the Caribbean. After all that, he'd only wanted his son out of spite and for the abundance of child support he'd receive. The poor kid had been nothing but a pawn in Shermer's chess match with his ex-wife. And I'd helped move the pieces.

Cliff Shermer tilted his head and scrutinized my face as Mariana tugged gently on my arm for us to leave.

"Something wrong, Simon?" he asked.

"Not at all," I said. "I was just thinking that it probably would've been wise for you to tell me about Kenny *before* you handed me a loaded gun."

Chapter 56

Mariana and I walked into the first bar we found, an open-air joint alive with good music and cool trade winds.

"You would like something to drink?" Mariana said, pointing to the bar.

After that last conversation with Cliff Shermer, I could have used a fifth of Irish whiskey attached to an IV. As difficult as it was, I pushed thoughts of him aside and instead recalled the old man in the Caribbean, the treasure hunter on Seven Mile Beach. After a few seconds, I felt my pulse begin to slow a bit.

"I'll have a rum," I said. "Neat."

Mariana started toward the bar then swung her head back around as she came to a realization. "I forgot, we have no money, Simon. We will have to go to an ATM."

"I'll go," I said. "You wait here. Get a table. Open a tab if you can, have a drink. I'll be back in a few minutes."

I pushed through to the bar. Waited as a young American bartender finished mixing a mojito. He asked what I'd like to drink and I asked for directions to the nearest cash machine. The directions he gave me seemed kind of roundabout but I thanked him and tossed him a small tip as he turned, picked up the house phone and dialed out.

I left the bar, rounded the block, turned right, then left, and found myself on the first truly quiet street I'd visited since we arrived in Venezuela. I inhaled the fresh night air deeply, relishing the break from the noise.

I crossed the street to the outdoor cash machine leaning up against a small Banco Central. I quickly scanned the block before pulling out my wallet.

As I fished for my debit card, it struck me again that I wouldn't find Olivia unless I could figure out the "why." Why had she been taken? If the late Kellen had anything to do with her kidnapping, then he'd been working for someone other than the Costa Ricans who'd held Mariana and the other women; that much was clear. But it was beginning to seem just as likely that Kellen had nothing to do with the Calabasas home invasion at all. He'd been killed because I was (inadvertently) getting too close to the sex traffickers, not because I was getting too close to figuring out what had actually happened to Olivia Trenton. Kellen was likely killed because I'd been following the wrong trail.

I'd been following that trail because of Olivia's missing day in Grand Cayman—the Tuesday following Olivia's night at the Next Level. I remained convinced that Olivia's missing day was key. But what could Venezuela's Minister of Foreign Affairs possibly have to do with an American teenager's missing day in the Caribbean?

It made no sense. If there was a plausible connection, I couldn't see it.

I was feeding my debit card into the machine when I heard the click of a gun being cocked a few feet from my ear.

I sighed, blew air through my lips in frustration, my blood beginning to simmer again. At that moment I never wanted so badly out of a place as I did out of South America.

In slaughtered English, the guy holding the gun on me said, "I desire to sell to you your life."

"Really." I summoned what little Spanish I knew, because I couldn't bear to hear him speak English again. *"¿Cuanto cuesta?"* I asked, reasonably enough. How much is it?

"Cinco mil."

I wasn't sure, but I thought that was about five thousand dollars. Then again, he was probably thinking in terms of Venezuelan bolívars. If that were the case, he wanted about a thousand dollars U.S.

"Es demasiado caro para mí," I told him. That's too expensive for me. *"Podría bajar un poco el precio?"* Could you lower the price?

"No!" he shouted as he smacked me on the back of the head with his gun. The strike smarted like hell, but at least I'd drawn him in closer.

The ATM was beeping, pleading with me to do something already. I peered into its monitor and studied our blurred reflection to try to gauge the distance between me and the assailant.

I placed my hands close together about chest high.

"All right," I said. *"Lo llevo."* I'll take it.

As I said it, I took a step back with my left foot; then I pivoted with my right, taking myself out of the line of fire.

I grasped the gunman's wrist, twisted it away from his body.

"This wasn't a good time to try this," I told him.

Fear swept over the gunman's face as he looked into my eyes and saw that I was no amateur. That was when I realized he'd probably received a phone call from the bartender who gave me the directions.

I was about to let him go when I heard an intermittent drip splashing the sidewalk beneath us. I looked down at the puddle, disgusted. "Really?" I said.

I ripped the gun from his hand, pushed his body away, and delivered a swift kick into his solar plexus, throwing him back against the cash machine.

I took a step forward, punched him in the gut. When he doubled over, I grabbed him by his shirt, lifted him up under his arms, and tossed him into the puddle of his own piss.

He hit the cement with a pained groan.

I leaned over him. "Get the hell out of here," I said calmly into his face. "And learn to control your bladder before you pull a gun on someone else."

He pushed himself up and started scrambling.

I watched him vanish around the corner, his boots still pounding the pavement well after he was out of sight.

I sighed again. Shook my head at the world.

Then I finished my transaction, gathered my bolívars, and headed for the bar so that I could throw back that glass of rum and maybe another.

Chapter 57

When I returned to the bar, the bartender I'd gotten the directions from was gone. Mariana was waiting at a small table, sipping a rum and Coke with a twist of lime. As I took a seat next to her, she slid over the rocks glass I'd ordered. I took a good, long swallow. Upon seeing me nearly finish the rum in a single shot, our waitress came over and asked if I'd like another. I handed her what was left of the rum, and asked her to get me an espresso instead.

"Any troubles?" Mariana said.

"None," I told her.

She reached across the table and grabbed one of my hands. "Good news, Simon. I was watching the television, and there is still a reporter covering the events here in Puerto La Cruz."

"And the president?"

"No, I don't think so. But this reporter, I asked the waitress about him. He is very—how you say?—antagonistic to the regime."

"Terrific," I said. "Did you recognize where he was reporting from?"

"I think so. An area not far from here. If he's not still reporting, we will find him in a bar. He is a heavy drinker, the waitress told me. He was drunk even on the news just now."

The waitress set my espresso in front of me. I fired it down, tossed some bolívars on the table, and stood.

"Then we'd better go now," I said, "before our reporter decides to pass out."

As we dodged revelers on the main boulevard, I scanned the throngs. Looking for a particular drunk in Puerto La Cruz during the second-to-last night of Carnaval was like searching for a specific bee in a swarm.

"There," Mariana shouted. "I recognize that intersection. The reporter was standing in the far right corner when he gave his report."

The Venezuelan police were out now, shoving people aside, walking purposefully against the flow of pedestrian traffic. Dressed in menacing dark blue uniforms, they were difficult to miss. Ask most locals in Venezuela, and they wouldn't hesitate to tell you that the cops presented a far greater threat to them than the common criminal.

"All right," I said. "This is a college town, so there are plenty of bars. Our best bet is to just drop by each one and start looking. You'll recognize this guy if you see him?"

"Better," she said, pulling me close to her again. As she dipped into my front pants pocket for the second time in hours, I could smell the sweet scent of rum on her breath and it dizzied me.

She pulled out my BlackBerry, opened the browser, and typed in a name. She clicked on a link and showed me a picture of the reporter.

"You're an angel," I said.

"And here I thought you do not believe."

I smiled. "I meant it in the metaphorical sense."

Before I finished the sentence, her lips were on mine and we kissed, long and deep, with the floats gliding by us, guys in windows throwing beads, women all over lifting their tops and exposing their breasts. Even so, it felt impossibly romantic.

When I opened my eyes, I held her to me. Glaring over her shoulder, I saw more police. They seemed to be advancing in a pattern.

Toward us.

"Let's go," I said, gripping Mariana's wrist and dragging her toward the first bar I spotted.

The bars were crowded, but not terribly so. The revelers obviously preferred taking their drinks outside, and in the chaos, it was relatively easy to enjoy a libation or two on the street.

As soon as we entered the bar, I headed toward the rear with Mariana right on my tail.

"Wait, Simon, I am looking."

"Look faster," I said, glancing over my shoulder. Through the open door, I could see the officers approaching the bar from the street.

I pulled Mariana with me as I crashed through the door leading into the kitchen, knocking over a young busboy and his gray tub full of dishes.

"Disculpe!" I shouted to him. Sorry. Or something of the sort.

Cooks fired obscenities at us; one stood between us and the door leading outside with a butcher knife held at eye level.

I removed the handgun from my waistband and leveled it at him as we hurried toward him. He dropped the knife on the tiles and scattered, ran straight for the freezer and hid himself.

Mariana and I burst through the door, and we were back outside. The back alley was empty except for a hooker plying her trade on a kid who couldn't have been more than fifteen years old.

We ignored them, ran as fast as we could down the alley. On the corner was an open steel door, steam billowing up into the night.

I pointed to it. "Another restaurant. Let's check it out."

"Wait," Mariana yelled as she tried to catch her breath. "Are we running from the police or looking for the reporter?"

I turned. In the distance, the door we'd exited from blew open, and three cops spilled out into the alley.

"Both," I said, then dragged Mariana into the blanket of steam.

Chapter 58

As far as I could tell, we'd lost the cops. Thirty minutes after I first spotted them, we were standing in a hot, crowded bar on the edge of the city, trying to rehydrate with tall bottles of Zenda mineral water.

Mariana offered to do a quick spin around the pub before giving up and heading back to Caracas.

I was standing alone, watching the door, when a Hispanic man of about my age stumbled into the bar by himself. He looked ready to drop, but he had a wide weatherman smile on his face. Other patrons seemed to know him, offering handshakes and hugs. Someone even broke into song.

I plucked my BlackBerry from my pocket and pulled up the picture of Jorge Tejata.

"There he is," I said to Mariana when she returned from the back of the bar. He was seated at a booth now, alone. For all the cheers upon his arrival, apparently no one wanted to actually sit and drink with the man. In fact, the party that had been at the booth promptly took off as soon as Tejata slid in.

Mariana said, "He is a bad drunk, from what I was told."

I shrugged. "Well, let's hope he's also a talker." I motioned her ahead of me since a self-invite from Mariana was bound to be more appealing to Tejata than a self-invite from me. "Let's drop in on him."

Tejata was a thin man, the kind of man who carried thin well, who looked both tough enough to play American football yet sensitive enough to cry during a romantic comedy. He wore a wrinkled yellow and orange aloha shirt, open; chest hair creeping out over a thick gold chain. He held a lit cigarette between his lips, but he seemed more focused on the pint of beer in front of him.

"Buy you one?" I said, pointing at his glass.

"Do I have to buy you one back?"

"Not at all."

"Then you can buy me as many as you'd like." He pointed to Mariana. "And get the lady one too while you're at it."

His English was excellent, even if a tad slurred from drink. With a wave of his hand, he summoned a young waitress and ordered a tableful of pints.

"To what do I owe your wonderful company?" Tejata was speaking to me but studying Mariana as though she were some kind of specimen. "Love your cheekbones," he told her.

"Your station is covering the missing American girl?" I said.

He looked at me. I'd apparently earned his attention *and* sobered him up, all with a single question.

Tejata said, "Who are you?"

"My name's Simon Fisk. I'm a private investigator of sorts. I was hired by the girl's father to track her down."

"The father's locked up, you know."

"I know."

"Hope you were paid up front."

"I was."

The waitress set a few pints on the table and said she'd be back with the rest in a few moments.

"So, what is it you want from me?" Tejata said between gulps.

"Information."

"What kind of information?"

"Information about the regime. The kind that might lead me to the Minister of Foreign Affairs, possibly all the way up to the president."

Jorge Tejata took it in as he stubbed out his cigarette. Narrowing his eyes, he said, "That's going to cost you more than a few pints of beer, you know."

I said, "What do you want?" Though I thought I already knew.

"The story, man. All of it. Beginning to end. Right here, right now. Then I'll take you to Vicente Delgado's doorstep in the hills if you want me to."

I took a sip of beer, pretended to mull it over.

"The girl *was* taken," I said. "Happened during a home invasion in Greater Los Angeles. Only the mother, Emma Trenton, was home with her. The father was in Berlin at a film festival. The assailants roughed the mother up, pumped her full of a sedative, then left the house with her daughter."

"How many of them?"

"Four. Spanish-speaking. All wearing black ski masks. One was carrying a bandola case with equipment; another had a laptop. They left a ransom note requesting eight and a half million, U.S. The father paid the ransom but they never had any intention of returning the girl. It was a setup from the start."

Tejata took a long pull off his beer. Sweat was beading on the fine line of hair above his upper lip. "Go on," he said.

"Two months before the kidnapping, the girl had spent winter break in Grand Cayman with three other girls. The girls were together the entire time, except for one day. I was just there, in George Town, a few days ago. Looks as though she met someone there, someone with enough dough to buy her an expensive diamond pendant."

"Any idea who?"

"I followed this American kid named Kellen down to Costa Rica. He'd hooked up with one of Olivia's girlfriends. When I started asking questions about him in San José, the kid turned up dead. A few minutes after I found the body, there was an attempt on me and an old friend who was helping me. Two assailants; one wound up hog-tied in the back of my SUV, the other was accidentally shot to death by his partner. The lucky one directed us north to a dense jungle near the Nicaraguan border. In a clearing, we found a camp with four men and more than a dozen women being held captive."

"They were sex traffickers," he said with a sideways glance at Mariana.

She didn't bat an eye.

"We rescued the women," I said, "but Olivia Trenton wasn't among them. It looked as though we'd hit a dead end."

"But it was not a dead end," Mariana told him. "I was one of the women being held by these men. I would listen to them, always listen, hoping for some information that might help me escape. A few days ago, I hear the men talking about a *mara* from somewhere in Central America. Honduras, I think. They had recently come into very much money because of some job that was done in the U.S. They had heard rumors that the girl was being handed over to one of the cartels in Colombia to work as a smuggler. I told this to Simon, and together we flew to Bogotá."

"I don't get it," Tejata said. "Seems like a hell of a lot of trouble to kidnap a mule."

"Of course it does," I said. "Long story short, we followed the trail in Colombia back to Los Rastrojos. We went straight to the top, to Óscar Luis Toro de Villa."

Tejata's eyes bulged. Seemed he'd all but forgotten the beers standing in line in front of him. "*El hombre malo?* How the hell did you get to him?"

"With a little help from an old friend in the DEA's Bogotá office. The DEA had an informant. We were able to locate one of Don Óscar's underground labs, where we captured his brother, José Andrés."

Tejata began to frisk himself, presumably for his pack of cigarettes. "What then?"

"From there, it was easy. My associate held on to José Andrés while I knocked on Don Óscar's door in Cali. I traded his brother for information. Los Rastrojos had indeed had the girl. But Don Óscar didn't do it to have her work as a smuggler. He had been threatened."

"*Threatened?* Don Óscar? By who? Who the hell threatens Don Óscar and lives to tell about it?"

"According to Don Óscar, it was Vicente Delgado acting on behalf of the Venezuelan president. Delgado threatened Don Óscar with closing his smuggling routes through Venezuela in order to get him to comply."

Tejata gave up his search for the smokes, leaned back in his seat, and put a pint to his lips. His hand was trembling, either from shock or excitement. Maybe a bit of both.

"Since we arrived in Venezuela," I said, "we've been looking for someone to lead us to Vicente Delgado, if not the big man himself."

Tejata slowly nodded his head.

"We started at the U.S. Embassy, which got us nowhere. Then we paid a visit to the president's supposed nemesis, the Archbishop of Caracas."

Tejata smirked. "Cardinal César Zumbado? He's no help to anyone. All he does is preach politics here in Venezuela. The Catholic Church in Venezuela is nothing more than another political party. If César's not yapping about 'sins of the flesh,' he's screaming his stupid red hat off about homosexuals and abortion."

My eyes dashed to Mariana. Something moved in her throat but she held up.

"And you?" I said.

"Me?" Tejata shrugged. "Me, I live what you Americans call an alternative lifestyle. As far as I am concerned, César Zumbado and everyone like him can go to hell and burn with their bogus devil." He lifted his pint. "Or not. I don't care."

I smiled. "Sorry for the confusion. When I said, 'And you?' what I meant, Jorge, was: Can you help us out?"

Tejata motioned to the waitress, then said to me, "Just one cup of coffee to sober me up, then we will go."

"Make it two," I said as I stood. "And make mine an espresso. In the meantime, I'm going to run outside and have a look, see if our uniformed friends are still hanging around."

Chapter 59

We were on a dark, desolate road back to Caracas not a half hour later when I first noticed the headlights behind us. I was driving Tejata's SUV with Mariana seated next to me in the passenger seat, Tejata himself sleeping one off in the back. I adjusted the rearview and tried to get a better look. Whatever was behind us, it was a large vehicle, at least as large as Tejata's, and as we descended a hill, I could see that there were two other mammoth vehicles just behind it.

"Wake up Jorge," I said to Mariana. "We've got company."

I gently pressed my foot down on the accelerator to see if they'd match my speed.

After a few minutes, there was no question; we were being followed.

"It's the military," Tejata said once Mariana had rattled him awake. "This is not good, Simon. If they catch us . . ."

I looked at him in the rearview. "Want to finish that thought?"

Tejata looked back at the vehicles following us again but remained silent. They were closing in on us; now they were almost on top of us.

"Jorge," I said, "I need your assessment before I can decide what to do."

When he spoke, his voice quivered. "If they catch us . . ."

"Yeah?"

"If they catch us, they will kill us."

"Are you suggesting we run?"

He glanced back at our shadows again. "To be perfectly frank, Simon, it does not matter. There is not another turn-off on this road for at least twenty-two miles."

I shifted gears. "Doesn't mean we can't try to make a break for it."

My foot pressed the accelerator to the floor as the red line on the speedometer climbed. The SUV coasted down one hill, then started up another, my stomach sinking and rising with the movement.

The last vehicular chase I had gotten myself into didn't end pretty. It ended with two dead on L.A.'s storied Mulholland Drive. I pictured the wreck, could almost smell the burning, bloodied flesh. Could hear Jason Gutiérrez's voice in my head as he begged me to pray with him.

As it turned out, none of my maneuvers mattered.

Because halfway up the next steep incline, I saw a string of bright lights ahead of us. Not merely a single vehicle, but a half dozen or more, parked diagonally in the middle of the road.

"Roadblock," I muttered.

I twisted my head from side to side and spotted nothing but dense jungle, nowhere at all to turn off.

In the rearview, I gazed at Tejata, his eyes wide and fixed on the scene just ahead of us.

"It's okay," I tried to assure him. "When they ask, you tell them I kidnapped both of you and jacked this vehicle at gunpoint."

"I don't think that's going to help," he said.

Chapter 60

I didn't know how much time passed, had no idea whether the sun had risen, only that it hadn't risen in this gray window-less room. I lay curled up on a cold cement floor, my clothing gone, all of it; the flesh on my chest, back, and neck was raw.

I didn't know how many lashes I'd taken, or who had delivered them, because I'd been blindfolded. I couldn't remember the questions I'd been asked, because I couldn't understand a single word that had been spat at me. Worst of all, I didn't know where Mariana and Tejata were, whether they were alive or dead or being tortured.

I only knew this was all my fault. I'd brought them into this. And for as many hours as I had left, their fate was on my head, even if it was no longer in my hands.

My father, Alden, had had a taste for locking me up in small rooms.

For using the belt as they'd used the strap.

He'd had a taste for blood, the fucker.

A slit of light appeared a few feet away before I heard a sound. Two men briskly stepped inside and lifted me roughly to my feet. One held me up as another removed the blindfold and placed a black hood over my head. Handcuffs were then locked tight around each of my wrists, and my arms were lifted into the air, stretched as far as they could go. The cuffs closed around something metal in the ceiling; then my body was let go and I hung.

My bare feet barely touched the ground.

My arms felt as though they were being ripped from their sockets.

I felt nauseated but had nothing left in my stomach but bile.

The footfalls of the two men dissipated down the hallway; then I heard the click of a light being turned on. I saw red through my hood. The source of the light was hot, probably a bare bulb hanging from the ceiling directly in front of me, most likely turned on from a gentle tug on a metal cord.

Despite myself, I groaned.

Someone cleared their throat as the door closed; I wasn't alone. Thoughts of Emma Trenton and her night of terror drifted through my boggled mind, and a fire lit in my stomach, my muscles tensed. The whole of my body filled with an impotent rage.

"Welcome to the Bolivarian Republic of Venezuela, Mr. Fisk."

The voice sounded young, coarse as gravel. He had a thick Spanish accent yet was clearly well educated, maybe somewhere abroad, possibly in the States. I tried to conjure a face to go along with the voice but ultimately came up with a question mark.

I took a solid blow to the center of my chest and immediately thought I'd been shot, was sure I was dying. I struggled for air, felt the bile rising in my throat, and fought to keep it down so that I wouldn't choke under the hood.

Found myself in a painful coughing jag.

I was very aware of my nakedness, felt more vulnerable than I could ever remember.

It was as though the man standing in the room with me could sense it. He stepped closer to me, grabbed my scrotum and squeezed.

All I could do was scream.

When he finally let go, the pain was so intense, I silently wished he would kill me.

He said, "You are a long way from home." He paused as though he expected me to fill the silence with something other than my pathetic whimpers. Then he said, "Why?"

We were alone in this room, me and him. I was sure of it.

Whatever I was cuffed to, I still had my legs. But I couldn't do fuck-all without my eyes. I needed him to remove this goddamn hood from my head.

"You coward," I rasped. It pained me even to speak, and I tried to conceal the discomfort. "When I get out of here, I'm going to hunt you down and bury you alive with nothing but a recording of my voice."

He laughed; it was a hideous thing, an animalistic shriek. "What on God's green earth makes you think you will ever leave this place with breath left in you?" he said.

I forced a smirk that pained my beaten face. "Why the hell else would I have this hood on my head? It's so I can't identify you." I paused for a breath. "Fortunately, though, I could never forget that smell you're giving off."

The hood was torn from my head so hard, I thought my neck might have snapped.

I blinked as I'd never blinked before, trying to force my eyes to adjust to the cruel light before he decided to deliver a fatal blow.

His face was only a few inches from mine, his eyes alight in the way only a lunatic's eyes can be.

He was even younger than I'd expected, and he was dressed like a civilian. Clean clothes, but nothing expensive. Around his neck he wore a large gold crucifix and cologne so pungent, it burned my nostrils. He had dark skin, a pencil-thin mustache and beard. His cheeks were evidence of a protracted battle with teenage acne.

"Should have kept the hood on," I said. "Don't need the last thing I see to be a Ven bitch with a face like a—"

Before I could finish, he drove a fist into my nose. My head was thrown back, and a white fuzz instantly clouded my vision.

"You fucking Americans, you like to hear yourselves talk, don't you?" he said.

Something warm flowed down the back of my throat and I tasted blood, nearly choked on it. More was streaming across the outside of my lips, though I wasn't sure what part of my face it was coming from.

I tried to take the kid's measure. Early twenties, around six-foot-two, thin but solid, roughly two hundred pounds.

He'd hit me with his right, which was still raised, still balled into a fist. On his right wrist he wore a watch, which meant he might have been a southpaw. If so, there was no telling what kind of punch he could throw with his left. Chances were I wouldn't be able to retain consciousness following one of those.

"Who sent you here?" he said.

I could hardly think due to an incessant ringing in my left ear.

He threw another roundhouse with his right. This time I saw it coming and was able to brace myself, but only so much.

His knuckles struck me close to my left temple. It was a punch that could have caused a brain bleed, could've killed me instantly.

One thing I was sure of: the way he threw that punch told me he was right-handed. He kept his right raised again, and I could make out the watch through my blurred vision. It was an expensive piece that didn't go well at all with the pale forest green shirt and khakis.

"*Who sent you?*" he shouted.

When I didn't answer, he popped me in the mouth, loosened at least two of my upper front teeth.

"Who sent you?" he said calmly.

I opened my mouth to speak but only felt blood pour down my chin, onto my chest, felt it drip all the way down my stomach and legs to my feet.

He took a step back to avoid getting any blood on him.

I tensed the muscles in my arms to see how much strength I had left in them.

Enough.

Maybe.

The kid dipped his hand into his right pants pocket and came out with the diamond pendant I'd had on me. Olivia's diamond pendant. I thought about the old-timer on Seven Mile Beach, mused how if I survived this, we'd probably have the same number of teeth.

"Where did you get this?" he said, dangling it in front of me with his right hand.

I was about to tell him that his henchmen had missed it during their home invasion in Southern California when something other than his fist finally struck me.

I narrowed my eyes and gazed hard at his wrist.

The watch.

I'd seen it before.

"Christ," I said, staring into his eyes. "The question is, where the hell did *you* get the pendant? And just out of curiosity, how god-damn much did you pay for it?"

Chapter 61

The kid seemed highly satisfied that I had finally figured out that he was the one with his arm around Olivia in the photo taken at the Next Level. He was actually smiling.

I smiled right back.

Or tried to.

He looked into my swollen eyes, said, "Are you not afraid to die?"

"Not particularly," I replied between heavy breaths. "What's there to fear? Simon Fisk ceasing to exist? Hell, I've only been alive forty years. I've been dead for hundreds of billions."

His head tilted to one side as though he might understand me better if he watched me from another visual perspective. "So you do not believe in the afterlife."

I stared back at him and grinned.

He seemed to take my response as an affront. When he spoke again, his voice had taken on an edge. "So you do not fear death. You obviously do not fear God. What *do* you fear?"

I thought on it seriously, said, "Flesh-eating bacteria."

Mirthlessly, he chuckled. "That is all?"

"Pretty much."

He stepped back to appraise me, no doubt trying to conjure something clever to say. It took a few moments, but then his brows rose and he opened his mouth to speak again.

When he did, he stepped forward, spoke directly into my face.

"Before this night is through, Señor Fisk, you are going to add me to that list."

While he watched my eyes for a reaction, I grabbed hold of the chains on my cuffs and allowed the blood that was flowing from my nose down the back of my throat to pool inside my mouth.

I didn't know exactly what he feared; all I knew from his actions was that he didn't care to get much blood on him.

So I spit no less than an ounce directly into his eyes.

He jerked back as though I'd thrown acid into his face. When he did, I pulled my body up just high enough to deliver a swift kick into the left side of his ribs.

As the kid doubled over, I lifted my bare lower legs and closed them around his neck in a scissor lock. When I had him, I squeezed.

He instantly felt the pressure and cried out, *"Let go, please! You're going to break my neck!"*

As I tried to work out just how the hell he was going to be able to get the cuffs off me without me losing my leverage, the door blew open and two uniformed guards charged in.

Their jaws dropped.

Must have been quite a sight, I supposed.

I scanned the two men; neither of them was carrying a gun.

"Off with the cuffs *now,* or this kid is dead," I shouted.

The guards hesitated.

I applied more pressure to the kid's neck with my left calf.

"Do it," the kid yelled. "Do it or my father will have you both *executed."*

One of the two dug into his pocket and pulled out a key; then they both began to approach.

"Slowly," I shouted. "One at a time. You on the right, you first."

The one on the right had the key. He took baby steps toward us and cautiously lifted his arm to unlock the cuff.

"One false move, and the kid's a paraplegic," I reminded him.

The kid hollered an instruction in Spanish, and the guard inserted the key into the lock and it turned. I kept hold of the chain so that I wouldn't lose my grip on the kid, but my arms were tiring, the muscles burning, my left forearm beginning to shake like a branch in the wind. Sweat poured from my forehead, stinging my eyes like tiny fires.

"Hand the key off and step over to the right wall," I ordered.

He did. Carefully, the left guard approached. With all the gentleness of the guard on the right, he unlocked the cuff.

Again I held on to the chain, but my arms wouldn't hold out much longer.

In fact, they weren't going to hold out at all.

My fingers slipped from the chain and my body fell, dragging the kid down by his neck. We hit the floor even harder than I'd expected. But I recovered immediately and interpreted the situation.

The guard on the left froze long enough for me to sweep his legs out from under him. He hit the deck.

I made it to my feet just as the guard on the right came within striking distance.

I dodged his right blow. As I did, I bent back the wrist on my right arm, keeping my hand close to my body. I stepped forward with my left foot and thrust my palm directly up under the guard's chin. I rotated my right hip and threw my body weight into the strike. When his head snapped back over ninety degrees, I realized I'd overcompensated for my injuries. As the guard hit the ground, I felt in my chest that I'd inadvertently killed him.

I swung my head around in time to see the kid flee the room. The other guard must have run out directly ahead of him.

I looked down at the fallen guard, knelt, and searched for a pulse—but he was gone.

I quickly undressed him. I then pulled on his pants and slipped into his shirt without buttoning it. His shoes were a bit tight, but they'd do.

As I ran toward the door, I looked back and saw the diamond pendant on the floor. I knelt down, stuffed it in my pants pocket, and took off.

Wherever I was, the place was deserted. The walls were an institutional green, the floor a yellowed linoleum covered in black streaks. Fluorescent lights flickered overhead, reminding me of a particularly eerie medical clinic in Minsk.

Through a cruddy window, I could see the sun slowly rising in a cloudless sky.

I checked room after room, looking for Mariana and Tejata. I shouted their names but received no response.

When I finally found Tejata, my heart nearly stopped. He was naked and beaten all to hell. As I ran into the room, I was certain he was dead.

But no, he was breathing.

I knew I couldn't move him, so I left him for the time being.

In the next room over, I found Mariana. She was fully clothed and appeared more startled than anything else. She looked fine and she confirmed it after a fleeting embrace.

"We need to get the hell out of here," I said. "But first I've got to find a phone and call an ambulance for Jorge. He's in a bad way."

She couldn't seem to tear her eyes from my battered face.

Finally, she said, "There is an office across the hall. I saw it when we were dragged in."

We shot across the hallway and rushed over to an empty metal desk. I picked up the phone and sighed with relief when I heard a dial tone. My racing mind tried to summon the emergency number in Venezuela.

"One-seven-one," Mariana shouted, pointing at a piece of paper tacked to the wall.

I punched in the numbers, and a female voice instantly came on the line.

"*Hola, Centro de Emergencia. Cómo se llama, por favor?*"

I searched my mind, but in this condition, the words weren't going to make it to my tongue. I handed Mariana the receiver, said, "Better you talk to her."

As Mariana spoke to the dispatcher, I spotted my thrift-store clothes balled up on a plastic orange seat. Beneath the clothes, I spotted my gun and the passports. I tucked the gun in my waistband, then emptied my pockets and stuffed the passports, my wallet, and BlackBerry into the pants I was wearing. I buttoned a few buttons on the shirt as I stared out the window.

At first I saw nothing but the onset of dawn.

Then I spotted movement. The kid and his guard were running toward a large black vehicle. It looked exactly like the Hilux I'd driven in Colombia.

I turned to Mariana and tried to hurry her with my eyes.

She said something into the phone, then set the receiver gently on the desk. "They will trace the call and find him," she said to me.

"All right, then," I said as we shot out of the office. "Let's go get the only guy in Venezuela who can lead us to Olivia Trenton."

She stopped me. "Where is he?"

"Just drove off in a black SUV."

"He was here?"

"Can't you read it on my face?"

"My God, Simon," she said as she studied the cuts and bruises again. "Who is he?"

I hurried her down the hallway.

"Apparently someone with a taste for the Caymans," I said through short, rapid breaths. "And a father with some serious influence inside the Venezuelan government."

Chapter 62

After running back into the room that held Jorge Tejata and grabbing his keys, Mariana and I darted into the parking lot. I took the wheel, turned over the ignition, and slammed on the accelerator, crashing through a small wooden gate at the entrance.

"Your face, Simon. Your neck, your back. What did they do to you?"

I thought of my father.

"Nothing that hasn't been done before."

The sun was fast rising over Caracas and as we sped along, more and more cars entered the roadway, heading toward the center of the city. Probably waiters and waitresses, bartenders and bouncers, all getting an early start on what was bound to be one hell of an eventful day. Call it what you wanted—Fat Tuesday, Shrove Tuesday, Mardi Gras—this would be the final and most chaotic twenty-four hours of Carnaval.

"We lost them," I said once I was absolutely sure of it. We'd been on the road twenty minutes without seeing their vehicle, and traffic was now slowing to a halt.

"We will find him, Simon. He is in Caracas. How far can he go?"

"Now that he knows we're looking for him? Anywhere. And worse, by now he may well have decided to kill Olivia and dump the evidence."

She placed a hand on my sore arm. "You must not think like that."

I wished I could share in Mariana's optimism, but there was just too much riding against us. Finding anyone on a day like today would be a near impossibility, let alone someone running scared. The kid, whoever he was, could don a full-length gorilla suit and not appear the least bit out of place. We could walk right by him a dozen times without being any the wiser.

Meanwhile, the Venezuelan police and military would be looking for us. We'd already had one close call and one capture. This time, they wouldn't be taking any chances. The cops and soldiers would have standing orders to shoot us on sight.

Truth was, Mariana and I should have been on a road back to Puerto La Cruz, where Cliff Shermer might still be with his yacht. He could possibly smuggle us out of Venezuela, perhaps as far as Grand Cayman. Without Shermer, we didn't stand much of a shot of getting out of the country alive. Our faces would be posted everywhere by now. There would be checkpoints at every border, from Colombia to Brazil to Guyana.

And here we were—instead of looking for a way out—moving deeper into the country, heading directly for its core.

But what choice did we have now? We knew the man responsible for Olivia's abduction. As far as I knew, I had been the only person to see his face. Maybe Tejata had, but he'd be in no condition to point him out for days, maybe weeks. And Olivia didn't have nearly that long.

I still didn't have the "why" in the palm of my hand, even though the picture had been steadily growing clearer. This kid, whoever he was, had been in Grand Cayman when Olivia and her friends arrived. He met the girls either near their hotel or at the Next Level, and he'd been infatuated with Olivia Trenton.

And she'd evidently been infatuated with him. Probably spent the night with him in her room at the Ritz-Carlton; it would have been why she wanted to be left alone. She'd spent that missing Tuesday with him too. Doing what, I didn't know. Except having lunch at

Hemingways and maybe taking a drive up to Rum Point, where the kid bought her that pendant from that old, red-faced guy named Barney, who'd wanted to blow my head off in his store.

As soon as we entered the land of skyscrapers, I parked and we exited Jorge Tejata's SUV for the last time.

"We'll need disguises," Mariana said. "Costumes."

I smiled at her even though it pained my entire face. "Maybe you do," I said, pulling the red beret out of the dead guard's pants pocket. "I've already got one."

Chapter 63

By the time the festivities kicked off, I looked like a genuine Venezuelan soldier (albeit one who'd just returned home from a bloody war) and Mariana was dressed as a blue macaw, her outfit so revealing, I'd never see birds the same way again.

We waded back into the ocean of people. I wore sunglasses, my red beret low, to hide at least some of the deep red swelling and bruises on my face. Most remained visible, of course, but there was nothing I could do. Because I needed to carry my gun. Seeing a soldier with a gun, revelers wouldn't think anything of it. If I were carrying a piece while wearing a full-length chicken suit, that might just set off some alarms.

We quickly took notice that I wasn't the only Venezuelan soldier trawling the streets. There were dozens of them, all appearing more alert than ever. It was possible that not every member of the military was looking for us, but after all we'd just been through, paranoia would supersede logic at every turn, at least until we were out of the country.

We began our search in earnest.

Before we knew it, an hour had gone by.

Then another.

And another.

There were plenty of kids his age—late teens, early twenties—on the streets, but none looked even remotely familiar, and we didn't have a name. I'd done a search on my BlackBerry to look for photographs of children of Venezuela's top-ranking officials, but there was nothing to be found. Venezuela wasn't exactly a bastion of freedom these days, and the press captured pictures only of the people, places, and events that the government wanted the electorate and the rest of the world to see.

"We're here again," Mariana shouted in my ear, temporarily freeing me of my thoughts.

"Where's here?"

She pointed.

I looked up. Saw the stark white face of the Caracas Cathedral, which we'd passed just an hour ago. We were literally running in circles.

As we stood at Plaza Bolívar, bells gonged from across the way. It was already noon; I could hardly believe it. Six hours had passed since we'd made our escape. And yet here we were, no closer to finding the kid.

I considered dropping in on Cardinal César Zumbado—maybe he could identify the kid if I described him in enough detail. But then I recalled that the archbishop was performing a wedding today—in the early afternoon, if I remembered correctly. He'd no doubt be busy preparing for the ceremony.

Besides, Zumbado hadn't been all that helpful or friendly to begin with. It didn't come as a complete surprise, not given the years I'd spent in Catholic institutions.

But maybe it should have raised a red flag.

Zumbado *was*, after all, a human being. Except for those who opposed me, most people I'd come into contact with over the past two years offered their help whenever I told them I was searching for a missing young girl. My friend Kurt Ostermann, a private investigator in Berlin. The lawyer Anastazja Staszak in Warsaw, and her brother Marek, the politician. A top Ukrainian law enforcement official named Martin Rudnyk, the South African Interpol agent Jess Kidman. An entire family of strangers in Belarus had taken us in when our car broke down and Ana and I became stranded in the freezing cold forest of Gomel.

Hell, the beautiful woman standing beside me was proof of the good in humanity. Mariana Silva had risked her life to help me find a complete stranger and return her to her parents. As had my old friends: Aubrey Lang, RN, in Costa Rica; and Samuel "Grey" Greyson of the DEA in Colombia. Cliff Shermer, bastard that he was, had given me a gun. Even the alcoholic journalist Jorge Tejata had put his life on the line for Olivia, or at the very least for her story. He was no doubt lying in a hospital bed right now being pumped with morphine and treated for broken bones and internal bleeding. Of all the people I'd come across since Edgar Trenton called me from Calabasas, only the archbishop and the bureaucrat Walter Brewer had been ice cold.

"Cardinal César Zumbado?" Jorge Tejata had said. *"He's no help to anyone. All he does is preach politics here in Venezuela. The Catholic Church in Venezuela is nothing more than another political party. If César's not yapping about 'sins of the flesh,' he's screaming his stupid red hat off about homosexuals and abortion."*

I turned my head and looked at Mariana. While she was staring at the Cathedral, holding her crucifix between her fingers, her eyes had grown moist again. As they had when we were inside the cathedral speaking to Zumbado.

"He's attacked the pope?" I had said to the archbishop just before Mariana became upset. *"Didn't the pope visit with the president recently?"*

"Not recently. Years ago, and only because I asked him to, in order to get the president's assurances that Venezuela will keep in place our strong laws against killing the unborn."

A few blocks later, we'd found ourselves seated at Restaurant Beirut, where Mariana told me her terrible story.

"Last year, one of our keepers drove me into San José to work for the weekend. . . . He brought me to this terrible apartment. . . . He said nothing, this big man. Just struck me with a closed fist, then threw

me onto the mattress and dropped his tremendous body on top of me. . . ."

She'd been touching her fingers to the small gold crucifix hanging around her throat, just as she was now, when she told me, *"I was pregnant, yes. But I could not have this baby, this product of a rape. . . . But I am Catholic, and the Church says that you cannot end a pregnancy, no matter what. Even with a rape, they say it is a gift from God."*

I'd tried to tell her it was okay, but she had pulled away, her head down, hair falling over her wet face. *"But it is not okay, Simon. I took the life. Every night I have to think about it before I go to sleep. I have to beg of God forgiveness for this. I have to pray. . . ."*

"Christ," I said, gazing up at the cathedral.

Mariana turned to me. "What is it, Simon?"

But I couldn't answer her. My mind had returned to the Trentons' estate in Calabasas. It was as though I were there now, standing in Olivia's room.

"She stopped taking the Paxil before or after the trip?" I'd said to her mother.

"After, I believe. Maybe just before, I'm not sure. But the doctor I spoke to—her pediatrician, actually—told me that her stopping the Paxil abruptly is probably what was causing the afternoon sluggishness and occasional nausea."

"Any vomiting? Maybe an eating disorder?"

"No, I don't think so. Just the nausea. It would come and go."

"Did she lose any weight?"

"No. If anything, she gained a pound or two since the trip."

That conversation had taken place only a few minutes after I got off the phone with my FBI hacker-turned-mommy Kati Sheffield.

"By the way, how are you feeling?" I had asked Kati.

"Fat, hungry, tired, fat, and nauseous."

"First trimester still?"

"Just started the second."

"It gets better, doesn't it?"

"I'll have to let you know; it's different with every pregnancy."

But even with all that, what really struck me—what really stood out in my mind as I stood there silently at Plaza Bolívar—was what Alysia had written to Olivia on her Facebook Timeline:

Don't freek but I made the appt. I love love love love love love love love you.

The hell with going to get tongue rings. Alysia had lied to my face about that appointment. Of course she would have, sitting there in front of her father.

Standing there, across from the Caracas Cathedral, Mariana continued talking at me, shaking my arms.

"Simon?" she was saying over the music. "Are you all right?"

The echo of the last of the gongs faded away.

"I'm fine," I said, gently pushing her away and making for the cathedral across the street. "Come on, Mariana."

"Where are we going?"

"You and I, we've got a wedding to crash."

I pulled out my BlackBerry. First I had to make a phone call.

As much as I hated to do it, I needed to ask for one last favor.

Chapter 64

T he Cathedral is closed," Cardinal César Zumbado called from the altar as we stepped through the tall double doors. He was dressed this afternoon in full regalia, red from head to toe, still preparing for the ceremony. He hadn't even looked up when we entered.

"Where is she, Your Eminence?" I called out from the rear of the church.

Finally, Zumbado looked up. Squinted but couldn't seem to make us out. "Who?" he boomed.

"The blushing bride."

I started up the aisle, with Mariana right behind me. The cathedral was empty except for the three of us, my words still echoing off the vaulted ceiling.

From behind the altar, the archbishop stared down at us. He cringed when he saw the cuts and bruises on my face but then quickly regained his composure. Calmly, he said, "I am afraid this is to be a *private* ceremony."

"Then would you kindly introduce me to the groom, Your Eminence?"

"Whatever for?"

"I'd like to give him a few words of advice before the nuptials."

The archbishop forced a wide grin. "I am sure his father is doing a fine job fulfilling that role."

"His father is a man of some esteem, I presume."

Zumbado hesitated. "He is."

"But not the president."

"Of course not the president."

"Which leaves Vicente Delgado, Venezuela's Minister of Foreign Affairs."

The archbishop remained behind his altar, a smug smile threatening to appear on his face.

Mariana squeezed my forearm. "Simon," she whispered, "I do not understand."

"The president had nothing to do with Delgado's phone call to Don Óscar in Colombia, did he, Your Eminence?"

The archbishop remained silent, but his eyes confirmed what I already knew. The Minister of Foreign Affairs had threatened Don Óscar without the president's authority.

"You are meddling in something that is none of your concern, Señor Fisk. Return to the United States and tell the parents that the girl is unharmed." He paused. "And please, inform her mother and father that she is happy."

"Happy?" I said. "Is that why her groom's father needed to have Olivia stolen from her home in the middle of the night?"

Zumbado lowered his chin onto his chest and said, "The situation, it was not ideal. But Minister Delgado was given no choice."

"No choice?"

"He is a God-fearing man. As is his son."

My fingers instinctively balled into fists. "Well, they'd both better adopt a healthy fear of man, as well," I said quietly. "Because I am not leaving Venezuela without Olivia Trenton."

The cathedral fell silent as the archbishop closed his eyes and held his palms together out in front of him. When he reopened his eyes, he seemed to have regained the courage of his convictions.

"They had *no choice*," he barked at me. "The girl was going to take their child's *life* if she remained with her parents in the States. She *told* Rafael. She'd made an *appointment*."

"He had no right—"

"He had *every* right, Fisk. Nay, he had a *duty* to protect the life of his *unborn child.*"

"My God," Mariana gasped.

Zumbado's face tightened. "To what lengths did *you* go, Simon, to protect *your* child?" He took a step around the altar and started down the three marble stairs. "Not far enough, apparently."

His words went off like a powder keg in my mind. Every last bit of me seemed to tremble. My eyes watered but I held my gaze on him.

Even as I dipped my hand into the back of my pants.

Even as I gripped the rubber of the Chief's Special.

Even as I pulled the handgun free and leveled it at the archbishop's head.

Chapter 65

Simon," Mariana cried, "what are you *doing*? The archbishop is unarmed."

"Sure," I said softly, motioning with my chin to the confessionals on either side of the cathedral. "But *they're* not."

Out of one confessional door on either side stepped a Venezuelan soldier armed with an Israeli submachine gun.

"Please, gentlemen," the archbishop urged. "Not in the *house of God*."

The two soldiers approached from opposite sides through the pews.

From behind the altar, two men dressed in formal black suits emerged: Rafael Delgado and his father, Vicente, Venezuela's Minister of Foreign Affairs.

"Drop the gun," Vicente Delgado instructed me. "Or I will order these men to kill both you and the woman where you stand."

There weren't many options. The Minister of Foreign Affairs had to kill us anyway. He couldn't allow this to come out. He'd manipulated the leader of a murderous Colombian drug cartel by pretending to act on behalf of the Venezuelan president. If Don Óscar didn't execute Delgado, the Venezuelan president would.

I eyed each of the soldiers. "These men betrayed your leader," I told them. "Drop your weapons and your lives will be spared. Keep them raised and you'll be made to face your president."

Vicente shouted something to them in Spanish, but all I could make out were the words *"el presidente."*

Mariana said quietly, "He told them to take us outside and kill us and the president will never hear a word of this."

My gun still leveled at the archbishop, I leaned over and whispered in Mariana's ear. "Tell them the president is already listening. He's already heard everything."

She stared at me.

"Go on, Mariana. Tell them."

When she did, everyone froze where they were.

"Now," I said to Mariana, "dip your hand into my front pocket."

"Which one?"

I shrugged. "I kind of like when you try both pockets."

She stood in front of me as she had twice before and dug into my pockets, pulling out my phone.

"Hold the BlackBerry up," I told her, "so that everyone can see."

She did.

"Mr. President," I said loudly.

"*Sí*, Comrade Fisk." The president's booming voice filled the empty cathedral, echoing off the walls like a ricocheting bullet from a .44.

The favor I'd requested before entering the cathedral had come through. I'd called Edgar on his cell phone and asked him if he was still in the company of Artie Baglin, his friend the director, who'd posted his bail.

"Put him on," I'd said.

"Put him on?" Edgar was understandably confused, but to his credit he didn't hesitate. "All right, Simon. Hang on." Then: "Artie, it's for you."

As soon as the echo of the president's voice faded, I said into the BlackBerry's speaker, "Do you have any orders for your men, Mr. President?"

"*Sí*, comrade."

The president then launched into a loud and protracted diatribe, during which both soldiers lowered their submachine guns then raised them again in the direction of Vicente and Rafael Delgado.

Mariana said into my ear, "The president ordered the Minister and his son to be arrest—"

Before she finished her sentence, Vicente and Rafael Delgado each produced a handgun and fired rounds into the soldiers' bodies, cutting them down.

Mariana let out a scream as the archbishop dropped to his knees, covering his head with his arms.

I turned to fire the nine-millimeter, but I was too late.

Both Vicente and Rafael had fled behind the marble wall and into the rectory.

"Stay here," I told Mariana.

Then I gave chase.

Chapter 66

The moment I ran out the back door of the cathedral, I took on fire. I dodged behind a Dumpster and hit the blacktop in a roll.

I stayed down. From beneath the Dumpster I had a clear view of the lot, including a tall statue of the Virgin Mary, which Vicente Delgado was using as cover. His son Rafael was nowhere in sight.

Rafael, I thought.

E-A-R-F-A-L-1

Clever girl. She'd used her crush but jumbled the letters.

The sound of heavy boots on gravel caught my attention. Vicente Delgado had taken off in a dash across the lot.

He was a diversion, I knew. He was buying his kid time to run. But it was the kid I needed. The kid was the only person I was sure could lead me to Olivia.

I aimed the nine-millimeter at Delgado's legs and fired. His legs were tripped up in a spray of bullets and blood and he hit the ground hard, his gun thrown several yards in front of him and well out of reach.

I got to my feet and ran toward the back of the lot, where I tucked my gun and hopped an eight-foot fence. Landed on a main street, re-straining my ankle.

I hobbled into the middle of the closed road, turning, peering into the hundreds of faces, visages painted like skulls, like devils, like horrible clowns, masked men and women everywhere I looked. Anxiety washed over me as I got caught up in the human tide, being pushed and shoved farther away from the cathedral.

I was vulnerable. At any moment I knew I could be shanked by a knife.

If I pulled the gun now, it would cause a stampede in which dozens of men, women, and children could be trampled to death.

I'd lost him.

Where are you, you son of a bitch?

A float with a giant Elvis Presley head was moving slowly toward my position, "Don't Be Cruel" booming from its enormous speakers.

If I could hop on the float, I'd gain the high ground; I could see farther, possibly spot the kid amongst the crowds.

But I no longer looked much like a soldier. My shirt was out, my beret gone. My face had swollen so badly, it must have looked like a Halloween mask.

Well, maybe I'd blend in after all.

A dozen Elvis Presley impersonators swiveled their hips and gyrated as the float went past. It seemed possible for me to grab one, borrow the wig and sunglasses. . . .

"Don't be cruel to a heart that's true."

One of the Elvises on the rear of the float, I noticed, was barely moving. He wore the wig and sunglasses but instead of the white BeDazzled costume, he was dressed in all black. A white shirt peeked out of his jacket.

"Don't be cruel . . ."

I gripped the edge of the float and pulled myself up.

As I hobbled toward the rear of the float, an Elvis jumped in front of me. Blocked my path, threatening me with his guitar.

". . . to a heart that's true."

I shoved him aside, hard, and he took a header off the float and onto the pavement.

That was when my Elvis spotted me.

"I don't want no other love."

As he reached into his jacket to pull out his weapon, I broke into a painful sprint and drove my shoulder into his sternum before he could fire.

"Baby, it's just you . . ."

The momentum took our bodies off the rear of the float, and we too landed hard on the blacktop.

". . . I'm thinking of."

His gun was kicked across the street by a passerby, so he grabbed for mine. I gripped his left wrist and twisted it till he screamed and dropped the gun.

Another passerby kicked my gun forward. I turned my head and watched helplessly as it vanished under the Elvis float, relieving me of my one advantage.

"Looks like it's just you and me, kid," I said through sore teeth.

With all his strength, he threw me off him and we both rose to our feet. He led with a left, which I blocked, then threw a right-handed uppercut, which I ducked. By doing so, he'd opened his body up, and I immediately cashed in, lunging forward and throwing three powerful hooks into the right side of his ribs. I followed through by delivering the edge of my right hand vertically across his neck.

He stumbled backwards, doubled over from the shots to his ribs. I took several steps forward to finish him.

As I did, Rafael quickly came up with a knife.

When he attacked, I stepped into his body, blocking the strike with my forearms. I grasped his wrist and twisted his thumb away from his body.

I took him to the ground with an armbar, then held him down with a forearm to his throat.

"I . . . can't . . . breathe," he muttered.

The knife dropped from his hand and clattered onto the street.

A wide circle had formed around us.

Pushing through the circle were several soldiers dressed in red, carrying automatic weapons.

The soldiers shouted at us in Spanish, but I couldn't understand a word of what was being said.

"Where's the girl?" I growled into Rafael's face.

"Gone," he rasped.

I applied more pressure to his windpipe.

"Where is she?" I spat.

His lips turned up in a demented smile. *"All . . . I want . . . is my . . . child."*

I stared into his eyes, which were beginning to bulge.

Meanwhile, the soldiers were moving in closer. I was running out of time.

"Then . . . her heathen parents . . . can have . . . her back," he gasped.

I froze.

So there was *a ransom all along,* I realized. *Only it was never money. He didn't love the girl. He only wanted the organism growing inside her.*

The music suddenly stopped.

A voice boomed from the crowd.

Soldiers stepped aside, and a large man dressed in red stepped inside the circle and cast a gargantuan shadow over the ground on which we lay.

"El presidente," Rafael cried. *"¡Socorro, por favor!"*

I watched the large man's shadow as he drew a sizable right hand from behind his back and produced what looked like a handgun.

From the other side of the circle, I heard Mariana's voice crying out.

I looked up and saw her running toward us.

I looked down at the kid again as he struggled for breath. His face was blue and turning bluer.

"Last chance," I said. "Where's the girl?"

The president barked something in Spanish. I heard my name spoken.

I looked up at Mariana for the translation.

"The president told the kid to tell you *now,* where is the girl."

I heard the cock of the president's weapon.

Mariana gasped.

I stole one last glance up at her.

"The president says to the kid, 'Tell him now, Rafael, or else I will shoot you in the head and pass your flesh around the shantytowns during supper."

Chapter 67

Twenty-four hours later, a private jet carrying only two passengers—Olivia Trenton and yours truly—touched down at Van Nuys Airport in the San Fernando Valley of Los Angeles.

There were no throngs of reporters there to capture the scene, as all access to the airport had been blocked off by the LAPD. When we stepped off the plane, there were only four individuals there to meet us: an FBI psychologist; Edgar's criminal defense lawyer; Emma Trenton; and her driver, Nicholas.

As soon as Olivia appeared at the top of the stairs of the plane, Emma ran toward her.

Olivia squeezed my hand, then hurried down the steps to meet her mother. From the last step, she leapt into her mother's arms.

A light drizzle began to fall, like tears onto the tarmac.

When I reached bottom, I shook hands first with the psychologist, who introduced herself as Dr. Stefanie Kurnz, then with Edgar's attorney, Seymour Lepavsky.

Nicholas approached and, after apologizing for disliking me, thanked me for bringing Olivia home.

"Oh, Simon," Emma said when she saw me. "Your *face*."

I forced a painful grin. "I've been getting that a lot lately."

Emma wrapped her arms around me and thanked me as though

I'd just saved the world. I knew how she felt, of course. As far as *her* world was concerned, I had.

An hour later, Emma and I were alone again, this time in the dining room of her estate, where we'd sat together not long ago. Olivia was upstairs in her room with Dr. Kurnz, while Lepavsky smoked a cigarette out on the back porch. A steaming cup of espresso rested in front of me.

Emma's green eyes were rimmed with red, her voice still hoarse. "I don't know what to say, Simon."

"You said everything you needed to say back on the tarmac, Emma."

"The FBI, they never would have found her. Am I right?"

I shrugged. "We'll never know. It all depends on how hard they would've looked. Children don't vanish into thin air. Every one that's missing is somewhere."

Including my daughter, Hailey.

Dead, I was sure. But somewhere. Somewhere there were answers to the questions I'd been asking for eleven years. Somewhere there was an explanation, and just now, I felt as compelled as ever to find it.

And with the Trentons' check, I could take as much time as I needed and focus only on the eleven-year-old case of the missing six-year-old girl. I'd find whoever was responsible, and I would make him answer for what he'd done.

To me.

To Hailey.

To Tasha.

To my entire family.

To my entire world.

Emma stared into the distance, watching leaves swirl outside the window. "It all seems like a nightmare now, Simon. Like it never really happened."

"That's the thing about nightmares," I said. "More often than not, they end."

She looked at me but said nothing; there was nothing to say.

"So this boy, Rafael—" She shuddered. "—he spent one night with my daughter in Grand Cayman. One night and she fell in love. When she got home, they kept in touch on the Internet—that's why she never left her room." She frowned. "That and because she was pregnant, which explains the nausea and the cravings and the weight gain, and why she stopped taking her antidepressants."

I said nothing.

"She told him she was pregnant. But she didn't know what she wanted to do yet." Emma's voice cracked. "She was too afraid to come to me or her father. She told only Rafael and her friend Alysia, no one else. Alysia told her to have the procedure, that she was too young for a baby, that if she kept it, she'd be ruining her life. Rafael insisted that she have the baby. He told her he'd marry her and they would live together in Caracas with his parents. Happily ever after."

"Then she finally decided," I said softly.

"And she told him." Emma held her head in her hands. "She should have waited until after she'd had the procedure done. Instead she told him that her friend had made the appointment."

"In her defense, she couldn't possibly have anticipated any of this."

"No," Emma said. "I just don't understand. I mean, what made that boy think he had the right . . .?"

Neither of us said a word. We both knew the answer to that question. It was the same answer we were given when doctors were murdered in cold blood, when clinics were blown into rubble.

"And the archbishop," she said, "how could he justify—?"

"We don't know that Cardinal Zumbado was complicit in the actual kidnapping," I reminded her. "From the confession the boy gave, Zumbado was merely an accessory after the fact."

"He helped hide my daughter," she said, staring down at her hands. "And Rafael's father . . . How could he—?"

"When something's drummed into your head from a very early

age . . . ," I said. "And if you're truly convinced the ends justify the means . . ."

"Vicente Delgado genuinely believed he was on the side of right," she said, her throat closing up on her. "To him, he was doing what we were doing. Trying to save a life."

Emma wiped some tears away and then held the back of her hand to her forehead as though checking herself for fever. "He was brainwashed," she said. "Both of them, he *and* his son. Brainwashed, indoctrinated . . . Whatever we decide to call it."

She closed her eyes.

"To be honest, Simon, I don't know what I would have told Olivia to do had she come to me."

I thought on it. "Sure you do, Emma. You would've done the same thing I would've done if it were my daughter, Hailey."

She opened her eyes and looked at me.

"You would have told her it was her decision," I said, "and you would have given her whatever guidance she needed. You would have supported whatever choice she made."

Lepavsky stepped in from the back porch. "You have a minute, Simon?"

I took Emma's hand. "Excuse me."

Outside, Lepavsky offered me a cigarette but I declined.

"I just got off the phone with the U.S. Attorney's Office," he said. "They're not prepared to drop the charges against Edgar."

"They really think Edgar used his daughter's kidnapping to hide the money, do they?"

"The feds discovered that Edgar had several offshore accounts set up in Grand Cayman. Apparently, he *was* hiding money. *Some* money. From his wife, though, not from the IRS. And not because of the coming divorce."

"No?"

"No. He was socking it away for his assistant, Valerie. She's three months pregnant herself. She and Edgar are going to have a kid."

I gazed at the sky. Thought about the old-timer on Seven Mile Beach. I took a step back, lowered my head, and took in the manicured lawn.

"Grass needs a good trim," I said.

"Gardener quit. Can you blame him? The Trentons aren't going to be able to pay staff for very long. Their majordomo's a real saint. He's agreed to stay on and maybe keep Nicholas. Everyone else, though, is out the door. Hell, I'm not even sure what the hell *I'm* doing here. I'm not going to take on a case like this pro bono. I figure I'll wait and see what Edgar can get for his Veyron. Car's worth about three million bucks."

I nodded absently.

Lepavsky shrugged. "And hell, maybe I can get his story. It's got to be worth a fortune, right? In this town, you can always find a payday if you're really looking for one."

My eyes remained fixed on the grass.

"Edgar's criminal case," I said. "It's just a matter of tracking down the ransom, then, isn't it? The eight and a half million? Proving Edgar didn't commit a fraud?"

Once more, Lepavsky shrugged. "Sure. Simple as that," he said.

A few minutes later, Dr. Kurnz came downstairs and announced that Olivia was doing well, considering the circumstances.

"She's more concerned about her dad right now than anything else," Kurnz said to Emma before turning to me. "Also, Olivia asked to see you, Simon. She said she slept most of the way on the plane and didn't have the opportunity to properly thank you."

"Sure," I said.

When I knocked on the door, Olivia didn't call me in; she opened the door herself and gave me a hug. She'd just showered, was as fresh and clean and beautiful as she was standing between her mother and father in front of Grauman's Chinese Theatre in the framed photo sitting on her nightstand.

This is what Hailey would smell like.

I tried to push the thought aside. But not far this time.

Olivia offered me a seat across from her bed. She was even more stunning in person than she was in the pictures I'd been carrying around for days.

I dug into my pocket. "Oh, before I forget, this is yours."

I handed her the diamond pendant.

"Please," she said, handing it back. "Keep it. I don't need it."

I was about to argue when I thought of the old treasure hunter. I'd give it to him. He'd never spend another day hungry again. Or thirsty, for that matter.

"Will you speak to the woman again?" Olivia said. "The one from Colombia?"

"I certainly hope so." I smiled, thinking of her. "That's the plan, at least."

"Please, *please*, give her my thanks," Olivia said. "I was in a daze when I met her, and I feel terrible now that I know everything she did for me."

"Of course."

"What is her full name again?"

"Mariana Silva."

"Mariana Silva. That's a beautiful name for a girl."

Not much catches me unawares these days, but those last three words caught me by surprise. "You're thinking of names," I said.

Her cheeks burned red and she turned away from me. "I don't know how to tell Mom and Dad," she said quietly.

I stood from the chair and sat next to her on the bed. I took her by the shoulders, turned her around, and held her close to me. "Just tell them," I said. "They'll understand."

Epilogue

Late that evening I arrived at Tocumen International Airport in Panama City. Technically, I was off the clock and had been ever since Olivia Trenton was returned to her home in Calabasas. But something continued to gnaw at me, and as much as I wanted to let it go, I couldn't.

With Edgar cleared, there were too many questions left unanswered. Emma remained sure she armed the alarm that night; so who unarmed it? Edgar maintained that he loaded the .38 Special himself with live ammunition; so who replaced the bullets with blanks?

Who gained access to Edgar's office in Burbank to steal the knife?

The more I thought about it, the more I became convinced—there was someone on the inside. Someone who could have "borrowed" the majordomo's keys and made copies. Someone who could have watched the majordomo arm and unarm the alarm and memorized the code. Someone who could have gained access to Edgar's gun vault to replace the .38's bullets with blanks. Someone who could have remained behind and hidden in Emma's home office after the rest of the staff left for the night.

Someone who could have snatched the pass to the studio out of Edgar's limousine and used it to get onto the lot at Carousel Pictures to steal the knife.

So after leaving Olivia's room, I asked Emma if I could have a look around her home office, specifically at the files for her employees, past and present.

Edgar had been right about his wife: she kept meticulous records. So it wasn't long at all before I located the file belonging to Raúl Corpas, the Trentons' former gardener.

Raúl and Luis were the only individuals who had been at the Trentons' house when I told them I was leaving for Grand Cayman. Of the two, only Raúl was of Latin American descent. Which meant that he had to be the one to pass the news along the chain to Delgado's people. There was no other explanation for how they came to be in Grand Cayman. Delgado's people had bribed and threatened and stolen evidence; there was no disputing it. It was how Barney the jeweler at Rum Point knew my name.

Less than an hour after finding the file, I had a taxi drop me off in Commerce, a city located in southeast L.A. County. Among other things, Commerce was known for having a large Panamanian American population. And according to Raúl's papers, the city had been his place of residence since 1992.

Raúl Corpas had lived in a large low-income housing complex just off the I-5 Freeway. Once I arrived there, it wasn't difficult to locate his apartment.

When I knocked on the door, a woman answered. Probably in her early thirties, she appeared frazzled in a bathrobe with a toddler hanging on her hip.

"Is Raúl at home?" I said.

"Raúl? You looking for Raúl?" Her voice rose sharply with every syllable, and the kid on her hip began to wail. "*Quiet*, Enrique," she said. Which didn't seem to help. "Raúl's not here, mister, and he's never coming back."

The way she said it made me think it wouldn't be a good idea if Raúl *did* come back.

"Are you his wife?" I said.

"Might as well be. We'd been living together eight years. This is his son I'm holding."

"I take it you've had a fight?"

"A fight? Yeah, you can call it that. Few days ago, Raúl gone and quit his job and called me from a pay phone, said he was going to be out at the bar shooting pool all night."

"He say why he quit?"

"The people he work for, they the family whose teenage daughter went missing. FBI was crawling around, wrecking his grass and garden and shit, he said. Told me he couldn't take it no more."

"And when he got home?"

"That's the thing. He never *came* home. I was worried as all hell, thought maybe someone killed him or he got picked up by the cops for some bullshit like public drunkenness. So I went upstairs to the sixth floor where my girlfriend Rosie lives to ask her to come down to the police station with me because I couldn't get answers and take care of Enrique at the same time. And you know what?"

"What?"

"Rosie's husband didn't come home either that night. He worked as a mechanic somewhere in Morningside. Left his job, too. So we went across the street to see our other friend, Franny. Franny's man hadn't come home either. And he wasn't no grease monkey. He was a paralegal over in Inglewood, wore a shirt and tie every day. All three just up and disappeared, along with one of their other friends from the block."

"Any idea where they went?"

"Where else they going to go? They went home."

"To Panama."

"You bet, Panama. Panama City."

Which was why I was now here. She hadn't noticed until well after he was gone, but he'd destroyed every picture of himself, taken or burned every document related to his identity, and left her and the kid in case anyone came around looking to rip his thieving head off.

So had the others. So all I had was a grainy Polaroid Emma had taken for his employment folder, along with worn photocopies of his passport and driver's license. It wasn't much. But it would have to be enough.

"By the way," I'd said before Raúl's wife closed the door on me. "Does your husband speak English?"

She stared at me as though it were the silliest question in the world. "Of course he does," she said. "Raúl speaks English even better than me."

The Trentons had had no idea; it was why everyone had spoken so freely when he was around. And how he was able to gather as much information as he did in order to plot what he'd thought was the perfect crime.

Seventy-two hours after landing, I was no closer to finding Raúl and his boys than I was when I left Commerce, California. I had spent the past three nights at salsa clubs like Habana Panamá, jazz clubs like Bar Platea, and lounges like Oz Bar, which catered to the city's elite. With the weekend come and gone, I was losing hope that I'd find them. It was possible they'd played it smart, decided to lie low for several months, maybe even hopped a train down to Argentina or Peru. If so, I'd never find them. If I never found them, I'd never find the money. And I wanted to find the money.

For the third night in a row, I was spending the wee hours of the morning walking around the Vegas-style casino at the Veneto Hotel, where I was staying. You figure, a few men who had never had money come into a ridiculous amount of it, and chances are they're going to try their luck at a craps or blackjack table sooner or later. But no, not these men. For all I knew, they'd double-crossed the Panamanian *mara* that hired them by never telling them about the ransom, which had been all over the television. If so, it could be that the four men I was looking for were already dead, their bodies weighed down at the bottom of the Panama Canal.

Almost 4 A.M. Time to call it a night.

Time to call it a trip.

Time to call it a case.

The U.S. Attorney didn't have enough to convict Edgar Trenton anyway, not if the eight and a half million was truly gone. The prosecutor would play hardball for another few weeks, see if he could talk Lepavsky into a deal, maybe a lesser-included offense with time served, just so that the Justice Department could save some face and preempt a possible lawsuit for unlawful imprisonment and malicious prosecution.

This wasn't about finding a stolen kid anymore; this was now nothing but a former U.S. Marshal chasing money in Central America. There was no nobility in that. At least none that I could see.

I pulled my BlackBerry from my pocket. From here, I'd head to Bogotá to see Mariana. If nothing else, I needed to give her her share of the earnings from the case. She'd put her life on the line just as I had. And she needed a break much more than I did.

Then I'd head north to San José to thank Aubrey Lang. I'd offer her a piece of the fee and she'd tell me where to stuff it and we'd laugh. Then I'd propose we set up a foundation for the kids of La Carpio. I couldn't get those slums out of my mind, but maybe I could get some kids out of those slums. At least I could try.

After my conversation with Aubrey, I'd head over to Grand Cayman and find the old-timer who spent his days hunting treasure. I'd watch him through field glasses for a while, and when I was sure no one but him could find it, I'd plant the diamond pendant a foot or so deep in the sand. Once I had caught the expression on his face, I'd head home to Washington, D.C., and once again get to work in earnest to discover what happened to my daughter, Hailey, all those years ago.

I knew now, I'd never let her go.

And I'd decided I didn't even want to try.

I took a deep breath of the oxygen-rich casino air and searched for Mariana's name in my phone. As I did, I came across that number I discovered in Jason Gutiérrez's Craigslist e-mail back in Eagle Rock.

I tapped the button to delete.

Then canceled.

Thought, *What the hell?*

With the phone in my left hand, I dialed the number, fully expecting to hear the familiar mechanical voice tell me, *The subscriber you have called is not able to receive calls at this time.*

Instead I heard a ring.

Not just in my ear but from somewhere in the casino.

Somewhere not far off; in fact, just past the row of slot machines stationed to my left.

I poked my head around the corner, and there he was, the gardener Raúl Corpas, and three friends at a table playing Texas hold 'em. The guy sitting next to Raúl set down his drink and picked up his phone.

"*¿Hola?*" he answered over the sounds of the casino.

I smiled, said, "I have a message for Raúl."

"A message?"

"Yes, a message. Tell him I'll see him soon."

"Soon?"

"In about thirty seconds."

I started walking toward them, reaching with my other hand into my jacket.

"Thirty seconds?"

"Thirty seconds," I said as I wrapped my fingers around the rubber grip of my Chief's Special. "Give or take a few."

Author's Note

Payoff is a work of fiction. In writing this novel, I endeavored to remain true to the laws and geography of the locations Simon visits in his efforts to find Olivia Trenton. However, I also took the liberty of altering facts and places whenever I felt such changes would enhance the story. All characters appearing in *Payoff* are either the product of the author's imagination or are used fictitiously. Accordingly, certain historical events, such as the death or resignation of public figures, have intentionally been modified or erased in order to create and intensify the universe in which Simon Fisk resides.